FOUND DROWNED

FOUND DROWNED

A NOVEL

LAURIE GLENN NORRIS

ADVANCE PRAISE FOR FOUND DROWNED

"A body washing ashore opens up a Pandora's box of ugly secrets in Laurie Glenn Norris's historical whodunnit. Set in the late nineteenth-century Maritimes, *Found Drowned* exposes the underbelly of rural life in scenarios rife with family feuds, domestic abuse, and madness. With its near-forensic attention to detail, this suspense-filled tale rubs away the blush of romanticism which often tints views of our past. Think the Age of Sail with a macabre twist."
–**Carol Bruneau**, award-winning author of *A Circle on the Surface*

"We're gripped by the plight of Mary Harney, a spirited young woman who goes missing. Is she escaping from her bedridden laudanum-soaked mother—or from the oily grasp of her raging father? In *Found Drowned*, the action, the characters, the trains and towns and waterways all captivate us—drawn with compelling nineteenth-century detail."
–**Linda Moore**, author of *Foul Deeds* and *The Fundy Vault*

"Few shadows from our collective past are as engaging and captivating as a good maritime Victorian murder mystery. In *Found Drowned*, Laurie Glenn Norris weaves a wonderfully mesmerizing tale of compelling characters caught in the darkest of miasmic uncertainties. Drawn into a time and place both warmly familiar yet coldly disturbing, readers will be unable to turn away from this skilfully told tale until reaching its surprising and satisfying finish."
–**Steven Laffoley**, author of *The Halifax Poor House Fire* and *The Blue Tattoo*

"Fortune is a strumpet. Laurie Glenn Norris leads us along a murky path strewn with bad luck, or good, depending on the angle of approach. In this nineteenth-century murder mystery Glenn Norris skilfully entangles our assumptions with the facts and keeps us guessing until the last page. This is an engaging read full of wit and intelligence."
–**Linda Little**, award-winning author of *Scotch River* and *Grist*

To Maureen, my only sister

Vagrant Press is an imprint of
Nimbus Publishing Limited
3660 Strawberry Hill St, Halifax, NS, B3K 5A9
(902) 455-4286 nimbus.ca

Printed and bound in Canada
NB1359

Editor: Kate Kennedy
Editor for the Press: Whitney Moran
Cover and interior design: Heather Bryan

This story is a work of fiction. Names, characters, incidents, and places, including organizations and institutions, either are the product of the author's imagination or are used fictitiously.

Library and Archives Canada Cataloguing in Publication

Title: Found drowned / Laurie Glenn Norris.
Names: Glenn Norris, Laurie, 1957- author.
Identifiers: Canadiana (print) 20189068590 | Canadiana (ebook) 20189068604 | ISBN 9781771087506 (softcover) | ISBN 9781771087513 (HTML)
Classification: LCC PS8613.L458 F68 2019 | DDC C813/.6—dc23

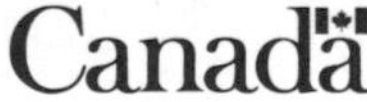

Nimbus Publishing acknowledges the financial support for its publishing activities from the Government of Canada, the Canada Council for the Arts, and from the Province of Nova Scotia. We are pleased to work in partnership with the Province of Nova Scotia to develop and promote our creative industries for the benefit of all Nova Scotians.

"Alas, then, she is drown'd?"
Hamlet, Act 4 Scene 7

BELL'S POINT

CAPE TRAVERSE, PRINCE EDWARD ISLAND
September 12, 1877

THE BOYS THREW STONES at it as soon as they saw the form in the distance. At first, with the sun in their eyes, they thought it was likely a calf. Once in a while one would stray from its mother, fall over a bank somewhere, and be washed to shore in the tide, its coat stiff with salt.

The seagulls had spied it first, their heads bobbing up and down, mouths open. Some of them had already landed and started to pick. When the stones began to fall around them with hollow thuds, the birds reluctantly scattered.

"See, I told you it wasn't no animal," Tom said as they got closer.

Jimmy ran on ahead of his friend.

"It's a girl," he yelled, dropping to his knees before the entangled figure.

"Jesus, don't get that close, Jim, you don't want to catch nothin' off her. Don't touch her!"

Tom backed away.

Leaning forward, Jimmy extended one chubby fist and lifted a clump of blond hair. A pair of blank, blue eyes stared back at him.

"She's dead as a doornail," Tom yelped, backing up again.

"Let's go git Dadda."

The boys ran across the beach and scrambled up the bank, their bare feet leaving tracks in the shiny red mud, while the screeching gulls descended once again.

The life I carried was like a tiny fish
encased in its own personal sea.

MERIGOMISH

NOVA SCOTIA
August 1876

MARY WATCHED RACHEL SCRUB Grandma Hennessey's kitchen floor. Rachel Connelly had been with the family for six months now, one of two housemaids the Hennesseys employed, along with Susan the cook.

"She's practical and clean," Helen Hennessey told her husband Patrick after she hired the girl.

Mary and her mother, Ann, with Little Helen, age four, and Harry, one and a half—"the two little ones," as Ann called them—were visiting Merigomish from Rockley for a fortnight. It was the first trip back home for Ann since she was a bride. The Harney children had never met their grandparents or Aunt Beatrice. Mary, almost seventeen, was especially shy around them even though she adored her aunt as soon as she laid eyes on her. The kitchen became one of Mary's favourite places to linger, however, and Rachel her confidant.

"Are you going to get married some day, Rachel?" she asked.

"I sure hope so. I don't wanna be scrubbing somebody else's floors all my life. Even though Mr. and Mrs. Hennessey are good to me," she hastened to add. "I know I'm some lucky to work here."

Rachel stopped to tidy the wisps of curly red hair that kept creeping out from under her dust cap. She was a short, big-boned girl with a creamy complexion, freckles on her nose, and strong forearms. Whenever she leaned across the top of the metal bucket to wet the floor, her pendulous breasts nearly filled its circumference.

There were lots of young men around who admired Rachel Connelly; she was not worried about ending up an old maid.

"I don't want to," Mary proclaimed with a defiant shake of her head.

"Every girl wants to be married."

"I don't."

"How come?"

Mary shrugged. "I just don't. I want to be by myself."

Rachel smiled. "People will make fun of you for being an old maid. And you'll have to live with your mother and father."

"No, I won't."

"And babies, don't you want to have your own babies?" Rachel continued. "I'm going to have three boys and then three girls. Boys should always be the oldest so that they can help their father out on the farm as soon as they can."

"I'd like to have babies but not a husband."

"It doesn't work that way, Mary." Rachel shook her head and whispered: "To get the babies, you need a husband or you'd be ruined. That's what happened to my cousin Agnes, she...no, never mind."

"Tell me?" Mary leaned forward in her chair.

"No, your grandmother would show me the door if I talked to you about such things." Rachel bent over the wash bucket once again.

"Do you ever feel all wrong?" Mary asked.

"What do you mean?"

"Do you ever feel like no matter what you do or say, that you're in the wrong, that other people are always right and you're always wrong, about everything? I can't seem to do anything right."

"Well, at home I'm the oldest and the only girl. So I'm usually right. Pa is always telling my brothers to mind what I say."

"I'm always the wrong one in my house," Mary told her.

"Who says?"

"Daddy and Grandma Harney. And Mumma agrees with them."

"I find that hard to believe." Rachel snorted.

"It's true. Grandma Harney says it all the time and Mumma doesn't say any different."

Tears welled up in Mary's eyes.

"Lots of women don't like to disagree with their husbands to their face and if you don't mind my saying so, your ma's a bit on the timid side, so I can't image her talking back to Mr. Harney at all, not that she should."

Rachel took a handkerchief out of her apron pocket and handed it to Mary, who buried her face in the clean cotton.

"Your ma has two babies to look after besides your father. You're getting older now and it's your place to help her all you can."

"I know," sighed Mary.

She wiped her face, blew her nose, and presented Rachel with the crumpled cloth.

"Look," said Rachel, cramming the handkerchief back into her apron pocket, "I'm just about done here. Wait till I scrub us out the door and then you can come and watch me bring in the clothes. It's been a good drying day and I'm sure they're about ready to come in. Then I'll have to help Susan get supper on."

"All right."

"I just love a nice clean floor," Rachel said, smiling. "Ma always told me that clean floors make a house feel warmer in the winter and cooler in the summer."

You know," she continued, "I lost my ma almost six years ago. She was so sick and she's better off now but life's not the same without her. Keep that in mind. You're lucky to still have your mother."

Mary nodded and wiped her eyes with the sleeve of her dress.

After Rachel wrung out the mop and threw the dirty water into the long grass at the side of the house, she and Mary walked towards the clothesline.

THE HENNESSEYS' HOUSE SAT CLOSE to the main road. Its yellow paint was new, just put on last year, and pink and white geraniums sat in clay pots in each of its five front windows, shown to advantage against the white shutters and crisp curtains. The three large hay barns, cow shed, stable, and numerous outbuildings sprouted up behind the house. It had taken Helen Hennessey twenty-five years, but finally the backyard was a tangle of shrubs and flowers surrounding whitewashed benches, reflecting globes in the cutting garden, and numerous feeders for blue jays, mourning doves, and hummingbirds.

When Mary wasn't spending time with Rachel, she was following her Aunt Beatrice and Grandma Hennessey around the house. Beatrice promised to make Mary and Little Helen each a new dress. She had started Mary's already from a pattern for a day dress in *Godey's Ladies Book*. Beatrice had made the same one for herself only three months before in navy blue. Mary's dress was to be lime green with black collar and cuffs and green buttons down the front. It would be her first ever grown-up dress and a change from the two blue frocks and aprons—one for school and the other to do her chores—that she wore all the time. She did have a cotton shirtwaist and a plaid skirt that she wore, summer and winter, to church, but they were quite worn. Now she would wear them for everyday and have something new for Sunday that would make the eyes of those LeFurgey girls bug out even more than usual. It was going to have a bustle in the back, Mary's first bustle, and a new lace-bordered petticoat and it would be long enough to skim over the tops of her boots, just like a proper young lady. She couldn't wait to wear it.

Like Mary, Ann had two dresses that she wore over and over. When she complimented Beatrice on her new pink walking suit, Grandpa Hennessey piped up, "You could have had clothes like that today too if you'd been smart."

Grandma Hennessey shushed him and he went back to reading the *Eastern Chronicle*. Later that day, Beatrice had gone through her things and given Ann two morning dresses and a walking suit, all in pretty jewel colours. Most of Ann's clothes were black and white.

"She looks like a damn Quaker," Grandpa snorted.

Aunt Beatrice was thirty-five years old and an old maid but she didn't seem to mind a bit. In fact, she said she preferred it that way.

"Life is short. I want to do all the things I can now. Looking after and catering to a man would only get in the way," she told Mary, who had asked her about it one day when her aunt was fitting the dress sleeves.

"I feel the same way, Auntie," Mary declared. "And I don't like men," she added.

"There's nothing wrong with men. I just don't want to live with one. Papa's more than Mother and I can handle as it is."

She looked over at her sister, who was at the kitchen window washing Harry's face for the fourth time that morning.

"But one thing I do regret is not having a child. I could eat the three of you up, you're all so sweet."

"Don't let them fool you, Bea. They're not as nice as they look." Ann grinned, drying Harry's face and tapping his backside as he ran away giggling.

"Sure they are," Beatrice said, bending down, touching her cheek to Mary's, and enveloping her niece in the scent of lavender. "Now stand straight, Mary, and let me try to fix this sleeve."

"This is too much, Bea," Ann said. "And that dress is too old for Mary."

"Oh pooh, Annie. You've kept Mary in children's clothes far too long. She's a young woman now and needs some nice things to call her own."

"I don't want her growing up too fast," Ann replied.

"Now go take that off again, sweetie, and I'll just stitch it up on the machine." Beatrice pinched her niece's cheek. "Oh, wait a moment. I want you to step on this piece of paper, so I can trace around your feet."

"Why?"

"Just for fun, to compare the size of your feet with mine. Good, now off you go."

Mary thought that Beatrice had the most interesting things. A Singer sewing machine that always smelled of the oil she doused it with, cardboard slides of side-by-side photographs that became one picture when you looked at them through a fancy viewer, and all the latest books and magazines. Along with *Godey's* she had both the *Canadian Illustrated News* and the *London Illustrated News* delivered by mail twice a month. And at the moment she was reading a new book just purchased from a Halifax bookstore. It was a collection of short stories entitled *Doctor Ox,* written by a man called Jules Verne. Best of all, she'd been reading *The Woman in White*, by Wilkie Collins, aloud in the library every evening once Little Helen and Harry were put to bed. Grandpa called it trash but Mary, Ann, and Helen hung on every word.

"That Sir Percival is up to no good, I just know it," Helen said looking up from her rug-hooking. "Why did poor Laura ever marry such a scoundrel?"

"Why indeed," Grandpa said, raising his eyebrows at Ann.

Grandma spoke softly, barely above a whisper, but Grandpa, Beatrice, and Ann minded her every word. She and Grandpa seemed to know what the other was thinking and sometimes even said the same things at the same time.

Grandma and Beatrice visited places like San Francisco and Boston and London, England, and sent Ann, Mary, and the little ones beautiful postcards, photographs, and gifts, wherever they went. But they had never been to Ann's home in Rockley.

Early in the morning on the day that the Harneys were to return home, Beatrice crept into Mary's and Little Helen's bedroom. The girls were still asleep and she put two brown paper bundles at the bottom of their bed. A half hour later the family was gathered around the breakfast table when they heard two squeals and then laughter. Shortly, there was clomping on the stairs and landing and Mary and Little Helen burst into the kitchen, still in their night dresses, with new boots on their feet.

"It's just like Christmas." Mary laughed.

"Like Quismis," Little Helen echoed.

The girls danced around the table holding hands and looking down at their feet. Little Helen's boots were shiny black leather with gold buttons up the side. Mary's were a white and black gingham pattern with black buttons and soles.

"Bea, this is too much," Ann said.

"Auntie! We knew it was you."

The two girls fell upon Beatrice, Little Helen hugging a knee while Mary wrapped her arms around her aunt's neck.

"What did Harry get?" Mary asked.

"Look on the sideboard."

There was a blue outfit with short pants, a coat, and a round-billed cap for the toddler.

"Oh sweet," said Mary.

"Ohhhhh swee," said Little Helen.

"Mary desperately needed a new pair of boots, boots that a young lady would wear, and I wanted to make sure that everyone had a goodbye gift." Beatrice smiled and lifted Little Helen up onto her knee.

"I'm sad to be going away," said Mary. "I wish we could stay longer."

"Yes, I know, dear. We all wish you could," said Helen touching her cheek.

"Could I?" Mary asked, looking shyly from her mother to her grandmother.

"No," Ann told her, "it's about time we all went home. You're certainly not staying behind. School starts soon and you have to be home for that."

Rachel was at the stove fetching the teapot. When her eyes met Mary's, she shrugged her shoulders.

"You can come again for a visit next year, Mary," said Aunt Beatrice.

"Me too, me too." Little Helen was jumping up and down.

"Yes, you too, sweetheart. You'll be a big girl of five by then," her aunt said.

"We'll see," said Ann. "Mary is needed a lot around the house."

"Travel, even just within one's own province, is the best education one can possibly get," replied Beatrice.

Patrick looked at his watch.

"Well, you two, sit down for breakfast now. We have to be at the station at eleven. I'm going out to see how the haying is coming along. I'll be back at half past ten to fetch you."

He got up, grabbed his hat, and left. Rachel rushed Mary's and Little Helen's pancakes to the kitchen table.

By eleven o'clock they were all standing on the platform of the train station. Patrick had paid for their train tickets from River Philip to West Merigomish return and for a buggy to take them to River Philip from Rockley return. This trip was the first time that Mary had been on a train. She found it exciting to watch the houses and trees and people as the train hurried along the track. She felt all grown up holding her ticket in her hand.

Aunt Beatrice hugged her tightly.

"Good luck, sweetie. Don't forget to write and let me know how your trip went. And here's another going-away present for you."

Her aunt passed her a brown paper–wrapped parcel. Mary could tell right away it was a book.

"Is it *The Woman in White*?" Mary whispered, and held it to her chest.

"Your very own copy," Aunt Beatrice whispered back, "plus another one I think you'll like."

Everyone except Patrick and Harry was crying when the Harneys boarded the train and took their seats. Watching out the window, however, Mary was sure she saw the big man run his right sleeve across his eyes. Everyone waved as the train pulled away from the station. Mary stood and looked out the window until Aunt Beatrice's walking suit was just a tiny pink dot, then she turned and dropped herself down onto the hard leather seat.

Ann sighed. "We'll be in Pugwash by suppertime."

Mary unwrapped her books. There was *The Woman in White*, marked at the place where Beatrice had stopped reading. The other book, *The Moonstone,* was written by the same author. Mary settled down to read. From time to time she looked out the window at the passing countryside. At noon they had the cold meats, fresh, soft rolls, and lemonade from the lunch basket that Susan had packed for them.

Later in the afternoon Mary fell asleep to the sound of her mother singing softly to the children. She awoke with a start when the conductor came striding down the aisle.

"River Philip next stop, all passengers for River Philip, next stop," he said. The train's whistle blew. Mary put her hands over her ears and looked out the window; they were coming into the station, passing the shacks scattered along the side of the tracks. A woman in front of one of the rundown buildings was bringing her wash in while rain started to spatter on the window.

"Good thing we have a ride waiting for us," Ann said. "Mary, wake up Little Helen and put her coat on, we'll be getting off soon."

The tiny River Philip train station was located at the edge of the village. By the time they walked out of the building, it was raining hard. Mary put her books inside her coat so they wouldn't get wet. People were running to escape the deluge. Some carried umbrellas, others held newspapers over their heads.

"Mary, stay under the awning or you'll get soaked," Ann warned. She scanned up and down the street.

"We can't stay out here for too long in the wet. We'll have to go back into the station to wait if he's late."

"There he is, Mumma, there's Mr. LeFurgey."

Mary waved at the large surrey coming down Main Street.

"Thank God," Ann said, shifting Harry from one hip to another. "Wait here, girls, he sees us. Let him stop and get the bags before you walk out. I don't want you to get run over by those horses."

"Mumma always thinks something bad is going to happen," Mary whispered to Little Helen and gripped her hand tightly. The child looked up with a frown and nodded.

"Whoa there," Fred LeFurgey told his horses, and the surrey came to a stop in front of the platform.

"Hello, Ann, hope you and the kids had a good trip. It was sunny here until about a half-hour ago and then it all clouded over."

"Yes, thank you, Fred," Ann replied. "It's good to be back safe and sound."

Fred jumped from the front seat and landed, with a thud, on the ground before Ann. He swept his cap off his head and bowed low in front of her. His handsome, grinning face was deeply tanned.

Besides running the farm with his parents, Fred had a delivery and cab service, taking people and packages from one place to another between Springhill and Pugwash. Once he was hired to go clear to Amherst. He was proud of his four-seat surrey and kept its red leather top and tan seats in immaculate condition. The iron-rimmed wheels and hand-operated brake were well oiled. Springs to reduce bumps ran the length of the vehicle's undercarriage.

In the past, when she had met him on the road, smiling and waving, or in Bailey's store, that time before Christmas, when he bought her a whole bag of ribbon candy, Mary pretended that Fred LeFurgey was her father, driving her to school every day in his fancy rig, the envy of all his LeFurgey nieces who regularly looked down their considerable noses at her. Seeing him up close now made her blush at the thought. Her mother's cheeks seemed to be a little pinker than usual too.

"Just let me get your bags and we'll be off."

His boots thudded across the wooden platform as he walked over to the luggage cart.

"Which ones are yours, Ann?"

"Those three on the top."

"Light as a feather," Fred said, grabbing the bags and lifting them off the cart. He walked over and placed them on the floor of the surrey.

"Up you go now, missy," he said, swinging Mary into the surrey's back seat. "The young people I carry like to sit in the very back." He winked.

"And you too," he added, lifting Little Helen.

"You're strong," she cooed.

Fred laughed and turned to Ann. Without speaking, he took Harry from her arms and handed her up into the front seat, then deposited the toddler into her lap. There were two empty seats separating him, Ann, and Harry from the girls. He settled in beside Ann, lifted the reins, and made a clicking noise with his tongue.

The main road to Rockley was lined with weathered farm houses, barns, and outbuildings. It was haying season and the fields were dotted with mounds of hay waiting to be taken in for the winter. The road ran parallel to the River Philip with fishing sheds of different sizes and in various states of repair scattered along the water's edge, only their roofs visible from the main road. Each shack, with a colourful punt tied up outside, contained ropes, wires, and nets used to trap trout, salmon, and gaspereau. Many of the sheds and punts were decades old and had been passed down through generations. Will Harney, Mary's father, had taken over the shed belonging to his uncle, John Dempsey. It was located just at the elbow of the river's widest bend, almost directly across the road from the lane leading to the Dempsey house where Mary and her family lived.

The rain was falling straight down but just a bit of drizzle touched Mary's cheeks. She liked the click, click of the water on the leather roof. She and Little Helen snuggled together under the blanket she'd found on the back seat. She felt warm and safe while watching the houses and fields go by and listening for snatches of words from the front seat that came to her on the wind.

He has such a nice voice, Mary thought.

This ride was a real treat since Ann and the girls usually had to walk wherever they went or take the old wagon which smelled of manure and mouldy hay.

Too soon for Mary, they reached the signpost for Rockley and she could see the red chimney and brown roof of their house. As the surrey got closer, she began to feel funny in the pit of her stomach. One time her mother had told her it was because butterflies were fluttering around inside. Mary's palms under the blanket started to sweat. She did not want to go into that house.

We'll have a life together, he said.

BELL'S POINT

Cape Traverse, Prince Edward Island
September 12, 1877

GILBERT BELL WAS ABOUT to leave the barnyard and make his way back to the upper field when he saw Sarah McPherson coming down the lane towards the house. She had walked the mile that separated her home from the Bells, across Gilbert's fields, picking cranberries as she came, to present to his wife, Catherine. As Sarah stopped to catch her breath, some of the fruit fell from the full pail and rolled around on the ground. She was not a small woman and the day was warm and sunny.

"Clothesline broke agin," she said, shaking her head. "If it had been fixed right the first time 'round that wouldn't have happened."

"Well, that was a devil of a storm we had last night, Sarah. You're lucky you've got any line left. Lucky it didn't blow clear into Charlottetown."

"True enough." She nodded. "The windows shook in their frames something terrible all night. It's a wonder we got any glass left in them at all. Neill told me to tell you that he'll meet you back up there as soon he's finished with my line."

"Thanks, Sarah." He grinned. "And just to let you know, I'll only charge you half price for those berries since you picked them yourself."

"Ha," she said, waddling to the porch door.

Gilbert couldn't remember the last time it poured rain as it had last night. It started all at once, right after supper, and lasted until dawn. Catherine didn't even have to call Jimmy, their youngest son, in from playing. He'd run through the kitchen door, his eyes big, exclaiming that the wind was blowing so hard it kept pushing him back as he tried to make it to the house. It almost took the porch door off the hinges before he got it shut.

Branches blew apples off the trees in the orchard. Gilbert had sent Eddie and Avard, his nineteen-year-old twins, out early that morning to collect the dead wood and assess the damage. They said that all kinds of apples had been swept away in the storm. That was not good for the winter store. It was going to take the boys the rest of the day to clean up the mess back there and to collect the downed apples. At least the horses could eat them.

Sam Thompson, the blacksmith, had arrived after breakfast with the new horseshoes Gilbert had ordered, and said that a lot of fishing boats had either broken loose from the Cape Traverse wharf or, while still tied, smashed up against it. The storm had also damaged some of the old fencing that Gilbert and Neill shared in the upper field and they had been repairing it throughout the morning.

Gilbert stopped short and shook his head in frustration. He had forgotten the maul he needed this afternoon for pounding the stakes firmly into the ground. The one Neill had brought along to do the job just wasn't sturdy enough. He retraced his steps back down the hill and into the tool shed. Gilbert was a tall man and had to stoop to get inside the door. Stepping out again with the maul over his shoulder, he heard shouting. Jimmy, with his friend Tom McPherson, Neill's and Sarah's youngest, were heading down the lane, likely on their way to Bell's Point to look around. A storm always churned up stuff in the water and washed it up on the beach. Stuff interesting to seven-year-old boys. Jimmy already had five wooden boxes neatly arranged under his bed and filled with shells, rocks, pieces of glass, and rope that he had scavenged.

He'll outgrow that soon enough, just like the twins did, Gilbert thought to himself. No harm in it, I guess, just something to make his mother yell when she has to keep fishing things out of his pockets before she can wash his overalls.

About all Jimmy ever found was trash that had been thrown into the Northumberland Strait from along the western shore of PE Island, or from Cape Tormentine in New Brunswick, or even further north.

"Quickest way to get rid of what you don't want," Gilbert mused aloud.

Most of it was worthless, but every once in a while someone would walk into Muttart's store trying to sell something or other that had washed up on the beach. Mainly, though, it was just kids who went looking for so-called treasure.

When Gilbert got back to the upper field where his land adjoined that of the McPhersons, Neill was already there.

"Took me no time to fix the old woman's line," his friend said, grinning. "She'll be disappointed, give her one less thing to go on about tonight."

The men were at the north boundary line that separated the two properties. Gilbert's great-grandfather Sherman Bell had started to clear the land shortly after arriving from upstate New York in the late 1700s. He died shortly afterwards, however, from blood poisoning, brought on from stabbing himself in the foot with a pitchfork while making a point during an argument. His wife had always said his temper would get the best of him. Forty acres of the original hundred-acre-plot had been sold off to Neill's great-grandfather and the two families had been friends ever since.

Gilbert and Neill worked together for about an hour, speaking only to give each other directions. The fence had been repaired in the spring but was getting old and fragile, and last night's wind had damaged it. Gilbert hoped to make do for another year before replacing it. Before pig butchering commenced, he wanted the fence fixed or he'd have a worse mess on his hands come spring.

The only sounds that registered for the men, besides the scrape of the shovel on rock and the thud of the post into the ground, was the humming of bees as they floated from flower to flower in the fields. At about three o'clock they stopped for a rest. Neill rubbed the sweat from his large face and receding blond hairline with a spotted blue handkerchief.

"Hot work. I thought that the storm would have cleared the air, but it's still pretty muggy," he said.

Gilbert turned to look down the pasture. The Holsteins were gathered for shade under the one large tree left in the field. There wasn't a cloud in the sky.

Neill leaned his shovel against a post and took makings out of his back pocket. "Want one?" he asked Gilbert.

"No, not right now, thanks." Gilbert stooped to pick up the water jug.

Neill was taking the first drag off his cigarette when a shout reached them from below. The men turned to see their sons running towards them, both yelling something that the distance held back from them.

"Now what?" Gilbert frowned.

They waited in silence as the boys ran up to them.

Jimmy flew into his father's legs head first. "Dadda, Dadda, come quick."

"Jesus, what's goin' on?" Gilbert asked, holding the boy out at arm's length.

Jimmy was trying to catch his breath as Tom yelled at his father, "You should see, you should see!"

He bent over, gulping for air with his hands on his knees.

"Take it easy, Tom," Neill warned.

Jimmy finally got his breath. "Dadda, come quick, there's a girl on the beach." He pulled on Gilbert's arm.

"She's deader than a doornail," Tom blurted out between gulps of air.

"Dadda, come quick, we've got to help her," Jimmy cried. "The seagulls will get her."

"All right, the two of you calm down and tell me what's going on," Gilbert said, passing the water bottle to Jimmy. "Have a drink first."

"This isn't another one of your stories?" Neill asked Tom.

"No, Pa, I swear...I swear it's true," Tom said, getting his wind back. "There's a girl on the beach, she's dead and all tangled up in the seaweed. We didn't touch her."

Tom spun around and looked at Jimmy.

"We didn't touch her," he repeated. "And we ran to get you and Mr. Bell right away."

"You better be telling the truth." Neill glared at Tom. "Don't be taking us away from what we're doin' here."

"It's not a lie, Mr. McPherson," Jimmy piped up. "She's really there."

"We'd better go down and have a look," Neill said, stamping out his smoke with his boot.

"All right then, you boys run ahead and find the twins. Tell them to hitch up Ned to the express wagon and to bring some of those old horse blankets out of the barn. Neill and I will be along right after you. You wait right there with them and we'll all go down to the beach at the same time."

The youngsters took off on the run. Neill and Gilbert gathered up their tools and water jugs and started after them.

"Do you suppose they're telling the truth?" Neill asked.

"They'd better be or I'll tan both their hides," Gilbert said. "But something's got them spooked, that's for sure. Everything washes up on the beach sooner or later. Remember me and Frankie found that man down there when we was kids? He had all his clothes still on, just missing a boot. And they never did find out who he was."

Soon they were in the field just above Gilbert's house and could see Avard leading Ned, the chestnut horse, out into the barnyard. Catherine and Eddie, holding the bridle, were standing beside the blue express wagon and Jimmy and Tom were running in circles around it.

"Those two are straining at the bit," Neill observed, "worse than old Ned."

"Eddie, you and Av run ahead and see what all the fuss is about, I'll finish the harnessing," Gilbert yelled when he got closer to the yard. "Go down to the point and wait for us there."

The boys ran out of the barnyard.

"Us too?" asked Jimmy.

"No, you stay here," Catherine said, grabbing her son by the shoulders.

"But Ma, we found her, it's not fair." Jimmy struggled to get away.

"You stay with your mother," Gilbert said firmly. "We don't need a bunch of kids running around down there."

"But we have to show you where she is," Tom protested.

"You can come along," Neill said, "but you're not going near it, whatever it is."

Catherine grabbed Jimmy by the arm and started to walk towards the house. He kept looking back and yelling, "No fair."

"Do like your mother says," Gilbert ordered.

"You come in the house with me." Catherine led him away.

Gilbert finished harnessing the horse and jumped on the wagon seat with Neill and Tom.

"Wait till you see, Pa, wait till you see." Tom could scarcely contain his excitement.

"Sit still, you," Neill warned him.

It took twenty minutes for the wagon to make its way along the path from the barnyard to the bank overlooking Bell's Point.

The twins were waiting at the edge of the bank.

"Didn't need Tom after all," said Avard, pointing to the seagulls gathered down the beach.

"Run and get them out of there. Put the rocks to 'em," Gilbert commanded.

"You stay in the wagon," Neill said to Tom as he jumped to the ground.

"Aw, Pa."

"Do as I say. No backtalk."

"Yes, sir." The boy crossed his arms and lowered his head in resignation.

In minutes, Avard and Eddie had chased the gulls away and stood over the spot.

"Yeah, it's a girl," Eddie shouted. "And you smell her before you see her."

The sun from the cloudless sky cast shimmering light on the table top-smooth water. The crashing waves that, the night before, had tossed large pieces of driftwood ashore and cast sea spray on windows more than a mile away, were now gone. Seaweed lay like a woman's necklace where it had been deposited along the bottom of the bank. When Gilbert and Neill got to the beach the smell hit them. Neill put his hand over his nose.

"You two stand back," Gilbert barked at his sons.

The men bent over the figure. It reminded Gilbert of a discarded puppet, all loose and disjointed. The girl was lying on her left side, her face to the sky. Her legs were spread wide as if she had been running and then frozen to the spot. Her right arm was stretched out behind. The top joints of three of her fingers were missing. Her left arm was hidden beneath her. A plaid skirt and chemise were wrapped around her waist. She wore a black and white stocking on her right leg; the other limb was bare. She smelled of salt and rot and dead things.

"Av, get me a couple of those blankets from the wagon," Gilbert said softly.

He covered the girl from the waist down with one of the horse blankets. Holding the other blanket in his left hand, he picked up a stick of driftwood with his right and folded the matted blond hair up over the top of her head. Throwing the stick aside he reached down again, his right hand covered by his shirt cuff and, running it over the girl's face, closed her eyelids. There was a large clot of blood on the right side of her face. Hundreds of flies moved through it, some getting stuck and mired down. Bits of flesh around her left eye had been torn away by the gulls and something had nipped at her nose and chin. Bile rose in Gilbert's throat. He stepped back quickly and spread thc second blanket over the first, covering the rest of the body. He turned to Neill, silent beside him.

"Let's get her into the cart and up to the barn. We'll have to send for the sheriff."

They carefully folded the blankets around thc underside of the body as they lifted, not wanting to touch flesh, and then moved slowly up the bank towards the wagon. The girl was small but heavy and they couldn't keep a firm grip on her. One limp arm escaped.

"What are we going to do with her, Pa?" Avard asked.

"We'll have to put her in the barn for the time being," Gilbert said as he and Neill carefully placed their bundle into the back end of the wagon.

"Tom, you run ahead and let Mrs. Bell know we're coming," Neill suggested.

"Yes, sir."

Gilbert turned to the older boys. "And you two run over to Muttart's and get the Captain to wire over for Sheriff Flynn," he instructed. "Tell him that we found a dead body on the beach, and he better get out here and be damn quick about it."

AT SEVEN O'CLOCK THAT EVENING, Doctor Henry Jarvis drove his shiny black phaeton down the lane to the Bells' farm. Men and boys milled about the barnyard or stood with arms crossed, leaning up against wagons and carts. They had already been inside the barn to look at the body but no one knew the girl. Now most of them were smoking and drinking tea from blue and white tin mugs. A few passed a flask back and forth. They looked up expectantly as Jarvis drove into the yard. Some waved their hands while others nodded in acknowledgment.

Jarvis grabbed his satchel from the floor of the vehicle and walked towards the middle of the group. He was a tall, spare man with thinning brown hair and grey side whiskers. He walked with a slight stoop which gave him a defeated look. His hazel eyes, nonetheless, snapped with a quick intelligence. A barrel-chested man walked out of the group and approached him, extending a calloused right hand.

"You the doctor?" the man asked.

Jarvis nodded. "I got a wire from Sheriff Flynn this afternoon about a body being found. I got here as soon I could."

"I'm Gilbert Bell. I expected to see Doc Price from Charlottetown," he said, inclining his head towards the barn.

"No, I'm the coroner for Prince County now."

"So where's Flynn?" Gilbert asked.

"I don't know. I thought he'd be here by now."

"Hasn't been any sign of him yet. Anyway, she's in the barn. Nobody here knows who she is. Must be from away."

"It's a woman then," Jarvis stated.

"A girl more like, not very old."

A balding, chubby man with a monocle stepped forward and extended his hand to Jarvis.

"Doctor, nice to see you again. You'll remember me. Hezekiah Hopkins, the apothecary from North Tryon. You'll likely need me to assist as I did before. You remember I'm sure."

"Yes, I remember. Thank you for the offer but I don't require your services," Jarvis told him, moving away.

The chemist let out an embarrassed cough and retreated back into the throng of waiting men.

Gilbert stepped on his cigarette butt then loped towards the barn to catch up with the doctor. The twins joined them as they reached the far end of the building.

"We put her in here," Gilbert went on. "We don't use it very much, just for storing tools and milk cans. Didn't want her in the way and spookin' the animals. Probably put the cows off their milking as it is. Animals can smell death a mile away."

The body was laid out on a small wooden table and draped with blankets. Jarvis placed his bag on the floor then gently pulled back the covering to look at the girl's face.

"The gulls picked at her a bit," Eddie said.

Avard poked him in the ribs. Gilbert shot them a stern look.

"Yes, I can see that," Jarvis said, holding the blanket up high on his side of the table, shielding the body from the view of the others.

"You know, I haven't had my dinner yet this evening," Jarvis said looking at Eddie. "Maybe Mrs. Bell or one of your sisters could make me a sandwich."

"We ain't got any sisters," Eddie replied, kicking at the barn floor.

"Go and tell your mother to make the doctor here something to eat," Gilbert said, nodding in the direction of the house. Eddie was resolved to stay put. "Go on. And stay there until it's ready." The boy walked out the door, dragging his feet.

Jarvis lowered the blanket, picked up his brown leather bag, and placed it on the table. The metal clasp clicked open and he started to rummage around with both hands. Then he stopped and looked at Avard.

"Just realized that I'd like a nice, hot cup of tea and a few lanterns in here. It's going to be dark soon, I'll need lots of light."

Avard looked at his father.

"You heard him."

"Don't do anything until I get back," said Avard, bolting for the door.

Gilbert shook his head.

"Don't let either of them back in," Jarvis said.

"I won't, they've seen enough for one day. And I'll just step outside myself so you can get to work. I'll bring in the lanterns when Avard gets them."

Gilbert headed for the door.

"Can you read and write?"

Gilbert turned. "Yeah, some, why?"

"Then I'll need you here with me for this."

"What the hell for?" Gilbert backed up towards the door.

"I need you as my clerk to write down what I'm going to tell you. I need to have notes taken while I'm performing the examination. I'm too likely to forget something if I wait until later to write it down. If Sheriff Flynn were here I'd press him into service. But tonight you're my volunteer."

Jarvis took a yellow notepad and a stubby pencil out of his coat pocket and handed them to Gilbert.

"What about Hopkins out there? He knows medicine. Wouldn't he do a better job?"

Jarvis grimaced. "I've dealt with him once before. He'd brag all over the province about what he saw. I don't want him involved. Just write down what I tell you. You don't have to look."

Gilbert nodded and flipped open the notepad to a clean page.

"Write down the date, the time, and where we are right now, your farm, Cape Traverse, PE Island," Jarvis directed.

The doctor removed his black topcoat, folded it, and placed it on a nearby milking stool. He returned to the table, rolling up his shirt sleeves. Tossing the blanket aside with a flourish, he bent over the girl and slowly ran both hands over her scalp, front and back, and along the top and side of her head.

"She has quite a cut over her right eye, doctor."

"I see that."

Jarvis took a pair of scissors from his bag and cut away the matted hair on the right side of the head. He poked an index finger into the hole.

"Looks like she got hit on the head, or hit something when she fell into the water," he said softly.

Jarvis opened her mouth and peered inside. He poked a finger in and moved it about, stretching the face wide.

"She threw up."

He stood upright and looked at Gilbert.

"Her lips, nose, and earlobes are eaten away quite a bit."

"Yeah, it's a damn shame. Like Eddie said, the seagulls got at her."

"I closed her eyes when we found her," Gilbert added. "It seemed the decent thing to do."

"It was."

The doctor reached down and pinched open the left eyelid then the right one.

"Ah huh."

"What?"

"The right pupil is blown," Jarvis said. "Look," he offered, standing back and still holding the lid open.

Gilbert stepped carefully towards the table and peered into the girl's pale face. He had forgotten that he didn't want to see anything. This close, the smell of rot and seaweed was overwhelming.

"Yeah." He swallowed. "What's that mean?"

"It means that she got a good bump on her head at some point before death."

Jarvis let the eyelid drop.

Gilbert suddenly remembered why he was there. "Am I supposed to be writing this all down?" he asked.

"In a few minutes. Good. Now." Jarvis lifted a knife from his satchel and cut through the leather belt. He snipped the bottom of the plaid skirt along its right side seam with the scissors then tore it the rest of the way up with both hands. He lifted the body gently, snatched the garment from underneath, and handed it to Gilbert.

"Put these aside, the sheriff will likely want to see them."

The girl's greenish-white skin became pink in the light of the sunset streaming through the cobwebs of the barn's tiny west window. Jarvis cut, then tore, the right side of her jacket and its underarm along the seam. He slid it off the body, then did the same with the shirt waist and chemise. Gilbert folded the sodden clothes and placed them in a neat pile on the floor.

The door handle rattled.

"Pa, let us in."

Jarvis, pawing through his medical bag, looked up.

Gilbert tuned towards Avard's voice.

"Pa, the door's stuck, it won't open."

"That's because I braced it shut. You two stay put for a while."

"Eddie's got the soup Ma heated up and I've got the tea, they'll get cold."

"Thanks, boys, just keep them out there for me. This won't take long," Jarvis called.

"What about the lanterns, sir?"

The doctor nodded. "Those I do need right now."

Gilbert yelled out the door while patting his shirt pocket. "Go get those two we use for milking, and don't forgot to bring some matches, I'm all out."

"Yeah, okay," said Avard, retreating.

Jarvis lifted a black cloth bundle from the depths of his medical bag. It was tied round and round with a light brown grosgrain ribbon. Studying the body, Jarvis methodically unwound the ribbon then placed the cloth on the table and unrolled it. Six small, ivory-handled blades, each held in place by grosgrain loops attached to the cloth, caught the fading light.

"My scalpels," he said. "While we're waiting for those lamps, here's what I'd like you to write down."

Clearing his throat he began, pronouncing each word slowly and stopping occasionally so Gilbert could catch up.

Outside, Avard and Eddie backed away from the barn and dropped the food and tea bundles on the ground beside the express wagon. Eddie started back to the house while Avard ran to fetch the lanterns. After they were delivered, he walked up to Neill McPherson and Rufus Dobson who were standing in the middle of the barnyard smoking. Rufus had a ring of flattened butts at his feet.

"Best you two wait out here with the rest of us," he told Avard, resting his cigarette-free hand on the boy's shoulder. "I don't like looking at a dead body at the best of times. She reminded me a bit of my sister's girl Ruby but she's working in Cape Breton somewheres now so it's not her. The way that some young girls act today, chasing after men, I'm surprised they don't end up dead more often. Still it's a damn shame. Did your father say how much longer they'd be? Lillian don't like to be at home alone after dark."

"No, Pa didn't say."

In the house, Eddie was answering questions as well.

"What, the doctor didn't even stop to have a bit of tea?" Viola McWilliams, the Bells' nearest neighbour, and the twins' godmother, commented when Eddie reported to his mother that he and Avard had failed to deliver the food. “Can’t say I’d have the stomach for it either.”

Catherine and three women who had escorted their husbands to the Bell farm were seated around the kitchen table.

“Poor little thing.” Sarah McPherson shook her head and sunk her teeth into another cranberry muffin.

“Catherine, how are you going to sleep tonight with that poor soul lying in your barn?” Beulah Hopkins asked, then continued on before Catherine could answer: “I don’t see why Hezekiah couldn’t have been in there with the doctor tonight.” She sniffed. “He’s a professional chemist and we came all this way so he could be of assistance.”

“I think it’s safe to say that the girl’s beyond a dose of physic now,” Sarah observed. Beulah sniffed again.

Catherine shot Eddie a warning glance. He turned his back on the table and bent down to pick up a piece of wood. He shoved it into the stove, then bolted, grinning, for the door.

“SUBJECT IS A YOUNG GIRL, approximately sixteen years old. Five feet, four inches tall, about one hundred pounds. Light brown hair and blue eyes. Head wound over right eye, approximately one inch in diameter and one half inch deep. Pupil of right eye dilated.”

Jarvis walked around the table.

“I’ll take those for a minute,” he said, removing the notebook and pencil from Gilbert’s hands.

He drew a circle under the handwriting, and inside that, a smaller circle which he shaded in with the pencil. He wrote the words “anterior of head” under the circles, then he handed back the notebook and pencil.

“Continuing dictation. Portions of the subject’s fingers, nose, and earlobes were bitten by fish and/or seabirds. Arms and legs scarred from time in the water. No broken bones or fractures.”

He paused again.

“Subject wearing black wool jacket and brown leather belt with a silver buckle, red, white, and black plaid skirt, white shirtwaist and chemise, one black and white striped cotton stocking.”

There was a tentative knock at the door.

Gilbert walked over, jerked the plank away, and opened the door a crack. Avard was there with a lantern in each hand. All heads in the yard turned towards the barn.

"Are they all still here?" Gilbert whispered hoarsely.

"They're waitin' to hear what the doctor says." Avard shrugged.

He handed his father the lanterns and then dug into his shirt pocket for a box of matches.

"Too goddamn nosey, the bunch of 'em," Gilbert said, slamming the door in his son's face.

"Put one of those at the end of the table and the other on that peg over there," Jarvis directed.

Gilbert positioned the lanterns then replaced the plank at the door and sat down on a barrel. The lanterns cast an orange glow over the girl's skin. The pencil needed to be sharpened and Gilbert had forgotten his jackknife in the house. It was warm and humid in the barn.

Jarvis stood over the body and cocked his head to one side. Starting under the ears, he traced his hands down both sides of the body.

"Continuing dictation. Body completely out of rigor. Subject likely dead for between twenty-four hours and a week."

Jarvis passed his hands down her chest, abdomen, and legs, then eyed the scalpels, touching one and then another. Finally he chose, then moved to situate himself over the body. He cut into the flesh along the bottom edge of the right collarbone.

"Now you may want to turn around, and get ready to take some more dictation."

Gilbert sat back down on the barrel, faced away from the table, and waited.

Jarvis worked silently for a few minutes then began speaking again. "Cut H-incision running from...damn," he whispered loudly. There was a long silence before the doctor finished his sentence. "Clavicle to pelvis."

Another silence.

A strong coppery smell filled the room. Gilbert bit down on the end of the pencil. He heard liquid splash onto the floor.

"Large amounts of water present in the subject's lungs. Removed, inspected, and replaced heart and lungs. Great loss of blood."

For a while, Gilbert heard only Jarvis's movement around the table.

"All right, Mr. Bell, I'm finished. You can turn around now. May I see that notepad for a minute?"

Jarvis had covered the girl with the wool blankets and tucked them neatly underneath her. There was blood soaking onto the table and the floor. Gilbert handed Jarvis the pencil and paper. "I didn't know how to spell some of those words you said," Gilbert told him. "I never went all that far in school."

"Not to worry, I'll rewrite the notes but will keep yours as well, just for the record. And I'm sorry about all the blood. Most times a body doesn't bleed a lot. But every once in a while—"

"It looks like you butchered a pig in here," Gilbert blurted out.

"If there's water I'll clean it up."

"Let's get some air first."

Jarvis nodded and wiped his hands, then the scalpels, on the top blanket. He replaced the instruments in the cloth, rolled it up, and wound the faded ribbon around it. After putting the cloth back into the satchel, he ran a hand over the metal clasp, securing it. Carrying his hat, coat, and bag, he headed for the door. Gilbert removed the plank, opened the barn door, and exhaled loudly. Avard and Eddie crowded around him, and everyone waiting behind them butted out their cigarettes.

"Pa, what's the doctor saying? Can we go in now?" Eddie asked, making for the door.

"Nobody goes inside. Stay here, the both of you."

When Jarvis stepped out into the night air behind Gilbert, the eighteen men and boys standing in a circle raised their eyes and lanterns to him expectedly. He tipped his hat then held a blood-smeared left hand out in front of him as if to ward them off.

"I can't say anything until after there's been an inquest and that needs to be done as soon as possible. Now I'd like to have a taste of that soup, if I may."

There were groans and a shaking of heads. Some curses.

"I'm sorry, gentlemen. That's all I can say at the moment."

Eddie ran back to where the food was left on the ground. The group gathered more closely around Jarvis, their faces pale in the lantern light.

"Do ya know what killed her, Doc?" someone asked.

"Yeah, do you know?"

"I have a good idea but can't say right now. Soon though, very soon."

Everyone started to talk at once.

"How are we going to find out who she is?"

"Where's Flynn, anyway?"

"Do you think she could have been done away with?"

"It's a damn shame. What's this world coming to with young girls washing up on the beach?"

"Well, come into the house with us, Doc," Gilbert said. "The wife can give you some hot tea." He raised his voice: "Flynn probably won't show up till morning now. Those of you who want to can come in and have a cup a tea,"

Only Neill and Rufus took Gilbert up on his offer. Bill McWilliams and Hezekiah Hopkins followed them to the house in order to collect their wives. The rest made for their wagons to head home.

"Let us know if you need anything, Gil," someone called.

"Yeah, let us know."

"Will do," Gilbert said and raised his hand, more in dismissal than thanks.

They walked in silence to the house.

"Your mother would have killed me if they all landed in the kitchen this time of night," Gilbert said to Avard as he opened the porch door.

After the other couples said their goodbyes, Catherine sat Jarvis down at the kitchen table, newly spread with a starched white cloth and linen napkins. Gilbert noticed that Catherine had changed into one of her church dresses and covered it with her best apron. He grinned. For a woman, a doctor as company meant that only the best they had was good enough.

"More soup, Doctor Jarvis?"

"No, thank you, Mrs. Bell, I'm full. It's lovely, though."

"More biscuits?"

"Thank you, but I've had three already."

"What kind of pie would you like, blueberry or apple?"

"I did save a little room for the blueberry, if you don't mind."

Catherine went to the pantry and returned with two pieces of pie. She placed one in front of Jarvis and gave the other to her husband.

"Rufus, Neill, what kind can I get the two of you? Sarah, anything else?"

Catherine was serious tonight, Gilbert noted, not joking with Neill as she usually did. A visit from a doctor was one thing, but there was also a dead girl out in the barn. And she would have had a time getting Jimmy to go to bed. Gilbert guessed that his youngest was, at that very moment, upstairs, lying on the floor of his bedroom, looking down the heat register, listening to every word being said.

"Sheriff Flynn must have had other business to attend to," Catherine said over her shoulder as she headed back to the pantry to cut into the apple pie.

"Yeah, we'll likely hear from him in the morning," Gilbert said, grasping a flowered teacup in his huge right hand and feeling like an idiot in front of the other men.

"I'd like to stay the night if it's not inconvenient," Jarvis said. "I need to talk to Sheriff Flynn and don't want to make another trip out here just for that."

The clatter of dishes ceased in the pantry. From where Gilbert sat he could see Catherine lower her head and shake it ever so slightly. Then, tucking a swatch of stray brown hair behind her left ear, she popped back into the kitchen and smiled.

"By all means, Doctor, you can sleep up in the twins' room. One of them can stay down here on the daybed."

"I'd appreciate it, Mrs. Bell, and I apologize for putting you out this way."

"No trouble at all, Doctor."

"Pa, I was wondering if maybe I should sit up with her tonight?" Avard said.

"Sit up with who?"

"The girl, the girl," he said, blushing as everyone turned to look at him.

"Certainly not," Catherine replied.

"Well, people always sit up with a body that's passed away." Avard frowned.

"Yes, but it's a young girl, your own age, and out in a barn," Catherine argued. "It's not decent."

"No, there's no need for that," Gilbert added.

"She's all wrapped up, not laid out nicely as someone would be in your parlour," Jarvis said, smiling at the boy.

"I think it only shows respect." Avard's bottom lip emerged.

Eddie snickered. Avard reddened again and looked at his brother with narrowed eyes.

"You're not doing it and that's that," Gilbert said, "but what I do want the two of you to do right now is to run over to Muttart's and wire Doctor Jarvis's wife that she shouldn't expect him home tonight."

The doctor nodded. "Yes, good point, thanks for reminding me."

Jarvis reached into his coat pocket and brought out the pencil and small notepad. He took a minute to write something on a yellow page, ripped it out, and handed it to Eddie. "Please forward it to Mrs. Dr. Henry Jarvis, St. Eleanor's. And here's a dollar to send it." The doctor handed the boy a crisp bill.

"It won't be that much, be sure to come back with the change," Gilbert directed.

"Keep it for your trouble." Jarvis spoke over their father's words.

"Thank you, sir," Avard said, heading for the door behind Eddie. Then he turned. "Will they still be up?" he asked.

"Muttart is awake until all hours, says his sailing days ruined his being able to sleep much," Gilbert said. "Just bang on the door till somebody comes and opens it. They're used to people coming to the house at all hours to send bad news somewhere."

"Pa, don't forget about the lanterns in the barn," Avard reminded Gilbert before going out the door.

"Watch yourselves and come right back," their mother called after them.

Rufus yelled at them as well. "Just wait a minute, you two, and I'll drive you over there. Thanks for the pie, it's getting late. Lillian will be worried."

"Yes, we've got to go as well," Sarah said, rising from the rocking chair in the corner. "Come on, Neill, morning comes early."

"I don't know what's got into Av," Gilbert said, taking his cup back to the stove for a refill after the others had left. "Imagine sitting up all night with a dead girl in a barn."

"He's always seen it done when somebody around here passes, seen it done since he was a little boy," Catherine said. "It's good of him to think of it, but it's not proper in this case."

She sat down for the first time since the men had come into the house. "What going to happen now?" she asked.

"Well, after Sheriff Flynn gets a look at her and I hold a coroner's inquest, she can be buried," Jarvis told her. "He may want to hold off on that for a few days, in case she can be identified, but it can't be postponed for too long. The body isn't in good shape." He looked at Catherine. "And it will only continue to deteriorate. Flynn will probably also want to have a look at her clothes, what's left of them."

"They're all right there in the barn for him to see," Gilbert said.

"And he may know of some girl who's missing," said Catherine, shaking her head. "I hope he does."

"I'll have to talk to Reverend Silliker about getting a spot in the graveyard just in case no one shows up to claim her," Gilbert said. "I'll drive over tomorrow, after Flynn's here and gone."

"Is there anything we can do to get her ready for burial?" Catherine asked.

"I think it's better just to leave her as is," Jarvis said.

Gilbert nodded. "I don't want any of you going near that body," he said, rising from the table. "Now I'll go get those lanterns. Don't want the barn to burn down on top of everything else."

"Doctor, I'll change Eddie's bed; he can sleep on the daybed there in the corner," Catherine said.

"Thank you, Mrs. Bell."

"Call me Catherine, please."

"And I'm Henry, to the both of you."

"You got any old rags?" Gilbert asked Catherine.

Catherine went over to the sink, opened the cupboard door below it, and reached in. "Will these do?" she asked, handing him the torn pieces of a large cotton towel. "I don't need them back."

"Good, they'll work."

Gilbert headed for the porch.

"I'll come out with you," Jarvis said.

As they walked across the yard, Gilbert diverted his steps to the barn's main entrance.

"Wait a minute," he said.

He stepped inside the door and brought out two galvanized buckets.

"Just need to go to the well."

He handed Jarvis the rags. In a few minutes he was back, water sloshing from the tops of both pails. They made their way to the barn. They could smell the sickening sweetness before they opened the door.

"Smells like spoiled apples," Gilbert said.

"The body's breaking down," Jarvis explained.

Gilbert placed the buckets on the floor and got on his knees.

Jarvis washed the table around the body.

"Now that she's out of the water she'll decompose faster," he said. He hesitated for a moment and then continued. "Gilbert, I'm going to have to rely on you for names of some local men to make up a coroner's jury. We'll need to decide whom to contact tonight and get word to them first thing tomorrow morning. And we'll need to hold the jury here where they can look at the body."

"Sweet Jesus."

"I know it's a lot to ask of you and your family but I'm obliged to impanel a jury. Hopefully it won't take any more than a couple of days."

Outside the barn again, Gilbert put down his bucket and braced the door with a board that had been resting on the side of the building.

"Don't want any animals getting in at her overnight."

He shoved the plank hard up under the handle and shook it.

"Nothing can get in there now."

When Gilbert got back to the kitchen Catherine was coming downstairs with a pile of bedding.

"Where's Henry?" she asked, trying out the doctor's first name.

"He stopped to see a man about a horse." Gilbert winked at her.

"For God's sake, if I must say it, Gilbert, don't be vulgar."

"All right, he's in the outhouse." He grinned.

Catherine put the pillows and blankets down on the chair by the stove and pulled the daybed out from the wall.

"The boys should be back soon," Gilbert said, walking into the porch and looking out the window.

Catherine sighed. "Gil, there's some mother out there tonight worried to death about her daughter."

"Maybe."

"The poor soul doesn't even know her child is dead."

"Don't think about that," Gilbert said. "There's nothing we can do about it."

The porch door opened.

"Getting chilly out there now," Jarvis said, taking off his boots.

"I heard your boys coming down the lane. It was good of them to go and send that telegram so late."

"Henry, are you sure there isn't something we can do for that poor child? Clean her up a bit, to get her ready to be buried?"

"Catherine." Jarvis sat down at the table again, reached for the salt shaker, and moved it from hand to hand as he spoke. "In order to find out what happened, I had to examine her. It's not something a lady should see."

"Oh."

"You can give her a nice funeral and decent burial if her family doesn't come forward. That's the most anyone can do for her now."

"Yes, that we can do. I'll make sure of it." Catherine looked at Gilbert.

"I said I was going to see Silliker tomorrow," he reminded her.

"And I've just told Gilbert that we need to hold the coroner's inquest here. That will take a couple of days, at the very most, I hope. That's a big thing you can do for her."

"He and twelve men are going to take over the barn." Gilbert shook his head.

"They won't be staying here, of course. But they will be here likely most of tomorrow and the day after if necessary. You will be paid for all of the meals you provide us and for the use of your premises. I apologize for such short notice."

Catherine turned, wide-eyed, to Gilbert, who shrugged.

"I'd better get upstairs to bed," she said. "Lots of baking to get to in the morning. Gilbert, show Henry to the boys' room, please. Goodnight now."

She walked into the hallway and up the stairs, her right hand massaging her temples.

Jarvis took the notepad and pencil out of his coat pocket again.

"All right, let's sit here for a few minutes and compile a list of names for the jury. You, Neill, and the two little boys will all have to testify."

At that moment Avard and Eddie came through the porch door.

"Lock that up for the night," Gilbert commanded.

Eddie reached up and drew the bolt into the slot.

"Now, have a seat at the table, the both of you," Gilbert ordered, "and help us come up with some names."

AN HOUR LATER JARVIS WAS finishing his transcription of Gilbert's notes, sitting in the boys' bedroom at a wooden table below a window that looked out over the Northumberland Strait. It was Eddie and not Avard who had come up the stairs after him, explaining that his brother had decided he wanted to sleep in the kitchen. Eddie was snoring softly almost as soon as his head hit the pillow.

Jarvis put down his pen and rubbed his eyes. It had been a long day. He wished he'd been able to make it home. Lucy and he had quarrelled again this morning, and he wanted to make it up to her. He probably should have sent that telegram himself.

It would be a few days before he was home. He'd stop off in Summerside and pick her up a little something. He had learned long ago that the way back into his wife's good graces was through the opening of his pocketbook.

Jarvis looked down at his notes. He hesitated for a moment and then wrote along the top of the next clean page:

Subject was approximately four months pregnant. Fetus deceased but intact.

Jarvis turned down the lamp and crawled into bed. The night was still and through the open window he could hear waves lapping on the beach. He thought about the body out in the barn.

His Elizabeth would be about the same age, if she had lived. If Frances had lived. Jarvis did not think about his first wife now as often as he used to. It was eighteen years ago, three weeks after giving birth. First her and then the baby. Frances had never been strong and she had lost a lot of blood. He should have brought in another doctor to look after them. He was too close to it all. Too close and too stubborn. He would not eat or sleep, and had hovered over them. His whole world had been in that narrow bed and he had lost it.

His parents had never wanted him to marry Frances Walker. They knew of her only through the letters he sent home from Edinburgh, during his medical training. But they disapproved of her background. "Beneath you," was how his mother, Anna, the wife of Prince Edward Island's Chief Justice Edward Jarvis, had phrased it. So they wed before sailing to Canada, just to be sure that his mother, who usually got her way, could not come between them. Then, two years after Frances's death, Henry married the young woman that Anna Jarvis had in mind for him all along, Lucy Harding, the daughter of an old family friend, a judge, from Gagetown, New Brunswick.

Frances's and Elizabeth's absence were always brought back to him keenly whenever he was faced with the death of a baby or a young woman. Tonight he thought about how he would feel if it had been his daughter who washed up some place where no one knew her, examined, speculated upon, and buried by and among strangers.

Jarvis sat up in bed and threw aside the covers. Moonlight streaked across the wooden floor. Using it as his guide, he felt his way back to the desk. He carefully reached for the lamp and turned its flame up slightly. Reopening the book, he turned to the page he had last written upon and slowly, while watching the sleeping boy, tore it from its bindings.

"THAT MUST BE FLYNN NOW," Gilbert observed as he rose from the table and looked out the porch window.

"Yeah, that's him. Likely want some breakfast, even though he's probably stuffed his face once already today."

Sheriff Darrell Flynn had to stoop slightly coming into the kitchen from the porch.

"Morning, Darrell. How's Beth?"

"The little woman's just fine, thanks." Flynn smiled and nodded at Dr. Jarvis, who rose from the table.

"Nice to see you again, Sheriff."

"Likewise." Flynn shook the doctor's offered hand enthusiastically.

"Darrell, can I offer you some breakfast?" Catherine asked, tapping a chair back with her fingernails. "I've got some toast and tea to keep you going until dinnertime." She headed for the pantry.

"That would hit the spot," Flynn replied and sat down.

"I couldn't make it yesterday afternoon when I first got your wire," he said. "I was just about to leave for here when some kids came flying in yelling about a fire up by the old creamery. There are a couple of fire bugs I've been trying to get my hands on for a while. They've been setting fires all over Summerside for the last three months. The little nose wipes claim they're doing the town a favour, getting rid of old buildings. I'd love to get my hands on them."

"Do you know who's doing it?" Gilbert asked.

"I've got a pretty good idea and heard lots of rumours, but I got to catch them at it. So tell me what happened yesterday. I know that there was a body found and thought I could wait till today. It wasn't going to get any deader, I figured."

Catherine returned from the pantry. She placed a jar of blueberry jam on the table and carried a wire toaster containing two thick slices of bread to the stove. Taking off one of the stove lids, she laid the toaster over the open flame. When the bread was browned evenly on both sides she put it on a plate in front of Flynn and poured him a cup of tea. He bobbed his head in thanks and reached for the last piece of ham on a serving plate in the middle of the table.

"It was about three o'clock yesterday afternoon," Gilbert began. "My young fella Jimmy and Neill McPherson's boy Tom found her on the beach."

By the time Gilbert finished his story, Flynn was wiping his face with one end of the tablecloth. Catherine's mouth was a straight line of disapproval as she leaned against the oven door, arms folded.

"Here's the boys now," Gilbert said, turning away from his wife to keep from laughing.

Avard and Eddie had finished the morning milking and each was bringing two full pails in for their mother to separate and churn. They placed the buckets in the far corner of the porch and covered them with pieces of cheesecloth.

"Boy, you two have grown since the last time I saw you." Flynn smiled and rose from the table. "All right, Gil, we'd better go out and have a look. Thanks for the lunch, Catherine."

"Cath, see that Jimmy gets out of bed pretty soon so Darrell can have a word with him." Gilbert reached for his hat and led the men outside. The twins trailed behind.

"So, Doc, what do you make of all this?" Flynn asked on the way to the barn.

"I believe that the girl drowned," Jarvis said softly so the boys couldn't hear. "Her lungs were full of liquid, which means she was alive when she first got into the water. Let's keep that just to ourselves for now. The official word will have to wait until the coroner's jury makes its determination."

"Know who she is?"

"No."

"So what do we have here?" Flynn asked no one in particular as they walked through the barn door.

"I'll unwrap her," Jarvis said, removing the blanket from the girl's head.

"That's good," Flynn said, waving his hand sideways. "So here's where the trouble is, eh?" He bent over the wound. "Looks pretty nasty," he observed. "Was she wearin' anything when she was found?"

Gilbert turned and pointed to the pile of clothing he had neatly placed on the floor the day before. "Right here," he said.

The sheriff lifted each garment individually and tucked them under his arm. "I'll take these back to Summerside with me," he said, then shook his head at Jarvis, who had begun to unwind the rest of the covering.

"Never mind that, I've seen enough." Reaching into his coat pocket, Flynn took out a toothpick and rolled it around in his mouth.

"You don't want to look at the rest of the body?" Jarvis asked, surprised.

"Nuh, it's pretty cut and dried from what I can tell. You said that she had no marks of violence on the rest of her, and that she had water in the lungs. This is clearly a case of drowning."

Jarvis covered the girl's head again. Avard made a motion forward to help. Gilbert, standing beside him, put out his right arm and shook his head.

"Yep, I see this quite a bit," Flynn said as he stooped his head to get back out the barn door. "Young girl runs away from home for one reason or another. Three weeks ago I got a telegram telling me to be on the lookout for some young thing that went missing from the Annapolis Valley. She turned up in Halifax a few days later, whorin' around the docks, and she's one of the lucky ones. I mind the time—"

The twins' eyes were wide. Gilbert shook his head.

"Huh? Oh," Flynn said.

"Tell us," Eddie urged.

"Not today," Gilbert interrupted. "You two have chores to finish. The first thing I want you to do is move the last of the ice from the ice house and bring it here in front of the door."

The boys walked across the barnyard.

"I'll be there in a few minutes," Gilbert yelled after them, then turned to Jarvis and Flynn. "Have to use up the last of my ice to try to keep the smell down. Thought if I dragged the old pig trough in there and filled it with ice, we could lay her on top of it. Now, what happens next?" he asked.

"Well," Flynn said. "I'll write up a physical description and wire it around the Maritimes, see if anyone is missing a girl. Somebody might come forward to claim her. If we don't hear anything in a week or so, after the coroner's inquest, you can bury her."

"A week or so!" Gilbert raised his voice. "I can't have her lying around that long. A person can barely stand the smell in there as it is and I've got to get back to work. Can't you take her off my hands, Darrell?"

"I've got no place to keep a body, especially this time of year," Flynn said.

"This is crazy. I thought you'd be able to help us out."

"Sorry, Gil." Flynn spit the chewed toothpick out on the ground. "Can't. You have to keep her here at least until after the coroner's jury anyway. But you know, you'd be surprised at the number of corpses that no one ever claims. Why don't you go ahead and bury her after the jury's done with her. She'll have to be planted sooner or later anyway, and if she has a family you'll be doin' them a favour."

"I'll go see the minister this afternoon," Gilbert said, relieved. "They have a section in the back of the churchyard for unknowns. We can likely bury her there."

"There you go." Flynn slapped Gilbert on the shoulder. "Now, do you suppose Catherine has any more of that hot tea on the stove?"

When the men came into the kitchen, Jimmy Bell was sitting at the table waiting for his breakfast while Catherine stood before the stove stirring porridge. The boy's eyes widened at the sight of the sheriff. His face was shiny and red from the scrubbing his mother had just put him through. His hair was wet and slicked back, and freckles stood out on his chubby face.

"Jimmy." Flynn's voice boomed. "I heard that you had an exciting day yesterday." He sat down and placed a hand on the child's right shoulder.

"Yes, sir," Jimmy responded, looking at his father.

"Just tell Sheriff Flynn everything you know," Gilbert told him.

"Before we start, Jim, I want to give you this." Flynn plunged a sausage-shaped finger into one of his shirt pockets, fished out a shiny piece of tin, and handed it to the boy. "For your good work yesterday. I hereby declare you an honorary sheriff's deputy for the province of Prince Edward Island."

"Holy smoke, Dadda, look, it's a real badge."

"You're a deputy now, son," Flynn said. "You're obliged to tell me everything you know."

The boy nodded his head, serious now.

"Me and Tom were on the beach looking for things washed up and we saw her. She was lying in the seaweed with her eyes open. Tom was scared to touch her but I went over to her and saw she was dead. I wasn't scared."

"Atta boy," Flynn said.

"As soon as we saw that she was dead as a doornail, we ran to get our daddas. Then they came and picked her up and brought her to our barn. Can I see her again now that I'm a deputy?"

Flynn laughed.

"No, you can't!" Catherine said, plopping a Blue Willow bowl down on the table in front of him. "Eat your breakfast."

Flynn ruffled the boy's damp hair. "Thanks, Deputy Jimmy. You've been a big help. Now I'm just goin' to have another cup of your mother's good tea and a piece of that pie I see in the pantry there, and then I'll be off."

"So you're going to be in touch with the mainland?" Gilbert sat down beside Flynn. "See if anybody knows her?"

"Yup, first thing," the sheriff replied, his mouth full.

THE JURY'S DELIBERATIONS COMMENCED, FIRST in the barn and then in the Bells' parlour. The jury members all went home for supper, but Catherine did give them dinner at noon and kept them supplied with hot tea, pie, and molasses cookies throughout the afternoon.

Gilbert started out early next morning for North Tryon. Before he jumped up onto the seat of the express wagon, he buttoned his coat and pulled the red knitted cap that Catherine insisted he wear further down on his head. It was chilly with the sun still low on the horizon. He flicked the reins over Ned's back.

"Off we go again, boy. No chance to get any work done today."

The road to North Tryon was lined on both sides by red and yellow maple trees. Gilbert liked this drive. It always made him think of his father, whom he used to accompany along here as a young boy. And, as his father had done years before, Gilbert usually stopped to talk to the men he saw out in their yards. But this morning he just waved and hollered "hello" or "how's she's goin'?"

"No time today," he said, urging Ned to go faster past each gate.

All anybody would want to talk about anyway was the dead girl in his barn.

Alexander Morrison's two-storey furniture factory was situated on the corner just before the right turn into the village. The lumber mill and the huge piles of wood, pulp, rough boards, and dressed planks fanned out in the large yard behind it.

Gilbert stopped on the road across from the factory, jumped from the wagon, and walked along the front of the building to where a man was standing before an open door. He was bent over the edge of a board, holding it between his legs and carefully smoothing it with a plane.

"Morning, Gil." Lester Chisholm looked up and smiled. "What you up to today?"

"I'm looking to buy a rough box, Les. Got any at a good price?"

"Oh yeah, heard you had some trouble up your way. Buryin' that girl, are you?"

"Yeah, as soon as I get the say-so from Doc Jarvis. These things take forever once doctors and the law get involved."

"That they do. Do you know yet who she is?"

"No, don't have a clue. So can I get a rough box?"

"Yeah, there's a few you can take a look at."

The clean smell of new wood met Gilbert as he walked through the door of the factory. Sunlight coming in through the upper-storey windows cast shafts of light over the open space, causing the fine coat of sawdust on the floor to look like winter's first snow. Though men and boys were all over, hammering, sawing, and working at the lathes, to Gilbert, the place had a silence that didn't come from inactivity and quiet but from the meditative movement of industry. He often thought that he might prefer this line of work to farming. At least this job didn't depend so much on the weather.

"I said this might do. I heard she was just a wee thing."

"She's quite tall," Gilbert replied curtly, angry that he hadn't been paying attention. Chisholm selected a wooden box, as high as his shoulder, from a number of them leaning against the wall and was holding it upright for Gilbert's inspection.

"She's about five foot five," Gilbert said, "so that's a good size."

"Hold it steady and I'll get a lid."

A number of lids were leaning against the opposite wall. Chisholm walked across the room, rearranged them for a few minutes, and then selected one from the back.

"I think this'll fit," he said, walking back across the floor with it under his arm. He placed it next to the box that Gilbert was holding up on its end. "Yeah, that'll do. I'll help you get it to the wagon."

After they had carried the box outside, Chisholm went back in for the lid.

"There you go," he said, placing it beside the box in the wagon. "That'll be two dollars, Gil."

Gilbert rummaged around in his shirt pocket and brought out two folded bills. "And I'll need a receipt," he said, handing over the money.

"Wait here."

THE NEXT MORNING JARVIS GAVE them his permission to take the girl to the churchyard. The jury had viewed the body under his direction and now was holed up in Catherine's parlour. Gilbert, Avard, and Eddie placed the body in the box. Gilbert secured the lid by winding a piece of old clothesline rope round and round the box and knotting it.

"Why don't you just nail it down, Pa?" Eddie asked.

"Doc Jarvis said not to until I get his say-so, just in case."

They carried the box out to the express wagon. Avard had picked some golden rods earlier and once the box was securely in the wagon, he placed the flowers on top of it.

"This gives her a bit more dignity," he said. "Ma always says dignity is important."

Eddie smirked and opened his mouth to respond but saw his father's stern look.

It was two miles to the Cape Traverse Methodist Church. The people they met along the way were eager to talk. Some even asked to see the body but Gilbert shook his head.

"No time," he told them. "Got to hurry up and get back to the farm."

"Fools! Why would anybody want to see a dead body? What do they think this is, a Barnum sideshow?" he asked no one in particular.

When Gilbert pulled on the reins and hollered, "Whoa," the five boys walking behind the wagon came to a halt as well and ceased their chatter.

"You'd better keep back now," Gilbert shouted as he jumped down to greet Reverend Silliker, who was waiting at the bottom of the church steps.

"Mornin', Reverend," Gilbert, Avard, and Eddie called out in unison.

"Good morning, all," Silliker responded, with the Scottish lilt that he had never lost despite the decades he had lived away from his home country.

"It's a lovely fall day, don't you think, boys?"

As was his practice when meeting any of his flock, no matter how many times a day he encountered them, Silliker shook hands all around.

"It's a sad task you've got today, Gilbert."

"Yes, Reverend. It's been a rough few days, what with all the coming and going and people about."

"Well, hopefully having the poor soul here will ease things for you a bit. And God bless you and your family for doing what you have."

"Where were you planning on putting her?" Gilbert asked.

"In the biggest shed there in the back. Roy McWilliams cleared off the table in there yesterday. She can stay there until she's buried. Do you need any help?"

"No, thanks. Me and the boys can handle it. All right to drive up behind the church here?"

"Certainly, just go along the path."

"Thanks, Reverend, and maybe you can keep those kids from following us back there. This is not a sight for them."

"Certainly."

Gilbert was about to drive away when he turned to Silliker again. "That shed got a lock on it?" he asked.

"I had Roy install a padlock earlier today. You'll see it when you get up there. Just close it. Roy has the key."

Silliker turned towards the children and raised his voice as the cart started to move up the hill. "All right, boys, run along now. There's nothing here for the likes of you."

"Awww, we just wanted to see the dead girl."

"Let the poor soul rest in peace. And no peeking around when I'm gone or I'll be paying your parents a visit. Now off with you. The lot of you should be in school."

There was kicking of dirt and some words of protest, but eventually the boys turned and left the churchyard.

Avard jumped from the wagon and let down the tailgate. Eddie pushed the box towards the back and Avard and Gilbert lifted it down.

"Eddie, run and open the door." Gilbert nodded his head towards the shed.

Eddie lifted the latch on the shed door and opened it wide. It bumped against a wooden table. "Not a lot of room in here, Pa. It'll be a tight squeeze getting the box through."

"Oh, don't worry, it'll fit," Gilbert reassured him. "We'll make sure of that."

The body rolled around as they tried repeatedly to wedge the box through the door of the shed.

"I think I'm going to be sick," Eddie said. "She's stinkin' to high heaven."

"Just a bit more. Christ, how did they expect us to get this through the door?" Gilbert panted, out of breath from the manoeuvring. "That so-called caretaker doesn't know what he's doing, if you ask me."

"Just one more push, Pa," Avard said.

Finally they got the box through the door and onto the table.

"There now," Gilbert said as he secured the padlock. "Just have to get the word to bury her."

"THE JURY'S GONE," JARVIS ANNOUNCED, walking into the Bells' kitchen at dusk, followed by Avard and Eddie. "Catherine, may I have a cup of tea, please?"

He sat down at the table and rubbed his hands up and down his unshaven jaw. There were dark circles around his eyes.

"It's over?"

Jarvis nodded.

"So were you right?" Eddie asked. "Did she drown, like you said?"

"It appears so, and now it's official. I just signed the death certificate."

Catherine placed the cup of tea on the table. "And finally she can be laid to rest," she said, and sighed.

A boat ride to celebrate. To end the day.

MERIGOMISH

NOVA SCOTIA
May 1859

"SUCH A LOVELY DAY," Helen Hennessey said as she looked up from her knitting on a warm spring afternoon. She loved to sit on the front veranda looking across her husband's fields, waving at neighbours driving up and down the road in front of the house.

"Yes," agreed Beatrice, who was sitting next to her, embroidering a pillowcase.

"Glad to be home, dear?"

Yes, very much. Although I do miss the busyness of the city. It can be dull here by times. But it's so nice to see you and Father again."

"And Ann? Do you think she's glad to be home?"

The Hennessey girls were both slim and fair, with green eyes. As teenagers they'd had an outdoor freshness about them. Helen had schooled them first around the kitchen table and then, later on, in the small library that Patrick had built onto the house. The girls loved their reading, their church charity work, and helping their father manage the financial end of the many family interests.

When Beatrice was nineteen and Ann seventeen, they were escorted from Halifax by Mrs. Cora Hill, a distant relative, to the Litchfield School for Young Ladies in Boston. Letters home were filled with accounts of the books they'd been reading, the theatricals they'd seen, sleigh rides and socials. Both girls scorned dances and card parties as frivolous pastimes, preferring the poetry evenings and lectures held near their Beacon Hill lodgings.

Now, they had returned to Merigomish, their schooling completed, but Helen was concerned about Ann.

"She seemed moody and out of sorts this morning. Do you know what's wrong with her?"

"We just got in yesterday, she's likely still tired out from the long journey. I know I am."

"You're sure nothing's wrong?"

Beatrice shook her head without meeting her mother's eyes.

"Well, please ask her if everything is all right and let me know."

"PATRICK, HAVE YOU NOTICED A change in Ann?" Helen asked as they prepared for bed.

"She seemed very quiet this evening, almost sad."

"I think something might have happened but Beatrice doesn't seem to know."

"Cora never struck me as a good choice to accompany the girls down there," Patrick said, taking off his socks. He paused for a minute then added, "She was always too casual for my liking. I remember her as a girl back in Truro. I never should have hired her to go to Boston with the girls."

"I'll keep after Beatrice to tell me what she knows, if anything."

WEEKS PASSED AND HELEN BECAME more alarmed.

"She's lost flesh since she's been home and looks drawn, don't you think, dear? Although she never complains about anything."

"She's taken to staring into space most of the time, and she can't seem to concentrate. I gave her last month's ledger to add up and had to do it over myself. She had her figures all wrong." Patrick shook his head.

Across the hall in Ann's bedroom, the sisters were having their own discussion.

"Where were you off to last night?" Beatrice asked Ann, who was lying on her bed with her face turned to the wall. "I know you left the house about 2:30, it's no use denying it."

"Just went for a little walk to the wharf. I needed to clear my head. There's no law against that, as far as I know."

"You've been going for a lot of walks lately. You looking for more excitement? Wasn't the States enough for you? God knows who you'd meet down at the wharf that time of night. Morning, I should say."

"Go to bed, Bea, and leave me alone, please. I'm fine."

"Well, you don't look it and I'm getting tired of Mother quizzing me about Boston every day. I wish she'd ask you herself and leave me out of it."

ONE RAINY AFTERNOON SHORTLY AFTERWARD, when Helen brought tea into the library for her daughters, she confronted Ann.

"You just don't seem to be yourself since you got back from Boston. Did anything happen there to upset you?"

Ann met her mother's eyes. "No, why do you ask?"

"Well, your father and I are worried something's wrong. How did you get along with Mrs. Hill?"

"Mrs. Hill showed us around Boston and we got to know it quite well," Beatrice replied for her sister. "But she never took us anywhere that was unsuitable. And the two of us always travelled together."

"And you never encountered any unsuitable company or incidents?"

Ann looked down at her book. "Of course not, Mother. And Mrs. Hill was always very kind to us."

Helen sighed. "Well, for the life of me, I can't imagine what's wrong with you."

"There's nothing wrong, Mother," Ann said, rising from the couch. "Now please excuse me. I think I'll lie down for a bit."

MERIGOMISH

Nova Scotia
August 1859

HELEN WAS SHOCKED ONE Sunday morning when a tall young man, unknown to the family, stepped forward at the gate of Merigomish Anglican Church and told Ann he'd like to see her home. Ann, however, did not look surprised. She smiled and turned to her parents. Patrick's mouth formed a straight line and he shook his head. To the astonishment of onlookers, Ann frowned, turned away from her family, and, without a word, placed her hand on the stranger's arm. He tipped his hat and he and Ann walked away together. Patrick made a move to follow them but Helen held him back.

"People will see," she whispered. "We'll follow them home and get to the bottom of this."

"But who is that?" Patrick said, louder than was necessary.

Marion Beaton and her daughter Florence, who had been standing nearby, hurried toward them.

"I know who he is," Marion offered. "That's Will Harney. He works for Mr. MacDonald, doing odd jobs around the place. He's been here for the last six months or so but this is the first time I've seen him in church. Nobody knows anything about his family. He doesn't seem to have any relations around here."

"He's from Tatamagouche and very handsome but is no better than he should be," Florence said, and giggled.

"Florence, hush," her mother admonished in a loud whisper, looking pleased.

Marion continued: "It's said he's not that hard of a worker but Mr. MacDonald likes to play cards and he's good company for him."

It was well known throughout Pictou County that Reginald MacDonald was a drinker.

"Thank you, Marion. Good day," Helen said, her face red with embarrassment.

Ann walking out with a strange man and defying her father in front of practically the whole congregation. What had gotten into her? Then she realized Beatrice was pulling on her arm.

"Come along, Mother. Good day, Mrs. Beaton. Florence, I'll see you Wednesday at choir." Beatrice pivoted her mother towards Patrick who was already across the road, pacing back and forth.

"I'm going to give that young man a piece of my mind," Patrick fumed. "How dare he not introduce himself to me before making off with my daughter? I have never seen such gall in my life."

"Very, very ill bred," Helen said.

"I saw him in town last week when I went to Murphy's," Beatrice told them. "He was walking down Main Street tipping his hat at everyone."

As Ann and her escort arrived at the front gate, Patrick picked up speed. "He's not getting away from me," he said over his shoulder.

The stranger was about to kiss Ann's hand when Patrick came to a halt in front of them. The young man stepped back and smiled widely. Ann paled when she saw the look on her father's face.

"Good morning again, Mr. and Mrs. Hennessey, Miss Hennessey. Thank you for permitting me to escort Miss Ann home."

"Young man, we have not been introduced and I don't know you from Adam," Patrick spouted in anger. "And I didn't give you permission to escort my daughter anywhere."

The stranger held out his hand, still smiling. "Will Harney, at your service."

"How do you know my daughter?" Patrick demanded, ignoring the offered handshake.

Will's arm fell to his side. "I didn't until I saw her in church this morning and so admired her that I thought I'd take the chance and ask to escort her home. I'm surprised that young men aren't lined up around the corner to do so."

He looked back at the blushing Ann and smiled.

"You've got a lot of gall, that's all I can say," Patrick told him, redder in the face than his daughter.

"Sir, Miss Hennessey's beauty made me forget the manners my good mother took such pains to teach me. I do apologize," Will said, bowing this time at Helen and Beatrice.

"Young man, I think we had all better step inside and get to know each other," Patrick said, leading the way into the house.

ROCKLEY

Nova Scotia
November 1859

"I SEE JOHN HAS had some visitors for a while now," Hiram Reid observed as he stepped up onto the wooden veranda of Bailey's store. He waved at John Dempsey, who was driving by with his horse and express wagon. John returned the wave but the young man seated beside him looked away. Calvin Bailey, the store's proprietor, was leaning on a broom that, a minute before, his wife, Jennie, had handed to him, demanding that he sweep the veranda.

"Visitors nothin'," Calvin replied, spitting a wad of tobacco over the veranda railing. "They're his family come to live with him. His sister Mabel and her son and his wife. They plan to stay, I guess. The young fellow's been lookin' for work, John said. His wife's a pretty little thing but I've seen her just the once on the day they came. There's going to be an addition to their family, I've heard."

"Well, new people moving in is always a good thing," Hiram said. "Now, I got a list of supplies the wife sent me for. I'd better not go home without them."

"I'D RATHER LIVE IN AMHERST myself," Will said after he and his uncle passed Bailey's, "but Ma wants me to stay here at the home place. Can't you talk her into staying with you and letting me and Ann move on? Rockley's pretty dull. I could use some excitement once in a while."

"I've tried, but as you know she's stubborn as they come. And you and her have never been apart that much since your father died. Give her time and I'll talk to her again. And you might as well stay until after the child's born. It makes sense, Mabel being a midwife will make it much easier for Ann when the time comes."

"Don't worry about her. That woman's like a cat. She'll always finds a way to get by."

John turned to his nephew to reply but decided against it. He didn't want to start another argument. He'd heard enough of them since the arrival of his sister and her son.

After their wedding, Will had told Ann that a whole new life was waiting for them in Cumberland County, that they would live with John for a while but would soon have a place of their own. Ann was eager to go to Amherst and get a fresh start. But they had been in Rockley three weeks now and Mabel wouldn't hear of her son travelling so far away to look for work. And that was the end of it.

ROCKLEY

NOVA SCOTIA
April 1870

"I DO BELIEVE THAT Mary is a bit simple by times."
Mabel was looking out of the window.

"Why do you say that?" Ann asked, coming over to the older woman's side.

"Well, what kind of ten-year-old spends her time doddling up the lane in the pouring rain."

Ann looked out of the window to see her daughter, sitting on her haunches, peering down into a puddle, with her dress trailing in the mud.

"Mary's making up stories in her head." Ann smiled and moved away from the window. "There's nothing simple about it. She's just being a child."

"People will think she's daft if they see her looking at puddles in the pouring rain." Mabel sniffed.

"Oh, lots of people daydream, I dare say." Ann shrugged her shoulders and walked out of the room. "But I'd better call her in. She'll be soaked."

Mabel frowned, shook her head, and went back to her ironing. "Doesn't even know enough to come in out of the rain," she said to herself.

ROCKLEY

NOVA SCOTIA
June 1872

WHEN MARY WAS TWELVE, Ann had a second child. They named her Helen Mabel and called her Little Helen to distinguish her from Grandma Helen Hennessey in Merigomish. Now it was two months after the birth, and Ann wanted to get some sunshine on her face. She suggested that she and Mary take a walk to Bailey's store.

"We need more flannel to make diapers," she told Mabel. "We won't be gone long and the outing will be good for the both of us. Will you keep an eye on Little Helen, please? I've just nursed her so she'll be all right for a bit."

"Oh, I suppose so," Mabel huffed, as Ann and Mary put their bonnets on.

But she didn't mind.

This baby girl's a beauty, and looks so much like Will, she thought. Once Ann and Mary left, Mabel picked up her grandchild and sang softly while rocking her back and forth.

Yes, she looked like her father, this one.

FRED LEFURGEY WAS PUTTING UP a shelf at the back of the store when Ann and Mary walked in. He ceased hammering and got off the ladder to greet them. Calvin excused himself to wait on a customer and Mary wandered off to look at the hats. Fred asked Ann about her health.

"I can't believe that Mary's your daughter," he added. "You look to be not much older than she is."

"You're very kind."

"Kind nothing, just stating the obvious."

Ann reddened and turned towards Calvin, who was back behind the counter. She placed a bolt of flannel down in front of him.

"I'd like two yards of this, please."

Calvin snipped the fabric six feet from the edge and then, holding it tight, tore a piece of it off the bolt.

"That's all for today," Ann said. "Mary, you can carry the parcel home."

"That's too heavy for such a little girl," Fred said, snatching the flannel away from Calvin and placing it under his arm. "I have my surrey right outside. I can drive the both of you home in no time."

"There's no need for that. We can walk."

"I won't hear of it," Fred told her, tipping his cap and making for the door.

Calvin looked at Ann and shrugged. "Looks like you got a ride home."

Hiram Reid opened the door as Fred, Ann, and Mary were leaving, and turned to Calvin with a smile.

"Nice to see Mrs. Harney out and about."

"Yeah, it is," the storekeeper agreed, "but Fred better be careful showing her too much attention. That husband of hers is a piece of work and he's in a bad mood, at least he was yesterday."

"Yeah, why?"

Calvin came around the counter and took hold of Hiram's arm, leading him to a corner away from the other customers.

"It was yesterday afternoon, when Harry Brown and I went fishing. I closed down for a couple of hours, Jennie being gone to her sister's. Harry and I were just on our way back in off the river. We got a lot of nice trout. I was about to step out to tie the punt up when we could hear this awful cursing. Will was over by the shacks yelling at this dog. All at once he picks up a sizable rock and throws it at the dog and hits it in the head. It goes down and he walks over to it and picks up the rock again and starts pounding the dog in the head with it. Blood was flying everywhere. We were yelling for him to stop, the dog was likely dead after he hit it the second time. Before we could get to him, he dropped the rock and started kicking it in the ribs. Harry and I grabbed a hold of him so he would leave the animal alone. He said the dog pissed on some rope of his. We threw the poor thing in the bushes. Will was in some temper. I never saw the like of it. Poor Harry was scared to death, you know how soft he is."

Calvin stopped, out of breath.

"Well, that's too bad," Hiram said after a pause. "I don't like to see any animal abused."

"Don't say anything about it. I don't want it to get back to the Harneys. Harry's not going to say a word. He's scared the young fellow will come after him. And you know, Hiram, it was almost as if Will enjoyed doing what he did."

WHEN FRED ARRIVED IN THE yard with Ann and Mary in tow, Will was standing on the doorstep smoking a cigarette.

Fred tipped his cap, helped Ann down from the surrey, and passed the roll of flannel to Mary.

"I see you met my wife in her travels."

"Yes, just now at Bailey's. Thought I'd help her and Mary home with their purchase."

"Much obliged, I'm sure." Will nodded. He raised himself away from the post and followed Ann and Mary into the porch.

Mabel had supper ready and the family sat down to eat.

"Mr. Bailey has nice hats in his store," Mary said. "I especially liked the blue one with the little veil—"

"I saw that last week there," Mabel interrupted her. "Way too old for the likes of you."

"Grandma's right," Ann said. "There were some nice boaters there we can look at next time."

"Will, would you pass the potatoes, please," John asked, reaching out.

Will ignored him.

"Will? Oh, never mind." John stretched across the table.

"Will, that's not very mannerly," Ann scolded him.

"Not as mannerly as the LeFurgeys, I suppose."

Ann shook her head.

"Fred was just being—" John began.

Will rose from the table, clattering his fork and knife on the plate. "He can go to hell, just like the rest of you." He slammed the kitchen and porch doors on his way out.

MARY WAS AWAKENED IN THE middle of the night by loud voices and Little Helen's crying. She got out of bed and tiptoed out into the hallway. Her parents were arguing.

"I better not see him in this yard again or I'll knock his block off," Will threatened.

"Oh, for God's sake, he was just being friendly, giving me a ride home," Ann replied.

"He wouldn't have bothered if he hadn't been encouraged."

"What do you mean by that?"

"You were likely making eyes at him."

"Don't talk so foolish, Will. Now I've got to nurse the baby, you've woken her up with all your yelling."

"Don't you walk away when I'm talking to you."

Mary heard a sound, a slap.

"How dare you."

Just then Mabel's bedroom door opened. Mary ran back into her own room. She opened her door a crack so she could see what was going on. Mabel raced into Will's and Ann's bedroom.

"Would you two stop it? I'm tryin' to get some sleep."

"He hit me."

"You deserved it, acting like a whore."

"Be quiet, you'll wake everybody up. And don't use that kind of language in this house," Mabel said. "You're married and you have to put up with each other."

Mary could see Mabel pointing her finger.

"Shut up, the both of you, and get back to bed."

ROCKLEY

NOVA SCOTIA
September 1872

"IS MARY IN THE house?" Will asked as he came through the kitchen door. "It's six o'clock. She should have been back with those damn cows by now. They're not going to milk themselves."

Ann was seated in a rocking chair knitting while Mabel lay on her daybed snoring softly. The supper dishes had just been cleared away. A cool breeze lifted the kitchen curtains and ruffled Ann's shiny hair as she looked up at her husband.

"She was late going to get them, Will. She'll be home soon. You know how Mary doddles by times."

"I'll just run up and see where she is." He turned and walked out the door.

Ann shook her head, placed her knitting on the little table beside the chair, and picked up the book lying there. Beatrice had just sent her a new book of poetry and she dipped into it whenever she could.

"No wonder that girl's so flighty," a voice called out from the daybed. "You've always got your head in the clouds or in a book, which amounts to the same thing."

Ann didn't take her eyes off the page.

"Grandma Harney, don't begrudge me one of my few pleasures."

The old woman muttered to herself and turned away, facing the wall.

"THERE YOU GO, BEAUTY, NOW you have one too." Mary placed the chain of goldenrod around the cow's neck. "Like the Lady of Shalott. Although you're not travelling down the river. She was very beautiful and the poem was sad. But you're just sweet."

Mary smiled at the thought of Beauty the cow mournfully sailing down the River Philip in a punt. She kissed her on the nose.

"All right now, we all have on our crowns or chains of gold. We must away to the castle before dark. There's evil about."

She hummed to herself as she led her charges along the path leading down to the barn. Her father had sent her up here more than an hour ago to fetch the cows and she had let the time get away on her again. She didn't want him to come looking for her. But as she rounded the last corner before the farm came into sight beyond the evergreens, she spied him making his way towards her.

"Taking your own sweet time again this evening, are you?" Will stood in the middle of the path blocking her way. "And what sort of getup is this?" he asked, surveying the flower-draped cows trailing behind her.

"We're...pretending," Mary offered, blushing.

"Pretending, eh." Will smiled. "I never knew a cow to pretend."

He walked up closer to her and looked down into her face. Mary could smell the liquor on his breath. She knew her father kept a bottle in the woods sometimes and drank from it whenever he had the opportunity. She had come upon him and his cache one time when she was picking berries. He'd made her promise not to tell anyone.

"Daddy just needs a little refreshment every now and then," he had told her, winking.

"Well, get on home now," he said, putting his hand on the back of Mary's head and hurrying her forward. "These poor things are straining to be milked. It's not good to let them go so long. I've told you that before. And stay and do the milking with your uncle. Don't just leave it to him like you usually do. You've got to learn some responsibility."

"Yes, Daddy."

"Now hurry along. I'll be back at the house shortly."

John laughed at the sight of Mary and the cows when they trooped single file into the barn.

"Well, the queen and her court have finally arrived," he said, bending down to kiss the top of Mary's head. "All right then, Queenie, help me get these ladies settled in for the night."

"IT'S NOT GOOD, A CHILD always making up stories in her head," Mabel commented later that evening when the adults were seated around the kitchen table. "It leads to lies, it does." She nodded her head and buttered another piece of bread.

"Oh, it's harmless enough and there's a difference between pretending and lies. I've never caught Mary in a lie," John reassured his sister.

"And it's a sign of intelligence," Ann pointed out.

"I just don't like the idea of her being bookish, like the rest of your clique," Will said and frowned at his wife. "Look at that Beatrice, never got a man because she thought herself too smart. And what good does book learning do when a girl is just going to grow up, get married, and tend house?"

"Too much reading's not good for the brain," Mabel declared.

Ann spit her tea out and burst into laughter.

"What...what does that mean?" Her eyes twinkled as she blotted at her apron with a handkerchief.

"Well," Mabel replied, "it turns your head. And it makes a woman forget her duties around the house. I can read, my ma taught me, and it comes in handy from time to time but I know where my first duties lie."

Ann shook her head and stood up.

"Well, I must get to bed," she told them. "My duty lies in getting a good night's sleep so I won't forget my place in the morning."

"I'M SO NERVOUS," ANN TOLD Mabel on a sunny Friday afternoon as she placed napkins and good cutlery on the parlour table.

"Why's that now?" Mabel had just finished dusting the room and was fluffing up the pillows on the sofa.

"Well, it's the first time I've hosted the Improvement Committee. The first time Will said it was all right with him. I hope he won't come home in a temper."

"Will doesn't like foolishness and I don't blame him." Mabel sniffed, "Glebe House Improvement Committee my—"

"It's for a good cause, keeping a decent roof over the heads of the minister and his family," Ann interrupted, smiling. "The Catholic Church does the same for the priest. And thank you for helping when you don't really have to."

"Don't be comparing the two," Mabel warned. "I'm helping to be sure none of my good dishes get broke. And I'll be working on my own knitting for my own church and not some Protestant rug."

Ann headed for the kitchen to bring in the food. She hoped she'd made enough.

"Oh God, let it be all right," she prayed.

Only four—Rita LeFurgey, Elaine Clarke, Elsie MacDonald, and Jennie Bailey—of the twelve committee members came to the meeting that day. The women were making hooked and braided rugs for the glebe house's parlour and hall floors. A new minister and his young wife were expected in the next month and there was a lot to be done before they arrived.

"That Washington pie is just delicious, Ann," Elaine said. "And that jam."

"Mabel makes the best jam in the county," Rita said. "Don't shake your head, you know it's true."

They heard boots stomping into the kitchen. Ann excused herself and left the room. She hoped to smooth the way by talking to her husband first. Her sweaty hands worried a napkin into a tight ball.

"You're home early today," she said to Will and kissed him on the cheek. She could smell liquor.

"Yeah, they let us go at a decent hour for a change. I heard talking when I came in. Are those old bags still here?"

"Shush. Lower your voice," Ann whispered, reddening.

"I thought they'd be gone by now. I'm getting hungry."

"We'll be done in about a half-hour, then I'll make you a nice supper and there will be lots of sweets left over from our tea."

"I don't want any leftovers."

"Just go have a smoke on the veranda, dear, and we'll be done in a little while. Please don't be mad."

Will left the kitchen. Breathing a sigh of relief, Ann went back into the parlour.

But the gathering wasn't over in a half-hour. The women decided to push on, finishing as much of their rugs as they could that day. Ann was looking nervously around her when Mabel suddenly got up from her chair. "That's it for me," she announced, and walked out of the room. Shortly after, Ann heard the noise of pans clanging and relaxed a bit. Mabel would make something for Will to eat. She didn't relax for long. All at once her husband was in the parlour. And he didn't look just tipsy anymore. He looked drunk. He surveyed the room, head held high.

"So, ladies, isn't it about time you all went home?"

There was a collective gasp.

Ann stood up, a lump in her throat.

"Dear, these are our guests."

"They're not my guests. Just a bunch of fat-ass old women who should be home looking after their men instead of running the roads."

Ann stood speechless, her mouth opening and closing.

"It's all right." Rita touched her arm. "It is time for us to go."

"I'm so sorry," Ann kept repeating as she followed the women through the house. "Please excuse Will, he's not himself."

She felt her face burning.

"Ill-bred, if you ask me," Elaine said, looking directly at Mabel who stood by the stove with a wooden spoon in her hand.

Ann, not able to stop the tears, stood on the doorstep wringing her hands as the women climbed into Jennie Bailey's buggy.

Rita turned in the yard, walked back to Ann, and put her arms around her.

"This is going to be all over the village," Ann whispered hoarsely, "what with Jennie witnessing it."

"Never mind that, Ann. People are so used to that one gossiping that they only half pay attention to what she says anymore. Now dry your eyes and go back to your family."

"I'm so embarrassed."

"Never mind."

Jennie had turned the buggy around and brought it up close to the porch.

"Mrs. Bailey, everyone, thank you for coming and please forgive me."

"It's not your fault," Rita whispered.

"Come on, Rita, I'm not staying around where I'm not wanted," Jennie said, not looking at Ann.

Rita got up into the buggy. She and Elsie were the only two who waved back as they rolled out of the yard.

"I can never show my face in Rockley again," Ann said to herself as she stumbled back into the house and upstairs to her bedroom.

"ANN, THERE'S SOMETHING I HOPED I would never have to tell you, but Will's got a dirty temper just like his grandfather, it runs in the family," John said in response to her account of the ladies' abrupt dismissal earlier that day. She sat crying and rocking Little Helen back and forth.

"Why does he act like he does, John? Why doesn't he care what anyone thinks of him, not even us, his own family?"

John looked over his shoulder. "Don't let on to Mabel that I told you but our father, who Will was named after, had some awful temper and Will reminds me of him."

"Does he? In what way?"

"To tell the truth, our pa was a mean bastard, excuse my language, Ann. Mabel and I don't talk about him. He's best forgotten really."

"Tell me about him."

"Well." John sat up straight on the edge of his chair and leaned in towards her. "You never knew what he was going to do next. He'd get mad at the drop of a hat. Our mother was a nervous wreck. I remember the time, I was about seven, I guess, and Mabel was twelve. One night he was mad over something or other and started throwing everything we owned out into the snow. Ma got a black eye for trying to stop him. She ran out of the house bawling, with me and Mabel behind. The old man locked and barred the door on the lot of us. It was February, freezing cold. We didn't get back in the house that night. I can see him yet, bold as brass, looking down at us from an upstairs bedroom window, where you and Will sleep now, sitting on a chair, holding his shotgun. Pretty near all of Rockley came out to see him. He had every lantern in the house lit and set behind him so he showed up real good, like one of those fancy silhouettes. He was just daring somebody, anybody, to try to get in. He'd have killed them sure as we're sitting here."

"Your poor mother. What did she do?"

"Nothing much she could do. We all stayed at the LeFurgeys' there across the field. They took us in. That's the only thing that kept us all from freezing to death. We were there for a couple of days. Then old Mr. LeFurgey, Fred's grandfather, came and talked Pa into letting us come back home. But every once in a while he'd run us all out again. You never knew when he was going to fly off the handle. I'm surprised he never killed us when he was wound up. My mother suffered terrible from ulcers her whole life. Even after he was dead."

"What a terrible way to have to live. Was he a drinker?"

"No, not really. Just full of meanness and hardness. And not afraid of a thing, human or otherwise. He had a team of horses, one he named Jesus Christ and the other was the Virgin Mary. People was afraid to go anywhere near them. Yeah, he was quite the fellow."

John reached into his shirt pocket for his makings and slowly rolled a cigarette. As he blew out the smoke he began again.

"When something got him into a temper he used to blame either the Lord or the Devil, sometimes both of them, and call on them to come and have it out with him. When I was little I slept with one eye open, scared to death that I was going to wake up and see one or the other of them standing over me."

Ann shook her head. "Will's not as bad as that, thank God."

"One day in the summer, I was fifteen, I think, he was out on the river fishing and got into a rage about a line or something. A bunch of us kids was on shore watching him. It was thundering in the distance. Just as the old man began to holler, calling up the Devil himself, a bolt of lightning hit him and lifted him clean off the punt, about ten feet straight up. Then he fell back into the water. He was dead before he landed, I'm positive. Took the rest of the day and half the night to find him and fish him out. And his whole body was covered with this dark red rash, lightning flowers, the doctor called it. Looked like the pattern the frost makes on a window. It was the Devil's mark if you ask me. Guess he finally accepted Pa's invitation."

"What a terrible thing for a child to see."

"Maybe so." John nodded. "But the house was a lot more peaceful after he was gone. And the neighbours around helped us out until I was old enough to take over the farm."

"What about Mabel? What was she like growing up? She must have been scared to death of your father too."

"Mabel was always cranky as long as I can remember. She does have a soft heart but you don't see it very often and she doesn't like to be crossed. And she's had her troubles and disappointments just like anybody else that didn't make her temper any sweeter. What with Pa being so mean and her losing Harold when she was still fairly young. And she lost a baby too. She was never the same after that."

"I never knew that. How did it happen?"

"A little girl. Just died in her sleep one night. About six months old. Will's little sister. Mabel did want more children, but time went by and then Harold died and it just never happened. And Mabel wouldn't marry again. Said if she couldn't have Harold she didn't want anybody else."

Ann sighed. "She and Will are just so difficult to get along with. It makes life harder than it has to be. And I don't know what I can do about it."

"Will wasn't always like he is now, you know. Before his father died he was always polite and well-mannered and a lot calmer than he is now. But he changed after that."

"Tell me about his father. I've asked him but Will won't talk about him."

"After Mabel and Harold were married, Ma and I went down to Tatamagouche to help them get their farm going. We were there about nine years, then Ma died and I came back up here. So we did live with them for a while. Harold was from Tatamagouche originally but had moved up to Pugwash to live with his grandparents. So Mabel and I knew him ever since we were kids. He was a grand fellow. Kind, and always helpin' somebody out. After his pa died, he wanted to go back to Tatamagouche to look after the farm. He and Mabel were courting then and she married him and we all went down together."

"So you knew Will as a little boy?"

"I did. And he was just like his father then. Real dear little soul. But it all changed when Harold died."

"Tell me about that."

"They were, Harold and Will, out in the woods cutting down trees. They went everywhere together, those two, Harold doted on him. Well, that day Harold cut his right foot with the axe and started to bleed something awful. Will was only twelve and didn't know what to do. They did get the leg up and leaning against a tree, then Harold told Will to go for help. Will ran as fast as he could. When he got back with the doctor and a couple of men, Harold was gone. Bled to death."

"How awful."

"Mabel said she would never forget the sight of Will running in the kitchen, covered with his father's blood, and talking like a crazy person. It took a long time to get him calmed down enough to know what was going on."

Ann winced. "Poor Will."

"He didn't talk after that for two weeks. He just laid in his bed, staring at the ceiling. She had to wrestle with him to get those bloody clothes off. Didn't go to the funeral either, Mabel couldn't budge him. After the two weeks he got up, nasty as hell. He was mad at his father for dying I guess, and he's been mad at everybody and everything ever since."

"I never knew. Will hasn't had it easy either. I'll try to remember that the next time he starts up with his foolishness."

"That's why I usually give him the benefit of the doubt even though he's a pain in the arse by times. And it's probably best not to mention to him what I told you. It'll make him mad."

"Yes," Ann agreed. "Well, he doesn't like to be seen as weak. And he's so hard to deal with once he gets an idea in his head."

She hugged the baby closer to her. What kind of a life had she brought this little one into?

"Now, you'd better get in the house. It's starting to get chilly out here and she should be in her bed."

Ann stood up, kissed John on the forehead, and walked around to the porch door. John sat back in his chair and rolled another cigarette.

I've never been so far out, so late.
His face in shadow.
My hand draped over the boat.
Shouldn't we be going back?

ROCKLEY

Nova Scotia
April 1876

IT WAS COLD AND damp when Will got down from his horse and tied its reins to the hitching post in front of Bailey's store. He was on his way back to Wallace for the week and needed some tobacco. The door of the store was open and he could hear laughter inside. He stopped in his tracks when he heard his name mentioned.

"Do Harney, do Harney," Calvin Bailey said, and then roared with laughter.

He hurried inside to see Jack Reid, facing away from him, walking towards the back of the store with his head held high in the air and his chest puffed out. Over the laughter, Jack didn't hear Will come in. At fourteen, Jack was a born mimic, able to walk and talk like just about anyone in Rockley. Mostly, it was something he did at home. His mother warned him within an inch of his life not to be making fun of people in public, but sometimes he couldn't resist.

Will charged down the length of the store, ignoring Jack's outstretched arms and Calvin's pleas. He punched Jack and sent him sprawling onto the floor. Then he picked him up by the back of his shirt and the seat of his pants and threw him against the back wall where he landed, among the shovels and picks.

"My God, you've killed him, you've killed him," Calvin shouted, running toward Jack.

"Throw a bucket of water on the little bastard and he'll come 'round. That'll teach him to make fun of me."

Will held the sore, reddened knuckles of his right hand in his left fist.

"I came in here for some tobacco," he declared, standing at the counter waiting to be served.

"Get out of my store and stay out!" Calvin yelled over the noise of the clattering tools as he attempted to disentangle the groaning boy. "You're not welcome here anymore. Get out!"

Will went behind the counter and grabbed two cans of tobacco from the shelves. As he walked around to the front again, he used his free hand to sweep everything from the top of the counter. Glass candy jars, bottles of pickles, a display of knives: all crashed to the floor. Without a word, Will walked around the mess and out the door.

"You'll pay for all that, don't think you won't," Calvin called out to Will's retreating back as he helped Jack to his feet. The boy's face was bleeding.

Will turned. "You'll squeal for your money, arsehole." Then he stomped out the door.

He brought his bruised hand to his mouth. Tears sprang into his eyes. He put the tobacco in his saddlebags and started down the road to Wallace.

"HE PUNCHED ME." JACK HELD his sleeve to his nose. "I can't see right. Everything's blurry."

"Sit down here and I'll run over and see if Dr. Creed is around," Calvin said.

"He better not have broken my nose." Jack flinched as he touched it gently. "Is it ever sore."

Calvin threw a towel in the boy's direction and ran for the door.

Jack knew he'd be in trouble when he got home, broken nose or not. He dabbed at his bleeding face with the cloth and began to cry.

JACK WALKED INTO BETTY REID'S kitchen, escorted by Calvin. He saw his mother freeze momentarily, then she walked towards him, arms reaching out.

Jack swallowed. He didn't want to cry in front of Calvin.

"Land sakes, what happened to you?" she said, leading him to the kitchen table.

Jack just shook his head, tears welling up in his eyes. "Will Harney punched me."

"God's teeth, why?"

"He came into the store and saw me walking like him and he got mad."

"Take that cloth away. Let me see what it looks like."

Jack removed the blood-splattered towel from his face. There was cotton wadded up in each of his nostrils. He leaned forward against his mother and felt her arms go around him.

"Doc Creed patched him up. He said he'd come and have a look at him in a couple of days after the swelling goes down a bit. He can't tell right now if it's broken or not," Calvin informed her. "The bleeding's stopped for good he thinks, but he said to leave the cotton in there for a while just in case. If it starts to bleed heavy again, send someone over to fetch him. He said he'd come right away."

"Jack, are you all right? Your face is a mess."

The boy nodded, his head on his mother's shoulder.

"Help me get him to his bedroom, Calvin, it's just off the kitchen this way."

Jack felt like a ragdoll as they removed his bloody shirt and sat him down on the side of the bed. His mother placed his pillow against the wall. "I'll get you one from our bed. Stay with him, Calvin, I'll be right back."

"You better not lie down straight just now, Jack," she said as she returned to the room. "It's not going to be comfortable but it's for your own good."

"Yeah, Dr. Creed said the same thing," Calvin offered. "Said for him not to lie down flat or to go to sleep until later tonight, and to put lots of cold cloths on his nose to help with the swelling."

Betty smoothed her son's dark hair and kissed his forehead.

"Just lie back now, but don't go to sleep. I'm going to get you a clean cloth."

Once Jack was sitting up in bed with his back leaning against the wall and holding a towel filled with ice shards to his face, Betty went to the stove to heat the kettle for a fresh pot of tea for her visitor.

"Now tell me what happened, Calvin," she said.

Afterward Betty sighed. "I told him, I don't know how many times, not to be making fun of people. I knew it would get him into trouble one of these days. Now his father's going to be mad as a wet hen when he gets back from Pugwash."

"Will Harney should be charged with assault, so he should," Calvin said. "There was no need of going at the boy like that. Just telling him off would have been enough. There's not sense in what he did."

"Thanks for bringing him home, Calvin, I appreciate that."

"Yeah, I better get back. The ol' woman says she can't watch everybody in the store at once. She thinks they all steal."

Betty smiled and rose from the table. "Well, I'd better go check. I don't want him to fall asleep. Once he's healed he'll get his punishment, but right now I'm worried about him."

"I think he's gotten punishment enough," Calvin observed, picking up his hat and heading for the door.

"Hopefully this will cure him of making fun of people," Betty said. "His father and brother encourage him in that foolishness and look what's happened."

BARNEY THOMPSON, FOREMAN OF THE Huestis Graystone Company in Wallace, was seated behind a desk, with a cigar clamped between his teeth, when Constable Pat Ryan walked into the office.

"You have an employee by the name of William Harney, I believe?"

"Yeah, Harney's been with us for the last few years. Does a lot of the dirty work around here. If any of it can be called clean."

"Is he here today? I have to talk to him."

Thompson grabbed his hat off a hook.

"I'll walk over with you."

"The rain we've had lately has kept the dust down a bit. Sometimes it's so thick it's hard to breathe around here," Thompson observed as the two men walked across the work yard. "Hope there's not going to be any trouble here today," Thompson said, looking sideways at the lawman. "Will can be pretty touchy at times. Has he done anything wrong?"

"He beat up a fourteen-year-old boy the other day."

"A kid. Jesus."

"Smashed his face up pretty good."

"Without cause?"

"That seems to be the case."

"There he is over there." Thompson pointed. "Hey."

A man halfway down a ladder with a bucket in one hand turned in their direction.

"Will, come over here for a minute," Thompson yelled.

Will waved in return and continued his descent. He carried the bucket over to where Ryan and Thompson were standing.

"Will, this man here would like to talk to you."

"Mr. William Harney?" Ryan asked.

"Yeah, who are you?"

"There's a warrant issued for your arrest on three counts. One count of assault on the person of Jack Reid of Rockley, one count of theft, and one count of destruction of property by Calvin Bailey of Rockley. You are to be remanded to Pugwash jail until the circuit judge comes through next week."

"Son of a bitch!" Harney stepped forward and pushed Ryan backwards with an open right hand.

"Hold on there," Thompson warned. "None of that foolishness here."

"That smartass kid got what was coming to him. And I didn't hit him that hard. If I'd wanted to I'd have knocked his block off."

Will spat on the ground at Thompson's boots.

"You broke the kid's nose. You're under arrest." Ryan produced handcuffs from a pocket of his long black coat. "Don't make it any worse for yourself by assaulting an officer of the law."

"The law, my ass." Will spat again.

"Take it easy, Will. Just do as he says," Thompson cautioned. "You'll get it all straightened around if you just stay calm. And you've still got a job here."

By this time the other men had stopped working and were staring at the three figures at the far end of the yard.

Will shrugged off Thompson's hand. "I didn't do anything wrong. Just stood up for myself."

"Well, you can tell all that to the judge in due course. Right now, you're coming with me." Ryan clamped the handcuffs on Will and turned to Thompson. "Can you lend me a horse and buggy for a few hours?" he asked. "I'll drive him to Pugwash, leave my own horse here, and come back for it later."

"No problem. I'll get one of the men to get it ready for you,"

"And if I could have a man of yours to come along with me, just in case of trouble, it would be much appreciated," Ryan added.

"I'll go with you myself," Thompson said. Turning to Will, he said, "And I don't put up with any foolishness."

Will's trial was held in Pugwash the following week. He was found guilty on all charges and would have spent six months in jail if John had not paid his fines. It cost him and Mabel fifty dollars to set Will free.

"I also paid Bailey ten dollars for the damage you caused and that tobacco you took," John told Will.

"Then you're a bigger fool than I take you for" were the only words Will directed to his uncle on the journey home.

THE NEXT MORNING, JACK'S FATHER, Hiram Reid, rode over to the Dempsey farm.

"I know he's home," Hiram told John when they met in the barnyard.

"I don't blame you for being mad," John reassured his neighbour. "I'd like to break his neck myself, but your coming here will only make matters worse."

"Jack has problems breathing through his nose. It's all twisted to the right side. Doc Creed doesn't know if he can fix it or not. His mother cries practically every time she looks at him. Jack's just a kid and Will hit him the same as he would a full grown man."

"We feel awful about it," John said. "Ann said for you to give us any of Doc Creed's bills and we'll pay them one way or another."

"Got some right here." Hiram reached into his coat pocket and handed the receipts down to John. "There'll be more if Creed has to operate."

"No matter. Send them along, we'll take care of it."

"Now tell him to get his arse out here."

Will had heard Hiram's horse come into the yard. He jumped out of bed, looked out the window down into the yard, and saw the two men talking. "That fool uncle of mine will give me up like nothing."

He ran to Mary's bedroom on the other side of the house, climbed out the window, jumped to the ground, and ran for the woods.

John sighed and turned towards the house. When he walked into the kitchen, Mary and Mabel were washing the breakfast dishes and Ann was rocking thirteen-month-old Harry while Little Helen sat at her feet.

"Hiram just came into the yard. He wants to talk to Will."

Ann rose to her feet. "Oh, John, he'll kill him." She handed the baby over to Mary and headed out the door.

"No more than he deserves, hurtin' that kid the way he did." John headed for the stairs.

"I think your mother was worrying about just the opposite," Mabel told Mary. "I'd be mighty careful if I was Hiram Reid, I would."

Mary sat down in the rocking chair. Ever since her father got home yesterday, he and Ann had been arguing.

He likely slapped her too. It looks like she has a bruise on her cheek, Mary thought as she rocked back and forth.

She snuggled her head down into Harry's warm body and closed her eyes. Her stomach started filling with butterflies.

"He's not up there anywhere," John said. "I looked through all the rooms upstairs." He slammed the door behind him.

"Must have seen Hiram outdoors and gone and hid somewheres," Mabel said as she put a plate away in the cupboard and pulled the curtain back from the window. Ann was out in the yard talking to Hiram.

"Mr. Reid, I know that what Will did to your boy was wrong and we're all very sorry because of it. But please, why don't you just leave and come back another time? Will is wound up at the moment and it's better if he's left alone when he's like this."

"I'm sorry to make trouble for you and your family," Hiram told her. "But some things just can't be let go. Your husband could have killed my boy. He and I have to have it out and it's better if it's just me alone. It was all I could do yesterday to keep my oldest boy, Smith, and a bunch of his friends, from going to Pugwash for the trial. They even talked about breaking in and lynching him on the spot."

Ann put her hand over her mouth and tears sprang to her eyes. "You are all such good people. I can't believe any young man in Rockley would actually think about doing such a thing."

He looked at her more seriously now. "When a young man gets riled up there's no telling what he might do. I told them I'd look after it so they're leaving it to me, for now anyway."

John came back out of the house shaking his head. "He's not in there. Don't know where he might have gotten himself to."

"It's no good lying for him, John."

"He's not in the house, I swear. He was in bed a half-hour ago but God knows where he is now."

"Do I have your permission to look around?" Hiram asked, swinging his leg over his horse's back.

"Yes," John said, "and I'll help you."

A second search of the house, then the barn and outbuildings, revealed no sign of Will.

"I'm goin' down to look around the shacks," Hiram told John.

"I'll get the wagon and follow you."

Will, hiding behind John's fishing shack, heard the rumbling of the express wagon as it splashed through the mud puddles that dotted the long lane to the main road.

"That idiot's leading him right down here to me."

He plunged back into the woods and headed toward the house. He didn't want to face Hiram Reid today. Not caught off guard like this. Will was sorry now that he had lost his temper and hit the boy. He knew he'd have to face Hiram for it sooner or later.

I jump too fast, he thought to himself. Gets me in trouble every time.

Hiram dismounted and took his rifle out of the saddle holster.

"There's no need for that now," John said, jumping down from the wagon seat.

"This is in case he tries any funny business. I don't want to make things hard for you, John, but the way I feel right now I could shoot him and not think twice about it."

John lowered his head and walked towards the fishing shack. His hands shook as he forced open the door. He had meant to fix that broken padlock but hadn't gotten around to it. He prayed that Will wasn't inside hiding like some scared rabbit.

"Your punt's here so he didn't take off down the river," Hiram observed. "Unless he stole somebody else's."

The two men walked down the shore in front of the string of shacks and then back up behind the buildings. There was no one else around to ask if Will had been there. But then Hiram spotted two boot tracks in the soft earth behind John's shack.

"Somebody's been here and not too long ago."

"Looks like," John agreed.

Hiram walked around to the front of the shack then strolled over to his horse. He put his rifle back in the holster, walked over to John's express wagon, and leaned up against it.

"You know," he said, taking tobacco and papers out of his coat pocket, "your nephew's both a coward and a bully."

"A person can't be one and not the other." John retrieved his own makings from his shirt pocket.

When they got back up to the main road, John turned to Hiram.

"If I get him to agree to talk to you and Jack, would you be able to keep Smith and the others from coming after him?"

"I'll do my best. My boys are reasonable. What they want is an apology. I don't know if Jack will ever breathe right again. Doc Creed is going to try and fix it, but there's no guarantees."

"I'll see what I can do and let you know as soon as I can one way or the other. Will can't hide out for the rest of his life."

JOHN DID HIS BEST TO convince Will to make peace with the Reids but he refused. The following Friday evening on his way home from Wallace, swaying in the saddle from his visit to the Wharf Tavern, Will was met just outside Rockley by Hiram Reid, Smith, and three of Smith's friends.

"I'm here to see that it's a fair fight and nobody gets killed," Hiram told them.

Will calmly got off his horse and tied its reins to a tree branch.

"Time that you had a fight with somebody your own size," Smith said, circling around Will and looking for the opportunity to land the first punch.

The men were the same height and of similar weight but Smith, almost twenty years younger, was quicker. He got Will down on his back and sat on top of him. He had punched Will twice when Hiram grabbed him by the arm. "That's enough, you've proved your point. Be the better man now and leave it at that. Your mother will see to that fat lip when we get home."

Hiram took satisfaction, as did Smith's friends, that Will had gotten the worst of it. And Smith was satisfied that he had avenged his brother. Dr. Creed had put Jack's nose back in place the best he could. Jack whistled a bit through it from then on, but after a while people didn't notice so much.

ROCKLEY

NOVA SCOTIA
August 1876

AS FRED LEFURGEY'S SURREY turned into the lane, Ann looked back at the children. Mary was staring straight ahead while Little Helen dozed, leaning on her older sister's shoulder. The time in Merigomish had gone so quickly. Ann wished Will had agreed to their staying for three weeks instead of just two, but she knew she was lucky to have gotten that much time away. It was good for the children to know her side of the family even if Will didn't care for either of her parents or for Beatrice.

Ann sighed and righted herself on the seat. Fred was sitting so near. She moved farther away, disturbing Harry's sleep.

"Glad to be back, Ann?" Fred asked.

"Mmm."

Fred looked straight ahead. He found it hard to meet Ann's eyes with his own. He had heard talk about her husband mistreating her. He hoped it wasn't true but at the same time longed for the opportunity to come to her rescue. He wished the drive from the River Philip station had been longer.

The surrey came to a stop in front of the Dempsey farmhouse.

"Home again, home again, jiggity jig," Little Helen called out, wide-awake now, and jumping up and down on the floor of the surrey.

Harry was squirming to get out of his mother's arms. "Down, down," he said.

"Looks like some people are glad to be back home." Fred smiled.

"And very tired," Ann said.

"Well, let me get your bags for you."

"Don't bother yourself, LeFurgey. I'll get them."

Ann and Mary both jumped. They turned to see Will striding up beside the surrey.

"Daddy, Daddy," Little Helen and Harry chanted.

Will plucked Harry off his mother's knee and deposited him on the ground.

"Thank you for getting my loving family home safely."

"Will, how's it going?" Fred replied with a smile.

"Just fine. How's the taxi business?"

"Can't complain." Fred grinned.

"Looks like you got a cozy little setup here," Will said as he grabbed the handles of the bags and jerked them off the vehicle.

In a panic, Ann jumped from the surrey and hurried onto the veranda. She wished that Fred would just drive away now. Why was he taking so long? She could feel her husband's mounting anger. Couldn't Fred feel it too? Wasn't he nervous? Please, just leave, she begged him silently.

Will walked over and dropped the bags heavily onto the floor in front of her.

"Be careful, please," she whispered.

"Well, I'll be off. Nice to see you again, Ann. Bye, kids."

"Bye, Mr. LeFurgey," Mary called out, sorry to see him leave.

Little Helen and Harry waved.

Fred drove the surrey ahead, beyond the house and into the barnyard, to turn around. He tipped his hat to Ann as he drove past them again and down the lane.

"Where's my boy?" Will called.

Harry came waddling up to him.

"Here he is," Will said, laughing and swinging the child up into his arms. "Come on, son, into the house to see Grandma."

The porch door slammed behind him.

Ann, slowly regaining her composure, was feeling suddenly exhausted. Her bottom lip quivered.

Mary stepped up onto the veranda carrying her case and grabbed the handle of one of her mother's bags.

Ann wiped her eyes. "Thank you, Mary. After you change your

dress, could you run out to the garden and get some peas and carrots and potatoes? I think I'll make a hodgepodge for supper."

"All right, Mumma," Mary said. "Come on, Little Helen, let's go upstairs and change into our chore clothes."

"All right, Mumma," the child repeated.

John rounded the corner of the house, carrying a hoe.

"Well, well, look who's back, all my best girls."

Smiling, he swept Little Helen up and placed her on his shoulders. She plucked the battered hat off his head and began to swing it around.

"Unca John," she cried, hugging his head and poking his face with the hat.

"How are things here? Did the quarry run every day?" Ann asked him.

"It was dull without you and the kids. Those two aren't much company." John lifted his chin towards the house.

"What about the quarry? Did it run?"

"Every day except one, when it rained. Rained hard, too. Will was there every day otherwise."

Ann breathed out heavily. Will missed so much work, often on the flimsiest excuse.

John took the case out of Mary's hand and stepped aside for her to walk ahead.

"I've asked Mary to get some vegetables from the garden for hodgepodge; perhaps you could show her the best ones to pick," Ann suggested to him.

"Mary can help you in the kitchen. I'll go to the garden myself as soon as we get these in the house."

They trooped into the kitchen. Ann, leading the way, removed the pins from her hat.

Mabel was sitting on her daybed, propped up by pillows and covered with blankets. She was holding Harry in her arms with Will standing beside her, grinning widely.

"Finally got back, did you?" Mabel asked Ann. "I don't know how much longer I could've kept this house going on my own. And I've had three calls while you've been running the roads. Never mind looking at me like that, John Dempsey, you know how poorly I've been these last few days."

"You've had but one call since they've been away and you weren't too poorly last night to eat half a chicken, a peck of potatoes, and two pieces of blueberry pie for supper."

"Oh, did you make a pie?" Ann asked her mother-in-law.

"Your beau's mother made it and brought it over to us." Will smiled at her.

"Who?" Ann sighed and motioned her daughters towards the stairs. It was this kind of talk that tired her out more than the long train ride, more than anything. She hated herself for asking a question for which she already knew the answer.

Will caught Little Helen up into his arms and tickled the giggling child.

"Rita LeFurgey, Fred's mother," Mabel answered. "It was good of her to bring it over. Seeing how long you've been gone, she likely took pity on us. But she sure skimped on the sugar. That pie was sour enough to make a pig squeal."

"You weren't squealing much last night at the supper table," John replied.

"Never mind, you," Mabel admonished him.

"Well, that was very thoughtful of Rita," Ann said. "I'll sit down after supper and write her a thank-you note and Mary can run it over. I'm going upstairs now to change and then start supper."

Harry's tiny arms shot out towards his mother.

"Here, take this one with you." Mabel lifted the toddler away from her.

"He's full of piss."

Ann walked across the room and picked up the child. Why did Mabel always have to be so vulgar? It was such a bad example for the children.

"Did Mumma's boy pee?" she asked kissing his cheek. Harry laughed and kicked his feet. "Upstairs we go," Ann said.

John trooped after her with the three bags.

"And what's for supper?" Mabel demanded, yelling after them.

"Hodgepodge!" John yelled back.

As they climbed the stairs, Ann turned around, grinned, and shook her head at John. He rolled his eyes.

"May as well laugh as cry," she told him when they got to the landing.

"YOUR MOTHER IS SUCH A lady, she knows about the niceties," Rita LeFurgey told Mary. "I don't get thank-you notes very often. And on such pretty paper."

It was stationery that Aunt Beatrice had given Mary's mother during the visit. Heavy and ivory-coloured with a pale blue border and envelopes to match.

"Can't get anything like this in Pugwash. Be sure to thank her for me."

The sun was setting when Mary walked back up the lane from the LeFurgey farm. The house looked peaceful as she got nearer. Its windows were on fire with reflections from the setting sun. She took in the familiar sound of the birch leaves quivering in the evening breeze. She decided to sit on the veranda awhile and listen. Since she was little, she had liked to pretend that the trees were inhabited by fairies who would come out at night to dance and play on the veranda. She could see them in their tiny, colourful clothing scurrying along the railing and bouncing up and down on the wicker chairs. Once or twice in the summer, Ann would give Mary permission to spend the night outside on the veranda and she would imagine that, after she fell asleep, the fairies would surround her and marvel at her size and her beauty. In her imaginings she was always beautiful.

In the dark, Mary had not noticed her father sitting there.

"Did you have a good time away?"

She jumped.

"Yes, thank you."

Mary settled into a chair across from him.

"We all missed you, especially me. I'm glad you're back." Will stood up, leaned towards Mary, and touched her hair.

"I missed everyone too."

"What's your Aunt Beatrice up to these days?" he said, settling back into his chair. "Still ruling the roost, I'll bet."

"She's so nice," Mary began, "and she has all kinds of beautiful clothes and books and—" .

"Yeah, she's nice all right." Will snorted. "And how's your grandfather's business? That old bugger must be richer than ever by now." Will laughed dryly.

"We didn't see him a lot. He was always working," Mary told him.

"Yes, I'll bet he was. The old cheapskate."

Mary sat back in the chair and closed her eyes. She didn't want to hear her father say mean things about Aunt Beatrice and Grandfather. She wanted to listen to the rustle of the leaves.

"Mary, you were away at the LeFurgeys' so long tonight that your Uncle John had to get the cows in and do the milking. That's your job."

Mary's eyes flew open. "I forgot all about it. Mrs. LeFurgey wanted to know all about our trip. I didn't even think—"

"Your Uncle John is in the barn right now."

She stood up.

"Now, before you go, come give me a welcome-home hug."

Mary turned to her father, holding her arms closely to her sides. He leaned down and kissed her on the cheek. She felt the butterflies rise in her stomach like they always did when Daddy was around. She didn't look at him. She was afraid to move, yet she wanted to run.

"Now get along."

Mary left the veranda and ran across the barnyard, wiping her cheek with her sleeve. Once inside the cool interior of the barn she felt safe and breathed deeply, taking in the smell of hay, manure, old wood, and leather. Fluffy grey kittens ran about on the dusty floor. She scooped one up and walked toward the stalls where John's fifteen cows stood.

Uncle John was seated on the stool next to Buckle, resting his head on the animal's flank. He had just begun to milk her when he spied Mary and, taking a teat in each hand, pulled them up and down at twice the normal speed required. He gave Mary a grin as Buckle turned to look at him, as if to ask what all the hurry was about. Mary giggled.

When the milk hit the bottom of the galvanized pail with a hollow thud, the kitten wiggled to escape from Mary's arms. Released, it skittered over to John, who turned one of the teats sideways and squirted milk in its direction. The stream went into the kitten's open mouth and washed over its face. Uncle John did the same to the other balls of grey fur who swarmed around him. There was silence in the barn for a minute or two as the kittens washed milk off their faces.

"This bunch is going to burst, they're drinking so much," John observed. "And they're still nursing off their mother. She's the one I should be giving all this to. I'm just about done here, Buckle's the last one needs milking."

Mary sat down on a stool across from her uncle, brought her knees up, and encircled them with her arms, balancing herself. The last rays of the setting sun carpeted the barn floor with thin lines of pink. The satisfied kittens wrestled each other in a corner. Except for the sound of their soft bodies on the floor and the milk filling the bucket, the barn was silent.

"I'm sorry I wasn't here to do the milking, Uncle John. I'm sorry you had to do it tonight after doing it all the time I was away."

"I don't mind. Tell me about your trip."

"It was wonderful. We read books together at night and ate in a real restaurant twice. I made a new friend called Rachel and Aunt Beatrice sewed us all new things. Did you see my dress and boots that I was wearing when I got back today?"

"That I did, and they're some handsome. You looked all grown up."

"I loved it at Grandpa and Grandma Hennessey's. I asked if I could stay a little longer but Mumma said no. I wish I could have."

"You will another time. I remember when I was your age. I wanted to see the world, travel. And I did a bit, but always found home to be the best. You'll learn that as the years go by. But I know what it's like to be young and restless."

"Who knows when I might ever go back for another visit. I'm almost seventeen and this was the first time I ever met them."

"It's hard to get away when you live on a farm, Mary. There's so much to do and not a lot of money for extras like travelling."

"I want to see things like Aunt Beatrice does."

"And someday you probably will. But you still have some growing up to do and your Ma needs you around here. And we'd all miss you something awful."

Mary folded her arms and pouted.

John reached out his arms and Mary walked into them.

"God knows, I understand why you'd want to stay at your aunt's for longer. All the criticizing and complaining you have to listen to all the time around here. But time goes by, and when you get older you can make some decisions for yourself. Not everybody goes on like your father and grandmother do. You'll see."

He kissed the top of her head and released her.

"Now you get to the house. It's time you went to bed. It's been a long day."

Mary ran across the barnyard and into the house. Her father and grandmother were now both sitting on the veranda. As always, Mabel was gossiping and complaining and Will was smoking and nodding his head. Mary mounted the stairs. Her mother was in Harry's and Little Helen's bedroom reading to them from the big Mother Goose book with the red cover. That too was usually Mary's job.

Her bedroom was at the end of the long upstairs hall. She passed her parents' room on the left, then her grandmother's. Across the hall were two rooms full of old bed frames, baby carriages, clothes that didn't fit anyone, farm tools, and anything else for which the family had no more use. No one knew for sure all that was in those rooms. John said that his grandmother Dempsey had, years before, started throwing things in there after her husband died and it had been added to over the years by other family members. Many times Ann said she wanted to clear one of them out and make a sewing room for herself but Mabel would not allow it. Both rooms were locked and Will had the keys. Beyond was Mary's bedroom. Uncle John slept in a room downstairs off the pantry. He said that was all he needed and that he didn't want to have to go up and down the stairs all the time.

In Mary's room a small table with a drawer and two shelves sat beside her bed. Two books lay on its top shelf, a bible sent from Grandmother Hennessey when she was christened and a copy of *Gulliver's Travels*. She placed *The Woman in White* and *The Moonstone* on the top of the pile.

Just then the door opened and Mary jumped away from the table. Her father stuck his head into the room.

"All ready for bed?" he asked.

"Not yet."

Will opened the door wider and walked into the room, looking around.

"Just wanted to be sure that you were all right. You've had a long day."

"I'm fine."

He smiled. "You looked fine in that new dress of yours today. All grown up."

"Aunt Beatrice made it for me."

"You're getting to be a real pretty young lady, Mary. Very pretty indeed," he repeated, backing out of the room without taking his eyes off her.

He turned and closed the door behind him.

Mary picked up a chair. She jammed its top up under the door knob, bracing it shut. Then she walked slowly to her bed, got under the covers, and curled herself up into a tight ball.

THE NEXT MORNING WHEN MARY went downstairs to the kitchen, Harry was seated in his wooden highchair wedged up against the kitchen table, banging a spoon on its tray.

"Just a minute, little man, it's almost done," Ann reassured him, stirring the porridge on the top of the stove.

"Mumma's boy is hungry this morning." She smiled at Mary. "Please get me a bowl from the cupboard, will you? And one for you and me too."

Mary brought the bowls over to the stove. Ann spooned a bit of porridge into one of them.

"Blow on that, please, until it's cool enough for him."

"Where's Little Helen?" Mary asked.

"I'm letting her sleep a bit longer this morning. She kept falling asleep last night as I was bathing her. She was that tired from all the travelling we did yesterday. Put a bit of molasses on that for him and stir it around."

When Mary presented Harry with his breakfast, he immediately began to slap his spoon on the surface of the cereal. Flecks of white flew about his head.

"Feed him, please, Mary. Yours will be cool enough by the time you're done with him."

Ann chatted away, and was, to Mary's surprise, drinking her black tea from one of Grandma Harney's good pink and white china cups, the little finger of her right hand raised. Most of the time she just grabbed one of the many chipped enamel cups in the cupboard. Mary looked out the kitchen window and saw her grandmother coming towards the house, carrying eggs in a twig basket. She had been out to the chicken coop and, as usual, didn't look pleased.

"This morning I'm going to make a couple of pies to take over to the church for the supper tomorrow night," Ann was saying. "Mrs. Murray asked me to make something before we went away."

Mary wrestled the spoon out of Harry's chubby hand for the third time. There was more porridge on her apron and the floor than had managed to find its way into the baby's mouth.

"Just a little more, sweetie," Mary begged. "Watch the train coming into the station." She made choo choo sounds as she moved the spoon, in intervals, towards him. Harry shook his head, placed his right arm across his forehead, and looked away.

"Good thing I wrote it down to remind myself," Ann went on. "I had forgotten all about it until I saw the note this morning. I think I'll make blueberry. Then I'll have Uncle John run me over to the church later. God bless him, he milked the cows and got them out to the field this morning. Your father went to work hours ago. He'll be gone for the rest of the week."

Mary had missed the cows while she was at Aunt Beatrice's. She'd be sure to fetch them in tonight and see to them. She was glad that her father was away. She had been relieved when he started working in Wallace. It meant he wasn't home at night as much.

She had given up on trying to feed Harry and was eating her lukewarm breakfast when Mabel came into the kitchen with the eggs. She immediately started with Ann over the china cup.

"You'll break that, clumsy as what you are. Just because you've been around your fancy relatives doesn't mean that you can destroy the few decent things I have. Those cups are for good."

Mabel shook her head as if in disbelief, and before Ann could protest she turned to Mary.

"I want you to dig some potatoes today. You can take Little Helen with you, keep her from bein' underfoot. Where is she anyway? Not out of bed yet?"

Mary got up from the table, leaving her mother and grandmother arguing in the kitchen. She climbed the stairs, washed and dressed herself and Little Helen, and fed her sister breakfast. Then the two girls walked up to the potato field on the hill behind the barn. Mary carried a hoe, two wooden buckets, one inside the other, and two feedbags, while Little Helen held the tiny hoe that Uncle John had made especially for her. The sun was warm and pleasant on their faces, and there was just enough wind to keep the bugs away. Little Helen, nonetheless, soon started complaining. First she was hungry, even though she had just had breakfast, so Mary gave her a bite of the buttered bread she had brought to hold them over until dinnertime. After that, the child said she was hot and sat down under the nearby alder bushes.

"Don't wanna work."

Mary sighed. "You don't have to. It's better if I do it myself, it's faster. Just sit there and watch."

Little Helen was soon dozing. Mary moved the hoe back and forth in the dirt in search of the blue potatoes that Uncle John had planted in June. She liked looking for the spuds. They were almost the same colour as the earth if she didn't look too closely. She would pretend that she was on a treasure hunt. Sometimes she would break into a potato with the hoe, revealing its creamy, blue-veined interior. She also made up stories about them. Sometimes they were married to the potato next to them and the smaller spuds were their children. Mary often felt guilty for digging at them roughly with the hoe, removing them from their warm earth bed.

Later on she heard voices down in the barnyard. Uncle John was harnessing Bill and Blackie, getting them ready to take Ann to the church with her pies. She stepped out of the porch door with two baskets, each covered with a white and red checkered dishcloth. Ann looked up towards the field and waved. Mary turned away and bent over the potatoes once again.

ST. GEORGE'S ANGLICAN CHURCH WAS an eyesore and everyone in Rockley knew it. Thirty years ago it had been just one of the many grand visions of businessman Lester Clarke. Chairman of the rectory board and said to be as rich as Croesus, Clarke wanted to construct a church he felt worthy of attendance by himself and his family. He had made good in the Boston States and retired at the age of fifty-five back to Rockley, the place of his birth, with many plans to boost the community. He started with the church. Parishioners couldn't be grateful enough that Clarke was using his own money to provide them with a brand new place of worship and the land for a massive cemetery.

Two weeks after the ten-foot concrete foundation wall was put in place, Clarke died in his sleep. Some people said it was his heart. Others repeated the story that he had been poisoned, slowly, by his spendthrift second wife. In any case, Clarke's was the first burial in the new graveyard. His widow and his money returned to Connecticut and the Rockley Anglicans were left with an impressive wall and no funds to build a suitable structure atop it. Finally, after years of pie socials and fundraising bazaars, they were able to cover it with a flimsy one-storey shed-roofed building and rickety wooden stairway leading up to the front door.

"Looks like my shithouse on top of the Roman coliseum," John said once when describing it to a man from Stellarton.

To deliver her pies, Ann climbed the many stairs to the front door of the church while John waited in the express wagon. At the top she read a note on the door directing her to the rectory across the road.

"I should have known." She sighed, turned, and took a step down from the platform. Then she tried to take another and couldn't. The heel of her right boot was wedged into a space between two loose boards on the top step. Then heel and boot separated.

Ann felt the weight of the two baskets pitching her forward. Her right leg dragged behind the rest of her body, the kneecap hitting each step on the way down.

"No, no, no."

The baskets were crushed beneath her and she heard glass breaking.

"Ann, are you all right?" John was kneeling beside her. "God, woman, you gave yourself an awful heist."

He tried to lift her left shoulder to turn her over.

"No, just a minute," she begged.

A sourness rose in the back of Ann's throat and she felt beads of cold sweat spring out on her forehead.

"Are you all right?" John repeated.

"I...I don't know. I just want to lie here for a minute."

"I heard glass breaking. You have to get up, you might be bleeding."

"Oh."

John gingerly lifted her left shoulder and got a basket out from under her.

"Jesus."

Then he realized that it was blueberry and not blood stains down the front of her dress.

"Oh," Ann said, turning to lie on one side. "My ankle hurts."

"Which one?"

"The right."

"It's curled up under you. Just a minute."

They heard a door slam and feet running towards them.

"Good heavens, what happened?" asked Mrs. Murray, the minister's wife, coming to a stop on her knees in front of Ann.

"She fell," John answered, indicating the church with a nod of his head.

"Oh, I knew this would happen one day, with those godawful stairs. I kept telling Earl to get them fixed but no, that would be too easy. Ann, come into the house so we can get a look at you. Do you think you can walk?"

"I'll try."

John placed both hands under Ann's left armpit; Mrs. Murray did the same on her right side, and together they managed to slowly lift Ann to a standing position.

"Oh, I can't," she cried. "I can't put any weight on my right leg."

"Wait a minute," John said. "Let's do this. Put your arms around our shoulders and we'll make a chair with our hands to support you."

He and Mrs. Murray bent forward and Ann put her arms around their necks.

"Now sit down," John said.

"You can't lift me," she protested.

"Oh, you're light as a feather, dear," Mrs. Murray reassured her.

They carried Ann across the road and up onto the Murray's veranda.

"To the left, the parlour," Mrs. Murray directed as they made their way through the front door.

They deposited Ann on the parlour sofa, and Mrs. Murray placed two cushions under her head.

"She'll be all right here, Mr. Dempsey. You run for Doctor Creed. I just saw him pass by here about a half hour ago so he's likely home. I'll make her as comfortable as I can until you get back. Where does it hurt, dear?" she asked as John slammed the door behind him.

"My right ankle and the inside of my right knee."

"Let's see." She lifted Ann's skirt and petticoat. "I'll need to run and get a hook to undo your boot, dear. I'll be right back."

"I'm so sorry about all this, Mrs. Murray," Ann said when her hostess returned. She started to cry. "The pies are ruined and I don't have anything else for the church supper."

Mrs. Murray smiled and began to unhook the buttons on Ann's right boot. "My dear, pies and church suppers are the least of your worries at the moment. This ankle's badly swollen. I'm going to wrap a cold cloth around it while we wait for the doctor. And we should get your leg raised above your heart. And please, call me Josephine. Oh good, here's Junior."

Through the pain, Ann saw a blond child come into the room. He stopped and stared down at her. She had never seen such eyes before. They seemed to bore right through her. In the background, she felt more than saw Mrs. Murray scurrying around.

"Stop gawking, dear, and go over to the churchyard and pick up Mrs. Harney's hat and bring it in to me. And be careful with it. Then take a shovel and box and scoop up those baskets and pies. Watch yourself, there's broken glass."

"What happened?" asked the child.

"Mrs. Harney fell down the church steps, thanks to your father. The doctor will be here any minute. Now off with you, and look lively. The Gardners' dog is already over there sniffing around."

As Mrs. Murray steered him towards the front door, the boy kept looking over his shoulder at Ann.

"It all goes onto the manure pile behind the barn. Thank you, dear.

"Now, let's look after that ankle," she said and headed for the kitchen.

WHEN WILL ARRIVED HOME FRIDAY evening, he found Ann sitting up on his mother's daybed while Mabel stood in front of the stove stirring a large pot of soup. John was at the kitchen table shining his boots.

"What's wrong with you?" Will greeted his wife.

"She's taken a lazy spell, that's what's wrong," Mabel stated before Ann could open her mouth. "Came in here last Monday bawling about her ankle being broken. And hasn't done any work since. I've been run clear off my feet."

"You haven't done a damn thing until today when you knew he was coming home," John corrected her. "That soup is the first thing you've laid your hand to all week."

"Ann was trying to deliver some pies to the church and sprained her ankle falling down the stairs," he told Will. "Doc Creed said she won't be able to walk on it for a while."

Will sat down at the end of the daybed and looked at his wife. "We should sue the bastards. How come you're here and not upstairs?"

"I can't go up or down stairs, Will. I can't walk at all, except with these crutches." Ann pointed at the wooden sticks leaning on the wall beside her. "And I have to keep my leg propped up or it doesn't feel right."

"Her knee's all swollen too," John added.

"She's been whining all week." Mabel shook her head.

"It was a nasty fall she took, Will," John said, getting up from the table. "We're lucky that she didn't break her neck."

"Well, well, well. This is a fine mess." Will shook his head. "What are we supposed to do with you now? Might as well take you behind the barn and shoot you." He grinned at Ann and slapped her on the knee.

"That hurts!"

"My apologies, madam." Will, still grinning, stood up and tipped his hat to her.

"We should sue the bastards," he repeated. "Get something out of this."

"Who are you going to sue?" Mabel asked him. "The Archbishop of Canterbury? That church has no money; they barely have a building let alone being able to pay you a settlement. Forget it. And that Mary's been no help whatsoever," she added. "Daydreaming like always. And sullen!"

"Aw, that's not right, Mabel, and you know it." John slammed the flat of his hand down on the table. "Why don't you let up on Mary once in a while?"

"Mary has been very good," Ann protested, raising herself up from her mound of pillows. "She's been at my beck and call all week, getting me things and helping me dress. She's kept the two little ones out of your mother's way and even made bread this morning. I told her how to do it."

"She's way past the time to learn to make bread. She's been spoiled all these years," Mabel scoffed.

"I'll see to Mary, Ma," Will said. "I know she tends to be slow but she's a good girl over all."

John had gone out to the porch but now he opened the kitchen door again. "She's out right now, getting the cows." He slammed the door behind him.

"How was work this week?" Ann asked Will.

"Good, good. For once they all left me alone to work in peace. Hey, here's my babies."

Little Helen and Harry had been playing on the kitchen floor and trying to get their father's attention since he came into the house. Now they both jumped into his arms.

"How's about a whisker rub for the pair of you?"

The children giggled and squirmed as he rubbed his five-day beard along their soft cheeks.

They're the only things worth coming home for, he thought as the two children sat on his back and he circled around on his hands and knees in the kitchen. They take me as I am, no complaining, no demands. Like Pa used to. Will tried not to think of his father. He let out a growl that caused more happy squealing.

"All right, such as it is, supper's ready." Mabel carried the steaming pot to the table.

"Stay out of the way or you'll get scalded." She motioned with her chin towards the children and plopped the pot down.

"What about Mary and John?" Ann asked.

"Little Helen, go out as far as the porch door and yell for Mary and John to come for supper," Mabel said.

"You get up to the table." Will nodded at his daughter. "They can get theirs when the chores are done. Now let's eat, I'm starved."

Ann folded her arms. "I'm not eating until Mary and John come in," she said.

"That's right, you're not," Mabel snorted. "I've got my hands full feeding these two. You'll just have to wait your turn. You can't be all that hungry anyways, all you've done is sit around and read all day."

Ann lay back and turned her face to the wall.

ROCKLEY

NOVA SCOTIA
September 1876

MARY WAS WALKING HOME from school when she stopped to listen to a squawking blue jay.

"You're funny," Mary told him. "And fat and sassy. What have you got to go on about?"

As if insulted, the bird turned and flew away into the forest. Mary decided to follow and took the path through the woods that would eventually lead to the hill in back of her uncle's house. She heard the thud of axes in the distance. Fifteen minutes later she walked out into a clearing, and there was Fred LeFurgey and Smith Reid, both stripped to the waist, chopping down a large tree. Smith saw her first.

"Mary, walk away to the other side of us," he said, pointing towards the hill. "This thing is going to come down in a minute and fall your way."

Mary didn't want to do as Smith said even if it was for her own good. Ann and Grandma Harney had both been frightened when Will got beat up last spring. But Fred turned and smiled at her, and he too pointed in the direction she was to go, so she reasoned it was him she was obeying. She had never seen a big tree falling to the ground so when she got a safe ways off, she turned back to watch. In a minute the tree began to sway, and both Smith and Fred stood on the opposite side from the cut and pushed it forward. Then they too got back out of its way. The tree fell, crashing down over the spot where Mary had stood minutes before. When the needles and dust finally settled, Fred called to her.

Mary walked over to them. Both men retrieved their shirts and were buttoning them up. Smith gave her a huge grin and nodded in acknowledgement. He really was quite handsome, she couldn't help but notice. She frowned at him, nodding her head, then turned to Fred and smiled.

"Why are you walking through here, Mary, and almost getting hit with falling trees?" Fred asked.

"I'm on my way home from school. I saw a blue jay and followed him in here."

"It isn't a good idea for a girl to be walking in the woods by herself," Smith said. She turned to look at him and shrugged her shoulders dismissively.

Smith blushed and Fred laughed out loud. "Mary doesn't seem to care much for your advice," he said and turned back to the girl.

"What did you learn in school today?"

"All about Henry the Eighth and his wives."

"Old Henry didn't bother cutting down trees like a normal person," Smith observed. "He was more interested in cutting the heads off his wives."

"Is that right?" Fred asked.

"Yes, he wasn't a very nice man," Mary said, surprised that Smith would know anything about it.

"Well, that's one way to get rid of 'em." Fred laughed again. Then he looked at Mary and was suddenly serious. "How's Ann—your mother these days? I heard she took a bad fall a while back."

"She's getting better. Thank you for asking."

"Well, we better get back to work here." Smith nodded to Fred.

"Yes, we'd better. It was nice to see you again, Mary. Tell your mother I was asking about her. Don't forget." Fred turned back to the fallen tree.

"I will. Goodbye, Mr. LeFurgey." She hurried away along the path.

"A sweet girl, that Mary," Fred observed to Smith as they cut the branches from the fallen tree. "Just like her mother. And she's almost old enough to be courted, give another year or so."

Smith grinned. "That father of hers wouldn't let me come within ten feet of her."

FOUND DROWNED

MARY DIDN'T GET HOME UNTIL almost suppertime.

"And where have you been, young lady?" Mabel was taking a pie out of the oven as Mary walked through the door. Little Helen and Harry were lying on the daybed with their mother. Ann's attempts to soothe the bawling infant seemed only to make him yell the louder.

"We could use some help around here once in a while."

"I'm sorry, Grandma. I was walking through the woods and it was so pretty that I didn't want to come home." She dropped her book and slate on the bottom of the daybed and took the baby from Ann's arms.

"I think he just needs another burp," Ann said, pushing the hair out of her eyes.

"I didn't get much sleep last night. I'll take a nap now that you're home."

Mary didn't tell them that for the last hour she had been on the hill above the house pretending to be Anne Boleyn in the hours leading up to her death. Mabel had no patience with such foolishness. Lollygagging is what she called it.

"You shouldn't be parading through the woods. It's not safe," her grandmother said, putting the pie on the windowsill to cool off.

"Yes, I know that's what he—" Mary started, then remembered herself.

"That's what he what?" Mabel asked.

"That's what Mr. LeFurgey said. I met him just after I reached the road. He saw me come out of the woods. He told me I shouldn't be in there by myself. Oh, and he also told me to say hello to you, Mumma."

"He would," her grandmother retorted, and turned to look at Ann in time to witness the blush spreading up her neck.

"Mary, take Harry upstairs and put a clean diaper on him, please," Ann said, hastening to change the subject.

As Mary mounted the stairs, she heard her mother say, "He was just being neighbourly."

"Will better not catch him being neighbourly, as you call it, or there'll be hell to pay," was the reply.

ANN WAS SITTING IN THE rocking chair, covered in a crazy quilt. Her right leg was stretched out in front of her, her foot resting on a wooden chair. Someone knocked on the porch door.

"Now what?" Mabel asked, looking up from the potatoes she was peeling. "Who the hell knocks around here?"

She disappeared into the porch. Ann could hear her speaking to someone and then Mabel returned to the kitchen with a telegram in her hand.

"It's for you," she said.

"Oh God, what does it say? Read it to me, please."

"Wait now till I find my spectacles," Mabel responded, retrieving them from the top of the warming oven. "It can't be good news," she said, putting her glasses on slowly. "It never is."

Ann clutched the quilt around her while Mabel broke the seal and cleared her throat.

"The writing's so damn small, it's hard to make out. It's from your sister." Mabel looked up from the message. "Your mother's dead." She stretched out her hand holding the paper.

Ann felt a ball of cold in the pit of her stomach and the surging noise in her ears was growing louder by the second and drowning out all other sounds. She saw someone standing, staring at her, moving slowly.

I can't focus my eyes, she thought.

The person seemed to be standing behind a wall of water.

"What?"

"Your mother's gone," said the person, kneeling down beside the rocking chair and placing something in her hand.

Instead of lowering her head, Ann lifted the piece of paper into her line of vision. Black marks seemed burned into the paper.

Heart attack this morning. Mother's gone. Complete surprise. Come home.

She burst into tears. "We'll write and tell them that you're in no shape to travel," the someone said, not unkindly.

Ann's mind whirled. Now, where everything had stood still, it burst into motion.

I have to go, she thought. She opened her mouth but the words couldn't come out.

"I have to go," she tried again, shouting. "Have got to get out of here."

She needed air, needed to get outdoors. Away from this person who kept talking to her. She waved her arms around and then braced them against the rocking chair, willing herself to move, to stand up.

The person put a hand on her shoulder.

"Just calm down, calm down. All this commotion doesn't help anything."

"I need to go home." Ann flinched at the hand and tried to bat it away. "Leave me alone."

The person grabbed her face and turned it towards theirs.

"Listen to me."

Ann shook her head and tried to rise once more from the chair.

"God forgive me," someone said and Ann felt a sharp slap across her face.

"You've had a shock. Just be quiet for a minute. Just sit there and be quiet."

Ann felt arms tighten around her shoulders.

"You can't go anywhere with that leg of yours," Mabel said softly after some time went by. "You can't even walk across the room, for God's sake."

"But I have to see Mother, I have to go, I have to—"

"Just wait. It's Friday. When Will comes home tonight we'll talk about it. Just rest now. Your sister can take care of everything in the meantime. Here, let me get you over to the daybed."

Ann cried herself to sleep. She woke up at suppertime still in shock and refused to eat. Will got home at ten o'clock that evening.

"No, you're not going and that's that," he declared to Ann after hearing the news.

"But Mother's dead."

"Yes, Ann, I know, and I'm sorry about that, I really am. Your mother was always pretty decent to me. And I wish you could go but it would be just too hard for you. And you couldn't go alone and you couldn't bring the kids with you like you did last time. You couldn't look after them. Wait 'til you're better and then we'll think about it. Now come here."

Will sat on the edge of the daybed, took Ann in his arms, and rocked her back and forth.

"I could go with Mumma," Mary offered, sitting in the rocking chair in her nightgown. "I could look out for her on the way there and back."

Will looked at her over Ann's bowed head. "Nobody's goin' anywhere," he said barely above a whisper. "Now never mind."

Early the next morning Will rode to Pugwash to telegraph Beatrice that Ann could not travel at the moment. In the afternoon Ann called Mary to her side.

"We need to write a letter to Grandpa and Aunt Beatrice to let them know why I can't be there with them. Theirs will be a very sad household for a long time. Just as ours will. Now get a pen and paper and I'll tell you what to write."

A week later Ann received a long missive from Beatrice describing Helen Hennessey's last days, the well-attended funeral, and how she and their father were holding up. "Mother's death has left him unable to concentrate on work and he's totally reliant upon me at the moment," she wrote.

After receiving Beatrice's letter Ann lay on the daybed, staring into space and making no attempt to walk.

What's the use? she thought over and over and repeated it to any family member within earshot, even Little Helen and Harry.

One afternoon a week later, Rita LeFurgey called carrying an apple pie. Ann was alone in the house. Mary was outside on the veranda reading to the children. John had driven Mabel to Pugwash on a midwife's call.

"Ann, my dear, how are you holding up?" Rita asked as she sat on the edge of the daybed. "I'm so sorry about your mother."

She had never seen Ann look so pale and drawn.

"Oh, Rita, my life's over, there's nothing left now that Mother's gone." Ann let out a ragged sigh.

"My land, dear, you're still a young woman. You have a husband and three children. You have to live for your children, no matter how upset you are."

"What's the use of any of it?" Ann responded, her eyes filling with tears. "No matter what we do, how we worry, how we work, we all end up the same in the end...dead." She turned away and faced the wall.

"See here, Ann, look at me," Rita insisted, reaching forward and touching her on the shoulder.

"Turn around right now and look at me."

She waited for Ann to face her again before she spoke.

"You're right, we all die. We have no choice in the matter. But we do have the choice of how we live. Would your mother want you to give up like this? No, she wouldn't. She would want you to live, especially for those grandchildren of hers I just saw outdoors. You have no choice, Ann, you need to live for them. After my parents died, I had to go on for my own family."

"It's so unfair." Ann gulped and wiped her eyes.

"Yes, it seems unfair but it's God's way. It's not for us to question."

Ann sat up. "Why would any God that loved us let this happen, let us lose the ones we love? It doesn't make sense."

"Everyone and everything that lives dies. That's how the world works. None of us can live forever, dear. God wants us with him."

"So why bother giving us feelings, making us capable of love while we're here? Why let us suffer? Life would be easier if we didn't have feelings. I'm tired of feeling."

She started to cry all the harder.

"Yes, life would be easier, I guess, but not as rewarding or as fulfilling. Feelings and love ensure, while we're here, that we're really alive."

"Rita, sometimes I don't even know if I even believe there is a God anymore. I'm sorry, but that's how I feel." Ann wiped her eyes with the sleeve of her nightgown.

"No need to apologize, to either me or God. He understands and he will give you the strength to get through this. Count your blessings, Ann. Don't forget to count your blessings," Rita counselled, "and with time you'll feel better."

Over the next several weeks Ann received messages from friends and relatives in Merigomish, Halifax, Boston, and San Francisco extending their condolences and sharing memories of her mother. She kept them in a birchbark container by the daybed.

"All she does all day is fawn over those letters," Mabel said to John one evening. "They should all be thrown out. She's just making herself sicker looking at them all the time."

"Leave her be for a while. The poor thing has had two shocks close together. She just needs time. She'll come around."

"I hope so, for all our sakes," his sister replied.

"MARY, I REALLY DON'T NEED anything to eat," Ann argued weakly when she saw her daughter coming towards her carrying a tray.

Mary placed it on her mother's knees. It held a large glass of milk and a tea biscuit covered with strawberry jam. Ann sighed and pointed towards the rocking chair. Mary sat down and her mother began to talk, picking at the food.

"You and your grandma doing the washing today reminded me of when I was a little girl. On wash day, Mother used to wait until it was Beatrice's and my bedtime to make our beds. First she would put the bottom sheet down and tell us to get in and then she would make the bed over us. I used to love the sheets fluttering down on top of me, so fresh and clean from the line. She would make the entire bed with us in it and tuck us in for the night."

Tears rolled down her face, and she added, so softly that Mary could hardly hear, "I always felt so safe when she did that." Ann closed her eyes and choked back a piece of biscuit. Finally, swallowing hard, she turned to Mary. "I'll never see her again."

Mary stood up and wrapped her arms around her mother's shoulders. How could someone stay so sad for so long? When was Mumma going to get up and walk again, go outside, go to church? Mary missed their talks about books and the sight of her mother reading in the rocking chair, and to the two babies. She didn't know what to do to make things better.

ROCKLEY

NOVA SCOTIA
October 1876

JOHN WAS SITTING AT the kitchen table, reading.

"The cows are all milked and ready for bed," Mary said. "Can I take your punt out for a while?"

"Yeah, just be careful and come back before dark," he answered, looking at her over the top of his newspaper. "Better put a coat on too, nights are starting to get a bit chilly."

"Got one right here," Mary answered as she skipped out the kitchen door.

The birds were beginning to bed down for the night and their calls echoed along the river. Mary walked down the lane and across the main road to the fishing shacks. There were a number of people out on the river tonight. She could see some young boys fishing down the way and a couple of girls being rowed around.

Mary liked being out on the river. Sometimes she would go so far up she could see the Pugwash wharf in the distance. She always wanted to row as far as the harbour itself but didn't want news of it to get back to Uncle John or he might not let her borrow the punt again.

Mary dragged the yellow punt down to the water's edge and into the river until it floated. She had just jumped in and picked up an oar when she heard a shout from the woods. She looked up to see her father jogging down the hill towards her.

"Hey, Mary, wait a minute." He waved to her.

"Sorry, Daddy, too late." She used the oar to put the punt, and herself, out of his range.

"Aw, for Christ's sake, Mary," Will yelled. A few people within hearing distance turned, their shouts and laughter skipping over the surface of the water. He walked back into the woods.

He's drinking, she thought.

Lately he'd been putting his arm around her waist and drawing her to him. The first time she was taken by surprise; after that, she pushed his arm away and they struggled whenever he made a grab for her. She noticed that he always did it when they were alone, and she avoided that as much as she could. He was her father and it was her duty to love him, she knew, but all she could feel about him was dread. Of what, she didn't really know. He had stopped coming to her bedroom since she braced the door at night. A couple of times he had called her name, pleading through the keyhole to be let in. But Mabel had caught him at it and warned that she didn't want to hear any of that foolishness again.

Mary brought the punt out into the current. She put the oars on the floor and let herself be pulled along. She closed her eyes, felt the wind at her back and her hair coming loose and blowing about her face.

"Hey...hey, Mary...what you up to? Better look where you're going."

She opened her eyes to see a punt coming up close on her right side, going in the same direction. In the middle of it sat Thelma and Theresa LeFurgey and at either end steering it towards her were Harold Mills and Smith Reid. Mary wished she had somewhere to hide.

"What are you doing out and about this time of night?" Theresa asked her, reaching out to grab the side of her punt as the boys brought the Mills's blue punt up alongside.

"Same as you are, to get some night air."

Mary could almost feel Smith's eyes boring into her. She tried not to look at him.

"Some night air." Thelma giggled. "Oh my."

"Want to come with us?" Harold asked her. "Smith and I are strong enough to row the three of you young ladies around. We can tie your punt to ours and lead it behind."

"No, thank you. I'll need to turn around soon."

"The current is strong tonight. Can you manage to get back on your own?" Smith asked her.

"Yes, thank you," Mary answered, determined not to look at him.

"You know, Smith, old man, I don't think she can." Harold grinned at his friend.

"You know, Harold, old man, I believe you're right."

To the squeals and protests of the LeFurgey sisters, Smith placed his oar down on the floor of Harold's punt and carefully stepped across into Mary's.

"No, stop," Mary said in a little voice. She felt like crying.

"I'm going to escort Miss Harney home, Mills." Smith picked up the oars from the floor of the punt. "Will you kindly do the same with your two lovely passengers?"

"That I will, sir," Harold assured him. "In fact, I'm going to start doing that right now."

Theresa flounced down into her seat and folded her arms.

"Now, none of that, Miss LeFurgey, or I'll have to put you out here." Harold laughed.

As the punt headed towards Pugwash, Mary sat with her eyes straight ahead and her arms folded. She could feel Smith's presence as he stood in the back of the punt and steered. They moved through the water together for a time, neither one speaking.

"What did you do that for?" she finally asked.

She felt shy and excited at the same time. She had never been alone with a boy before and Smith Reid was more than a boy.

"I didn't think that you could handle this punt all by yourself."

"I've been out in it dozens of times. I can handle it alone."

"Yeah, I've seen you out on the river a lot," Smith admitted. "I just thought I'd be a gentleman and escort you home."

"But we're not going home," she observed.

"Well, I didn't want to cut things short," he said after a minute, then added, "I've probably spoiled your evening as it is."

"We're coming up to the ferry dock. It's time to turn back now," she told him.

"Look up there to the left on the rocks," he told her, pointing, although her back was still turned to him.

"Aren't they something?"

"It's just a couple of cranes," Mary answered, turning away and trying to sound uninterested.

"No, not cranes, Mary, those are two blue herons. They're feeding at the end of the day. They mate for life, you know."

Smith wasn't sure if he was correct on that last point but thought it wouldn't hurt just to add it to the conversation. He found that he wanted to impress her, like he had never wanted to impress anyone before.

"They are very pretty, there in the sunset," Mary admitted.

"Let's get closer."

"No, let's not bother them. Leave them be. And please, let's turn around. I have to be getting home before it's dark or I'll get in trouble."

"With your father." Smith slowly turned the punt around.

"Yes."

"Are you angry with me for making trouble for your father last spring?"

"Not as much as I used to be, and I was never really angry so much as scared. When your father came to the house looking for Daddy that time I was really afraid and so were Mumma and Grandma. Grandma wouldn't ever say but I could tell."

"Pa thought it was for the best to talk to your father himself. To try to stop things from getting out of hand."

"They still did, though. You beat him up."

"I know. I was mad and wanted him to pay for hurting Jack. I'm sorry he was your father, though. Can you forgive me?"

"I suppose so."

"Mary, why don't you turn around so it's easier for us to talk?"

"No thanks, I'm all right the way I am."

The punt turned the bend in the river and they could see people gathered around fires in front of some of the fishing shacks. Mary prayed that her father wouldn't still be there waiting for her.

"Mr. Reid, would you mind going to shore along here and getting out? I don't think people should see us together without a chaperone. It's not decent."

"All right, Mary, I will, on one condition."

"What?"

"That you call me Smith from now on. Will you? I don't know why you're so formal anyway. I'm not that much older than you."

Mary was silent for a time.

"Yes, all right."

"So say it. Say my name. Turn around and look at me and say my name or I'll take this punt right over to the landing."

Mary was silent again. Then she stood up slowly, turned, stepped over the seat, and sat down facing him.

"I'll call you Smith from now on," she said, looking right at him. "But you're not being much of a gentleman about it, threatening me."

He grinned. "I'm gentleman enough when I want to be."

He started to move the punt over to the shore. Mary watched him. She liked that he was tall and his hair dark and curly.

In a few minutes the punt bumped up against the river bank.

"Okay, I'll get out here and take the path home. You be careful taking this back out." He passed her the oar and they stood looking at each other for a moment, the punt softly rocking. Then Smith jumped out onto the shore.

"I'd like to see you again sometime, Mary," he said. "Could I?"

"No, I don't think so. Daddy wouldn't like that at all." She pushed the punt away from shore.

Smith tipped his cap and walked off into the darkness.

Her hands were shaking as she steered the punt towards the landing. She felt scared and happy at the same time. Her father would be so mad if he knew about tonight. He hated Smith and his whole family. And he had told her before that he'd beat her if he ever found out she was having anything to do with any boy.

Mary brought the punt into the landing and dragged it up onto the shore. She was humming as she tied it to the post in front of Uncle John's fishing shack. She looked over to the bonfire. She knew that the group of laughing men over there were telling stories, and this being Saturday night, likely sharing a bottle or two. She wondered if Smith was among them. Just then, out of the corner of her eye, she saw someone get up from the doorway of the shack and stumble towards her. Her father waved a bottle around in his hand.

"I've been waiting and waiting for you to get back...worried that something happened to you. You shouldn't make me worry like that, girl."

He walked up to Mary and put his hand on her head, his fingers in her hair. "We worry about you. Me and your mother do. Especially me. I think about you a lot, Mary."

She raised her arm and dislodged his fingers from her hair.

"Look at that bunch over there," he said, pointing towards the fire. "Assholes."

He placed an arm around her shoulder and walked her towards the path leading to the main road.

"I thought I'd better stay and watch for you so none of those idiots would get any ideas. You don't know how a man's mind works, girl."

"Well, I'm all right now that you're here," Mary said, ducking from under his arm and starting to run. "I'll go ahead and get home so Mumma won't be worried anymore."

Will loped ahead and caught up with her. He grabbed her by the shoulders and turned her around. His arms pinned hers to her sides.

"Stop it."

She struggled to get away.

He walked her towards the woods, backed her up against a tree trunk, pressed his whole body flat against hers, and fumbled with the collar of her dress.

"Please stop. Stop," she pleaded. She could smell the whiskey on his breath and the sweat from his shirt.

Will placed one hand over her mouth and put the other around her waist.

"Just once, Mary. Just once."

She managed to bite the hand he had over her mouth. He removed it, yelling with pain. She pushed him and stumbled away.

"Stop it, Daddy. Why are you acting like this?"

Mary ran up the side of the bank.

Will tried to catch her but couldn't. "Oh, the hell with it," she heard him mutter to himself.

SOON AFTER THEIR PUNT RIDE, Smith found out that Mary brought in the cows each evening, and he began to walk over to John Dempsey's property at dusk a couple of times a week, hoping to run into her. After a few of these meetings she agreed that they could talk while she brought in the cows, and they became friends. Smith wanted more and finally persuaded Mary to start kissing him goodbye when they parted.

"I don't like kissing," she told him at the beginning.

"Everyone likes kissing," he had said. "You're just being shy."

Mary surprised him, however, in other ways.

"Whoa," he exclaimed, grinning as she moved a hand down his body, towards his belt, the first time they embraced.

"Isn't that what I'm supposed to do?" Mary blushed and hid her face.

"Yes, but all in good time," he told her gently.

"It's not right?" she asked, her head hanging.

"Yes, but at the proper place and time," he said. "Not that I don't like it. But I'm surprised I don't have to show you."

ROCKLEY

Nova Scotia
November 1876

DOCTOR TIMOTHY CREED CALLED on Ann ten weeks after her accident. Mabel greeted him at the porch door with a bright smile.

"So good of you to call on us," she said, removing her apron with one hand and offering him the other.

"If I knew you were coming I'd have made myself more presentable."

Timothy Creed was thirty-five years old, tall, with light brown hair, a chin dimple, and a charming young wife. Three years ago, fresh out of the Dalhousie School of Medicine, the day after he opened his practice in Rockley, he received, by telegram, a summons to attend Mrs. Mabel Harney. When Creed arrived at the farm the patient was on the veranda waiting for him, dressed in her Sunday best. There was a lovely tea table set with pink china, and fruitcake and dainty squares laid on. He was invited to sit down and Mabel commenced to welcome him to the neighbourhood with gossip about the locals and much fluttering of eyelashes. She mentioned a headache when he inquired as to her health and she undid the two top buttons on her shirt waist to show him the difficulty she had turning her neck from side to side.

It didn't take Dr. Creed long to realize that he had been lured there for a social call. He wasn't told until afterwards, no new Rockley physician ever was, that Mabel Harney made a point of acquainting herself with all the young doctors who settled in the area.

"I'll be a sick woman come morning," Mabel had declared to her neighbour Fannie Burbine upon hearing that Doctor Creed was in need of patients.

Now she motioned for him to come in.

"Never mind your boots. I'm just about to get Mary to do the floors if I can find her." She led the way into the kitchen and offered him a chair.

"I'm here to see Ann. I met your brother over at Bailey's store this morning and he told me that she still wasn't walking. I thought I'd take a look in to see how she was doing."

"Oh, she's fine." Mabel rolled her eyes. "Just likes being waited on, that's all. That's what's wrong with that one. She's set up camp in the parlour. Says she can't make the stairs yet. I'll go see if she's decent."

Mabel hurried down the hallway and was back in less than a minute.

"Her majesty will see you now."

Dr. Creed smiled and shook his head.

"It's the second door on the right. Used to be a proper parlour. Now it's a damn sickroom," Mabel yelled from the kitchen.

"Hello, Ann," Dr. Creed said. Ann watched as he seated himself on a faded green armchair.

"Dr. Creed, I'm surprised to see you," she said, sliding herself up higher on the sofa.

She was wearing a flannel nightgown and wrapped in a black shawl. She was covered up to the waist with a blanket. Suddenly she felt too warm.

"I wanted to see for myself how you were doing."

"That's very kind of you. I'm still not able to put any pressure on my right ankle and the side of my right knee still hurts a lot. And on top of that my heart has been beating something awful lately. Did you know that my mother passed over a month ago? My heart started up right after that."

"Yes, I heard. Accept my condolences. Now, let's have a look. I'll call Mrs. Harney into the room for a moment."

As Mabel stood silent, her arms folded and her foot tapping, Doctor Creed pushed the front of Ann's nightgown up to her knees, placed a hand on her right kneecap, then felt around to the inner side of her knee. She winced.

"It still hurts a lot there," she said.

He touched the area gingerly. "You've bruised the bone. That's why you have so much pain and why it's taking so long to heal."

"If it's bruised, why isn't it black and blue?" Mabel demanded.

"Because now only the bone is bruised, the skin has healed," Creed answered, winking at Ann. "The only cure for that is time. Now the ankle."

He lowered her nightgown to her knees and pressed on the top of the right ankle, using his forefinger.

"Does this hurt when I apply pressure here?"

"No, not really."

"You did have a bad sprain but the swelling is gone now, and the bruising around the toes and on the bottom of the foot is as well. So what's the problem?"

"I just don't feel like I'd be steady on my feet. I'm not sure I can ever walk again."

Creed sighed, placed the nightgown over Ann's feet, and stepped back while she drew the bedclothes up around herself. He walked over to the table, rummaged around in his bag, and withdrew a stethoscope.

"Sit up for me. I'm going to listen to your heart and lungs."

Ann removed the shawl, unbuttoned the collar of her nightgown, and bent forward. Doctor Creed stood behind her, slipped the stethoscope down the neck of her nightgown, and placed the instrument on her back. She gasped from its coldness against her skin.

"Well, your lungs sound strong and clear. Now for your heart."

He moved around to face her and got down on one knee beside the couch. Ann held her collar open. Creed placed the stethoscope high on her left breast. The room was quiet except for the ticking of the grandfather clock in the corner.

"All right then."

Creed removed the stethoscope from around his neck. He sat down and looked at his patient.

"Could you bring the doctor some tea?" Ann asked Mabel.

After Mabel left the room, Dr. Creed shut the door behind her and sat back down.

"So, Ann, how are you feeling in general?"

Ann liked Doctor Creed but she didn't want him to know the truth. She had a difficult time admitting it even to herself: that she didn't care anymore, about anything. And what kind of a wife and mother didn't care? She didn't want to be a wife to Will. She didn't want him near her. She didn't want to clean the house or cook. She didn't want to look after the children. There was so much to do and she was just so tired.

"I feel sluggish and run down but at the same time I'm jumpy, nervous."

"Have you been up and dressed since your fall?"

"No."

"You've got to start getting dressed each day. It will make you feel like your old self."

"It might."

"And you haven't been out of the house since your accident?"

"Oh my, no, I'm much too crippled for that."

"You're not crippled, Ann. You've just had a bad fall. Have you used the crutches that I gave you? I don't see them. Where are they?"

"Oh, they're out in the kitchen somewhere. I just haven't felt strong enough to use them. Will and John carried me in here last week. And everyone has been so good helping us out. Rita LeFurgey is looking after the two little ones this afternoon. She takes them a couple of times a week so I can get some proper rest. And Mary's a big help to me."

"Ann, your muscles will weaken with no exercise. Starting tomorrow, I want you to walk around the house, using your crutches or not, every day for ten minutes. And start going outdoors every day too. It's getting cooler now but the fresh air will do you good. You've got to get back on your feet, Ann. You'll feel better when you're looking after your own home once again."

Ann didn't know how she could possibly look after anything. She had no idea where to begin. And it didn't matter. Everyone had been getting along without her for weeks now. And this house was not her home. She had never had a home of her own.

Suddenly there was a kick at the bottom of the door. Dr. Creed opened it and Mabel came in carrying a large tray bearing a Blue Willow teapot, three matching cups, a sugar bowl, cream pitcher, and spoons. She placed the tray on the table beside the doctor's bag.

"Be right back with the biscuits. They're just about ready," she said.

"As you can see my mother-in-law is very good to me," Ann said, stone-faced.

"As she should be," Creed replied.

After tea, as he rose to leave, the doctor withdrew a small bottle from his bag and handed it to Ann.

"Your heart sounds like it has a bit of a flutter," he said, "so I'm going to leave this with you. It's powdered laudanum. Put a small amount of it in a glass of water or some spirits and it will help you sleep and calm those nerves of yours. It's bitter, so be sure to add sugar to it as well. Mabel, make sure that she takes this each evening before she goes to bed."

"Yes, sir," Mabel said, clearing away the tray.

"THE DOCTOR'S CALL MADE NO difference whatsoever," Mabel told Fannie Burbine in the yard of St. Peter's Catholic Church the following Sunday.

"Beyond limping around the house a couple of times, that one doesn't try to walk at all. She's determined to be sick."

Fannie shook her head. "I don't see how you can put up with it, Mabel, I really don't."

"Clear, sheer laziness is what it is. And it's beyond me how my Will let himself get mixed up with that bunch in the first place. To top it all off, as you know, they're Protestants."

"You warned him and warned him, it's his own fault if he didn't listen to you," Fannie told her friend.

"Yes, he burnt his arse now he has to sit on the blisters."

"Will is a bright boy, he could have gone places." Fannie put her arm through Mabel's and the two women walked towards home.

ROCKLEY

Nova Scotia
December 1876

"I CAN'T ACCEPT IT," Mary told Smith.

"Why not?"

"It's not proper taking Christmas gifts from young men. We're not promised."

"No, we're not promised to each other and I don't expect a thing in return. I'd just like you to have something pretty. I was at Bailey's last month when he unpacked it from a shipment just in from Halifax and it reminded me of you. I asked him to keep it for me until I could buy it."

"It is very nice."

"Open it up."

Mary slid her fingernail into the slit between the two sections of the silver locket. It opened up like a clam shell. There was a tiny photograph of Smith in one section of the locket, looking solemn with his hair combed down close to his head, not blowing around in curls like it was now as she gazed up at him. On the opposite side there was a space for another photograph.

"Thank you, Smith. I'll treasure it. But I don't have anything for you."

"There's nothing I need, Mary, as long as you'll wear this. Do you like it?"

"Yes, very much. But I can't let anyone see it. Daddy will be mad and take it away from me. But I'll always have it with me."

Mary stood on her tiptoes and kissed him on the cheek. When she got home she pinned the locket to her chemise and hid it under her clothing.

On Christmas Eve afternoon Mary and Uncle John trudged through the woods beyond the back pasture looking for a tree.

"Some nice white spruces here, Mary," John said. "And this is the real straight one that I thought would do. What do you think?"

"I think that one's better," she said, pointing to a tall tree just at the edge of the grove.

They walked over to where it stood and Uncle John waded around it through the knee-deep snow.

"It has a couple bald spots," he observed, wrinkling his brow.

"I think it's sad because it's skinnier that the other ones," Mary told him. "I think it needs a home."

Uncle John grinned and chopped down her pick. He lifted it onto the sled and Mary walked along behind him and their tree. When they got home Uncle John nailed the tree to two boards and then nailed the boards to the floor in the parlour, while Little Helen and Harry danced around with excitement. Mary decorated it with candles and helped the little ones make bows out of red tissue paper.

"Oh, go ahead, but it's going to be a big mess and you're cleaning it up," Mabel grumbled as she allowed the children to place pine boughs on the whatnot and on top of the photograph of her Uncle Oliver and on the mirror above the sink in the kitchen.

For Christmas morning they would receive the colourful mittens that Mabel had knitted and the gifts sent by Grandpa Hennessey and Aunt Beatrice.

"I'm just too tired to make anything for anybody this year," Ann declared.

"The way your hands shake now," Mabel huffed, "you're not able to thread a needle or knit a stitch anyway."

"Fetch me my purse, Mary," Ann directed.

Digging out some money, she handed it to her daughter.

"Here, that should be enough. Go to Bailey's and get some ribbon and penny candy, and a few apples and oranges. We'll put them in the little ones' stockings on Christmas Eve."

By nine o'clock that night, the house was quiet. Little Helen and Harry had been so excited about Father Christmas that it was difficult to get them settled down. Harry was frightened about the prospect of a strange man coming into the house, magically, as Uncle John had described, by way of the stovepipe, but Mary finally got him to sleep with a few more Mother Goose stories.

"Father Christmas would be the last person in the world to hurt you," she whispered in answer to the child's worry. She placed the covers over him more snugly and made her way downstairs to the kitchen. Harry and Little Helen had had their baths before bed and now it was Mary's turn.

The water in the galvanized tub was still warm but she wanted to heat up another kettleful. Mary primed the pump and filled the kettle with cold water. Then she lifted one of the lids off the stove and stirred the smouldering ashes. They burst back into flame and she put in a piece of wood. She'd make sure the fire was banked again before she went to bed. While she was waiting for the water to heat, she sat at the kitchen table and, by the lantern light, read the *Chignecto Post* that Uncle John had brought home from Bailey's store that day. Looking at the Amherst and Pugwash stores' advertisements for fruits, candy, Christmas geese, and the latest fabrics for holiday dresses and coats, Mary wondered what Aunt Beatrice had sewed herself for tomorrow. Then she remembered that whatever Beatrice wore, it would be black. Grandma Hennessey had been dead only three months and Aunt Beatrice, like the rest of the family, was still in mourning. The paper's front page featured a Christmas serial about a lost puppy. As she read she moved her fingers along the rope-like design on the locket's smooth surface. It was now round her neck, hanging from an old chain she had found in her mother's jewellery case.

Mary had read halfway through the story when she heard the water starting to boil in the kettle. She took the chain off and laid it on the table by the paper. She walked to the stove, picked up the kettle, tipped it over, and let all the lovely hot water spill out into the tub. As she swirled it around with her hands to distribute its heat, the lamp light cast a glow over both the room and the water. After placing the kettle on the seat of the chair beside the tub, she removed her clothes. Letting them fall to the floor, she eased herself down into the tub. The water rose to her neck. She closed her eyes and lay back.

Wouldn't it be nice to do this every day, she thought and then giggled to herself over the extravagance. That was something rich people could do maybe, but even they probably never took a bath every day.

Mary leisurely washed herself all over with a washcloth and the last of the Pear's soap that Aunt Beatrice had given her in August. Then she stood up in the tub and reached over for the kettle to wet her hair. She was facing the kitchen window that looked out over the barnyard. She glanced towards the window and froze. There was someone looking in, watching. Her father. She felt an involuntary chill deep in her body. For a moment they stared at each other, motionless, then Mary let out a sob and slid back down into the tub. When she looked up again, he was gone.

It won't take long, he reassures me.
I've heard it can be pleasant,
like going to sleep in a warm bath.

ROCKLEY

NOVA SCOTIA
January 1877

"MUMMA, MAY I TALK to you about something?"

All the way home from school Mary had practiced what she was going to say to her mother about Will. Since Christmastime he had stayed away from her. But just before he went back to Wallace on Sunday, he...Mary tried not to think about it. She was half tempted to tell Smith about him bothering her, but shame and fear of what might happen stopped her.

Every Saturday evening, now, she took a pan of hot water up to her bedroom and, with the top of a chair fitted securely under the doorknob and the curtains closed, gave herself a sponge bath.

Ann was alone when Mary came into the parlour.

"Of course, dear. Come and sit beside me. Grandma Harney took the little ones over to call on Fannie Burbine."

"You look tired, Mumma."

"Yes, I've just woken up. Now first, can you mix me up sugar and some of Uncle John's rum in a glass? You know where it is in the kitchen."

Mary hesitated. "Do you need it right now?"

"Yes, Mary, I do. Go and do as I say and then we'll have a nice chat all by ourselves. And don't forget to bring a spoon."

Mary's hands shook as she poured the rum into the tumbler. Maybe I'll wait and tell Mumma another time. What could Mumma do anyway? It would only lead to a big fight with everybody yelling at me. But it's not fair, it's just not fair.

When Mary returned to the parlour, Ann bent over the side of the sofa and felt around beneath it. She retrieved a small bottle, undid the cork, tipped the bottle over, and shook some yellowish-white powder into the tumbler, then stirred it around with a spoon.

"Here, put this back under there for me." Nobody needs to know about it. It's my spare."

Ann was going through more medicine than her doctor could keep up with, and often sent Mary to fetch it from Bailey's store.

"Dr. McGee's tonic is the best. Get that if he has it," she always instructed. "Along with what Dr. Creed gives me it helps so much, you'll never know."

There was a half bottle of Dr. McGee's tucked away behind the pillows Ann rested against.

Mary looked at her mother's brown teeth and watery eyes and didn't think that she was being helped at all.

"Now, what is it you wanted to talk about?"

Ann nudged over closer to the back of the sofa and patted the cushion. But Mary knelt on the floor.

"Oh nothing, I just wanted to sit with you for a while."

"Are you sure there's nothing, dear?"

"Yeah."

"You know, your father was just saying the other day that he was worried about you. Said you seemed moody lately and out of sorts. Is that what's wrong?"

Mary felt her temper rise.

"If I'm moody, it's Pa's fault not mine."

"Your father only wants the best for you, dear."

"No, he doesn't."

"What do you mean?

Mary shrugged and hesitated before speaking.

"It's hard to talk about. I don't know how to say it. I don't want you to be mad at me." She felt a spot of cold in the pit of her stomach. She had never spoken out loud about what her father did before.

"Why would I be mad? Is it about your monthly visitor? We talked about that, it must be two years ago now?"

"No, not that." Mary shook her head.

"Then what?"

Mary bit her lip. Tears smarted her eyes.

"It's Daddy," she blurted out. "He's always trying to touch me. It scares me."

"What do you mean," Ann asked, taking the last gulp of her drink.

"He tries to touch me and kiss me when nobody's around. And last week he tried to get me to...to...."

"To what?" Ann was sitting bolt upright now.

"To touch...his pants." Mary was crying now.

"I don't know what you're talking about, Mary." Ann folded her arms across her chest, still holding the empty glass.

"And at Christmas I was taking a bath and he was looking in at me through the window and after that he tried to get into my room."

"How can you say such things?" Her mother was fully awake now. "I don't believe you. You're lying." She turned her head away from the girl.

Mary was pleading now, her heart pounding.

"No, I'm not, Mumma, I'm really not. He's my father, why is he doing things like that? Is it something I'm doing? Let me know, please."

"You're lying to hurt me." Ann slapped Mary across the face. "I don't ever want to hear you talk that way again. I'm ashamed of you."

Ann folded her arms.

Mary was crying and holding her cheek as she rose from the floor.

"Get out." Ann pointed towards the doorway.

Mary ran from the room. Mumma doesn't believe me, just doesn't believe me at all. Now she'll tell Pa and he'll tell Grandma and I'll really be in trouble. I should have known better.

Mary made her way up the stairs to the hallway, her heart pounding.

"Maybe I should just run away," she yelled before slamming her bedroom door.

Ann sat and looked at the wall for a long time. She had heard Will at Mary's door, sometimes in the night. She had been awakened by the noise of her daughter running up the stairs on Christmas Eve. She had often seen the look in Will's eyes as they followed Mary around the house.

He wouldn't do something like that, she reasoned.

She reached back behind the pillows and grasped the bottle of tonic. She released the cork and took a long drink.

ROCKLEY

NOVA SCOTIA
April 1877

"SHE'S LATE AS USUAL," Mabel complained. "That girl seems to think she can do as she pleases around here. She needs to be shown who's boss. She just turned seventeen. Time to start acting like a young lady."

"Leave her alone, Mabel," John warned from the porch where he was taking off his boots. "Just saw her walking in the lane as I was coming from the barn. She'll be here in a minute. Boy, it's some cold out for this time of year."

Mabel stood stirring chicken soup in a large pot. John kept talking.

"It's damp and it looks like we're going to have another dump of snow before long. Saw Doc Creed coming in the lane behind Mary. Must be delivering more of Ann's tonic."

"Tonic my arse," Mabel said. "It's been a good five months now and I don't see how that stuff has done her any good at all."

"It calms her nerves, she says." John sat down at the kitchen table.

"Calms them! I'd say it makes them worse, if anything," Mabel countered, bringing a cup of tea over to her brother.

"Ann was never totally right in the head to begin with but it's gotten worse since she fell," Mabel said. "And she hasn't done a day's work since. And pretending that she can't walk. She should be ashamed with two little ones to look after, and leaving an old woman like me to do all the work. She's not even a fitting wife to Will any—"

There was a noise in the porch and John put a finger to his lips. Mary came through the kitchen door with parcels in her arms.

John was about to greet Mary when Mabel started in.

"And where have you been? I sent you to Bailey's over an hour ago. What took you so long? You're supposed to be looking after the little ones while I get supper ready."

"You're not my Ma," Mary said standing in front of her grandmother. "You can't tell me what to do."

Mabel sprang away from the stove as if stung.

"How dare you, you little skate...so high and mighty. Wait til your pa hears about your sass. He'll soon put the kibosh to that."

"Pa won't listen to anything you say against me."

Mary raised her head in the air and walked past Mabel towards the hallway. Her grandmother grabbed her by the arm, and slapped Mary across the face.

John jumped to his feet. Mary's shocked look dissolved into tears and the parcels she was carrying fell to the floor as she ran from the room.

"That'll teach you to sass me," Mabel yelled after her.

"Mabel! Mabel, you're way too hard on the girl," John said, stooping down to retrieve the groceries. "There's no need to be hitting her like that."

"I don't like the way she's been acting this last while back. Full of sass."

Little Helen ran into the kitchen from the parlour.

"Mumma wants to know if the doctor came yet."

"Tell her majesty that no he ain't," Mabel barked. The child scurried away.

There was a knock on the porch door and the sound of stamping boots. John opened the kitchen door to find Doctor Creed brushing flakes of wet snow off his black greatcoat.

"Getting messy out there," he said.

"Have a seat, Doc. Mabel will get you a nice strong cup of tea."

Creed stepped inside. "How's Ann doing this evening?"

"Herself is the same." Mabel frowned. "She's still holding court in the parlour. I'll bring your tea in to you in a few minutes."

Lying on the couch and wrapped in a blanket, Ann had been awakened by someone far away, yelling in the distance. Her mind fought to come to the surface of consciousness. She blinked her eyes, straining to focus them.

"Little...Helen...?"

"Yes, Mumma."

The child was sitting on the floor in front of her with a doll in her lap.

Ann licked her lips. So dry, she thought to herself.

"What's dry, Mumma?" the little girl asked.

Ann hadn't known she'd spoken aloud.

"Mumma is," she replied. "Could you run and ask if the doctor has arrived yet?"

Little Helen ran out the door. There was more yelling and she returned.

"Not yet, Mumma."

"Then you go run and play with Harry."

The footsteps receded.

Ann tried to raise her head but gave up and flopped back down on the pillow. She scratched at both arms with her fingernails, bringing out long welts. Her arms and legs were always itchy now. She tried to remember the dream she'd been having before she woke up. She had been in a room filled with books. She and a man were in the room alone. She struggled to remember. Was it even a dream? A memory?

Suddenly, there was a man standing in the doorway. She narrowed her eyes again.

"Ann?"

She ran her dry tongue over her teeth and smiled widely. She'd been waiting so long. She extended her hand to him. He pressed it in his own and stared at her.

"I need another bottle of my tonic."

"I just gave you two bottles last week to see you through my being away. I haven't even left for Halifax yet, and now you need more?"

"My nerves have really been bad lately. I had to take more medicine than usual to calm myself down."

"Why are you still down here in the parlour? And have you been doing any walking? I've been telling you for months that you need to. There's no reason why you shouldn't be able to walk up and down stairs by now. You need to strengthen that leg."

Mabel appeared in the doorway with a teacup. She set it down on the table.

"I can't climb the stairs, my leg still bothers me."

The doctor sighed and shook his head. "I just don't believe that after all this time, you can't walk normally. You'd feel better and be able to get a proper rest if you were in your own bed."

"Yes, and you'd be out of the way in the bargain," Mabel told her.

Ann felt tears in her eyes. Couldn't they see how sick she was?

"I'm just so tired and I can't sleep, not unless I have some tonic. And to settle my stomach. It feels upset all the time."

"This is what we're going to do," Dr. Creed directed. "John and I are going to carry you up to bed and you're going to sleep there from now on. And I'll give you some more laudanum, but just a bit. You need to get weaned off it now. You're using it as a crutch and you'll get less and less until you don't need it anymore."

"But..." Ann started to plead. Dread welled up inside her.

Creed turned to Mabel. "Mrs. Harney, ask your brother to step in here."

He turned back to Ann.

"It'll be all right."

He stood watching her with arms folded. Ann sank back down into the cushions.

"Ah, here he is. John, Ann is going upstairs to rest. We'll make a chair with our arms for her. Never mind pouting, Ann. Put an arm around each of us. This is for your own good. Stay still now."

"She's light as a feather, eh, Doc?" John grinned.

"She's lost too much flesh," Creed said. "She'd be less nervous with a little more meat on her bones."

"Everything makes me gag." Ann groaned, her head swaying back and forth as they carried her up the stairs.

"It's the first door on the left down the hall," John said as they reached the landing with their bundle.

"I don't want to stay up here," she said as John eased his shoulder against the bedroom door to open it. "I want to sleep by myself. I said, I don't want to stay up here."

Manoeuvring a path through clothes, bottles, and dirty dishes, they made their way to the unmade bed and gently deposited Ann upon it.

"Let me yell for Mabel to come fix up the room," John said, kicking a pile of clothes out of the way.

"I'll get some fresh air in here." Creed moved to the one window in the room, a big two-over-two with a crack in its right lower pane. He strained in the effort to open it.

"It's painted shut," Ann said, turning listlessly to look at him.

"Damn." Creed backed away, shaking his head.

Mabel came charging through the door with John on her heels.

"This place is a mess, Mabel. Don't you ever clean up in here? You'd think Will was a kid instead of a grown man."

"It's because he is that I don't," she said. "It's not up to a mother to clean up after her boy once he's married. It's his wife's job then and her majesty hasn't done a damn thing for months now."

"I'm not well," Ann said, close to tears.

Mabel dismissed her with a wave of her hand. She bent down and started picking clothes up off the floor.

"These bedsheets should be changed," Creed said. "Where's Mary? She could help with this."

Mabel yelled down the hallway. Mary opened her bedroom door a crack and looked at her grandmother.

"Come and help me clean up this mess in your father's room and behave yourself, we have company."

"Yes, Grandma."

The door closed again.

"And be quick about it, Missy," Mabel bellowed. "Useless as a five-wheel wagon," she said storming back into the room.

"Ann," Dr. Creed said, "your pulse is racing. I'll give you something to make you sleep. In the meantime—oh, here's Mary. Young lady, run down to the kitchen and get your mother some of that lovely soup that your grandmother was making when I came in. She needs a full stomach to help her sleep better."

"Yes, sir."

"Move Queen Victoria over to the armchair there so I can make that bed," Mabel commanded.

Minutes later, Mary came back carrying a bowl of soup on a tray.

"Thank you." Creed smiled. He took the tray and placed it across Ann's knees.

"Eat as much of this as you can," he instructed.

Mabel made the bed while Ann slurped the soup. She took four spoonfuls then placed the spoon inside the bowl.

"That's not very much."

"It's all I can stand right now."

John and the doctor helped her from the armchair into the clean bed.

"Do you need me for anything else, Grandma?" Mary asked.

"Pick up all this mess on the floor then go get the broom and give this floor a good sweeping."

"Yes, ma'am."

Creed walked back over to the bed. "Now, Ann, I'm going to give you some laudanum to help you sleep and will leave the rest of it with Mrs. Harney to look after."

He turned to Mabel and John.

"She needs a good night's rest."

Mabel sighed loudly and headed downstairs with the bottle.

John held Ann's hand until Mabel came back into the room.

"Here's your nightcap," she said, thrusting a full tumbler at Ann.

"Thank you, Mabel." Dr. Creed smiled encouragingly. "I'll just make sure that Ann is comfortable here and then I'll be on my way."

Ann grabbed the glass and greedily drained it.

I'm all right, she thought, as she drifted off to sleep.

ROCKLEY

NOVA SCOTIA
September 1, 1877

WILL AND MABEL HAD decided that it was time for Mary to start earning her keep. She was old enough and strong enough, they reasoned, and it shouldn't be too hard to find her a position. Well-to-do families like the Pineos or the Clays in Pugwash were always looking for good, respectable girls, so there'd be no need for her to return to Rockley School.

"She's got her grade nine," Mabel said to John one evening. "That's a lot of schooling for a girl. More than is needed, truth be known."

"We really can't afford to keep her, with her not contributing nothing to the household. More reading and writing's not going to help her anyway," Will agreed.

Mary didn't want to go to a stranger's house to work. And she didn't want to stop going to school, since Smith was to be the schoolmaster.

"I plan to be a doctor someday," he'd told Mary one evening as they followed along behind the cows. "That means going away to Halifax for a long time. I want to start next fall, at Dalhousie."

"You're so smart, you'll do it," she replied.

"I've been going with Doc Creed sometimes on his rounds, learning as much as I can. He says I can work with him when the time comes. But I'll need to teach school for a year to save some money. My parents just can't afford to pay for everything. Room and board are high down there."

He stopped in his tracks and, blushing, grabbed Mary by the arm. "Do you think that you might like to live there some day?"

"In Halifax? I don't know. What's it like?"

"It's grand. Lots of people around and so many buildings. They're wonderful to see. The best is the statue of the lion commemorating two Crimean War soldiers. I've been to Halifax twice and spent a lot of time looking at it while Ma and Pa were calling on friends. It's just up the street from the Waverley, a new inn where we stayed the last time we were there."

"I wish I could see it someday," Mary said.

"Per—perhaps I could show it to you," Smith offered. "Someday maybe we could visit it together."

"Maybe." Mary smiled up at him, then quickly lowered her head.

"I'll be a long time studying medicine." He was still holding on to her arm.

"We need to get these cows home before they come looking for us," Mary said, slipping out of his hold and continuing along the path.

They walked along in silence for a few more minutes.

"You'd better start back now," she said, just above a whisper. "We don't want Daddy to see you. It's Friday and he might get back early from work."

"I don't care if he sees me or not. I'm not scared of him and I'm tired of just meeting you here. I want to court you proper. He's going to have to know some day."

"You might not be scared, but I am. I'm afraid of what he might do if he ever caught us walking out together."

"He's got a mean streak," Smith said.

"He's got a bad temper and yells a lot."

"Does he yell at you?" Smith asked, reaching for her hand again.

"Sometimes." Mary grimaced.

"I'd better not hear him do it."

"He's my father, he can do as he likes with me." Mary blushed and turned away.

"No, he can't. He's not allowed to be cruel, as much as he wants you to believe he can," Smith said. "Doesn't your mother stand up for you against him? Ma lets Pa go only so far to discipline us."

"Mumma just started to talk to me again after months of ignoring me," Mary said.

"Why's that?"

"Oh, we had a misunderstanding a while back and she never spoke to me for a long time. She was so mad at me."

"But why?"

"It was...I just told her something she didn't like. Now, you need to go, we're getting close to the house," Mary warned him.

"All right, I'll go. But I'll see you tomorrow?"

"Yes." She smiled up at him. He bent down and kissed her.

Mary turned and ran down the hill.

ROCKLEY

Nova Scotia
September 8, 1877

"ALL RIGHT, I'M LEAVING now," Mabel yelled from the kitchen where she was pinning on her hat and waiting for John to bring the horse and wagon to the porch door.

Mary, with Harry in her arms and trailed by Little Helen, came down the stairs.

"Your father will likely be home sometime this afternoon," Mabel continued. "Since he didn't get back last night, he likely worked overtime. Cut up some of that beef and use it with the potatoes and carrots I cooked last night to make a hash for dinner. You can heat it up again for supper if you want to."

"Where you going, Grandma?" Little Helen asked.

"To Oxford to sit with Kay Brown. She sent a message early this morning. She wants me to come now. Hopefully it's not a false alarm like the last time. I don't expect to be home until about this time tomorrow, if even then."

"We'll be all right, Grandma," Mary reassured her.

"You're going to have to be. Mary, you watch these two. Don't let them get away on you. John will be home as soon as he drops me off and does a few errands. And watch that one upstairs."

Mabel reached out and touched the top of Harry's head. The toddler smiled.

"You and Little Helen mind Mary. I'll be back as soon as I can."

"And while I'm there," Mabel continued, "I'm going to ask around if anyone needs a good, dependable girl. I'll get you a position yet, Mary, just you wait and see."

Little Helen ran in circles around her grandmother.

"We'll be good, I promise we will."

"See that you do and stop that, you're going to make yourself dizzy." She turned to look at Mary one last time. "And you stay around the dooryard, don't go sneaking off when your Uncle John gets back."

"I won't."

"Hmmm," Mabel replied on her way out the door.

They all trailed behind her into the yard.

"Bye, Unca," Harry called, waving.

Uncle John waved in return. "I'll be home as soon as I can, Mary. Watch the fires, and you two mind your sister."

The children waved as John's wagon went down the lane. Then Mary turned to the youngsters. "I have a whole day planned for us. First we're going to play hide-and-seek then go for a walk and pick some cranberries. Then it'll be time for dinner. How does that sound?"

"Just lovely," said Little Helen, clapping her hands together.

Mary laughed and kissed both children on the top of the head.

"Little Helen, you hide first and Harry and I will try to find you. But mind you're to hide in the barn or around the house somewhere. Don't go in the woods, or the fields or down the lane. Harry, let's count to ten. Go on, Little Helen, run and hide."

The child giggled and off she went.

A half hour later, Harry called a halt to the game.

"Had 'nough," he proclaimed, flopping down on Mary's shoulder.

"You're right, that's enough for now. Wait here while I get a couple of bowls for picking berries. And I'll get a hat for you, little man. The sun is bright today. Don't want that noggin of yours to get burnt."

After picking cranberries and eating a dinner of beef hash, Mary and the children took a tray up to their mother.

"Well, what have you three been up to?" Ann asked as she moved the food around the plate with her fork.

After eating a little she snuggled down and patted the bed for Harry and Little Helen to join her.

"Your Uncle John's not back yet, is he, Mary? Get my purse and bring it here."

Mary fetched the green-fringed bag. Ann, after rummaging around in it for a minute, brought an old white silk change purse up from its depths. She opened it, drew out a dollar, and gave it to Mary.

"I need you to go to Bailey's for more of my tonic. Tell him that my leg is paining badly today and I just need something to get me through it."

"Are you sure? You know that Grandma and Daddy don't like you taking it anymore. You can have a little bit of Dr. Creed's medicine tonight."

"Yes, yes, I'm sure. Hurry now before Uncle John gets back. Me and the little ones will take a nap while you're gone."

Mary reluctantly left the room, squeezing the money into her palm.

WILL HAD BEEN SURE HE'D get that job at the Lower Cove stone quarries. Job Hibbard, from the Seaman Company, was travelling around the county looking for workers, and when Will had talked to him in the Wallace general store just the day before yesterday, he'd practically promised him the job. He was all set to get home on Friday night, could hardly wait, in fact, to tell them all that he'd got a new job, a better job, and would be away for a while. He would likely get home only once a month, if that, and he'd send money when he could.

He had smiled to himself at the thought. I'll be the next best thing to a single man again. Might meet some pretty little Frenchy girls down that way.

But now he didn't have a job at all, anywhere. Barney Thompson had yelled at him when Will was slow getting back to work after the dinner break.

And I got mouthy, that's all, he reassured himself.

Confident that he would no longer have to keep himself in the foreman's good graces, Will told him off, said that he was going to be working for the Seamans and that he didn't need the Huestises' two-bit job anyway. Then he laughed in Thompson's face. He was fired on the spot. Will shrugged, picked up his things at the hotel, and hitched a ride with a man going to Pugwash. Once there he'd made his way to the Wharf Tavern. He'd go in for a little snort with the week's pay he'd just gotten, maybe even buy something for Ann and the kids and still be home earlier than usual. But it was there, as Will was coming through of the door of the tavern, that he met Job Hibbard coming out.

"So I'm ready to head for Lower Cove any time," he told Hibbard.

"What? Oh yes, hello, Harney."

"When should I report for work? I'd like to have a few days at home before I start, if possible."

"Harney, I hate to tell you this but all the positions are filled. I just signed up the last man a few minutes ago. We might have a place for you in the spring but nothin' right now."

Will stared at the man, his mouth open. "You said you weren't signing anyone up just yet—just going around—seeing who was interested," he stammered.

"Yes, I know, but I found some good men here and decided to hire them while I could." Hibbard looked away.

"And I'm not one of those so-called good men?" Will asked, taking a step forward.

"I'm sorry, Harney, maybe in the spring." Hibbard began to walk away.

Will grabbed him by the lapels of his coat. "The spring, my arse. I need a job now. I've got a family to support."

"You have a job with Huestis, don't you?"

"Not anymore." Will let go of Hibbard's coat, pushing him backwards. "I quit to work for you."

"Well, that wasn't very smart now, was it?" Hibbard smirked. "Don't count your chickens before they're hatched, as my mother always said. And if you lay another hand on me I'll have you arrested." He straightened his coat and walked towards his horse and rig across the street.

"To hell with you and the Seamans both," Will called after him. "You know how they made their money? Rum-running and bringing whores up from the States, that's how. The goddamn stuck-up bastards."

Will kicked the dirt at his feet. "Goddamn, goddamn, goddamn. I can never get a break. I can't get a jeezless break."

He walked into the tavern and sat down at the bar. "Give me a bottle," he instructed the bartender.

At dusk, after starting two fistfights and with all his money gone, Will was thrown out the back door of the tavern. He crawled under the doorstep and spent the night there.

MARY SAW HER FATHER STUMBLE up the lane around seven o'clock that evening. She and the children were sitting on the veranda. They had had their supper and were now in their nightclothes pretending, sleepily, to read the Mother Goose book to her and didn't see or hear their father. And Mary, hoping he didn't spy them, kept quiet as he made his way through the porch door and into the house. She had been worried about both him and Uncle John. It was hours after Grandma said her father would be back. And Uncle John had not come back by suppertime as they expected. It was not like him to be so late.

Mary noticed that Will wasn't singing when he came into the yard as he often did when he drank too much and was happy with himself. But he walked like he did when he was drunk. She knew what that meant, he was in a bad mood. She had been hoping to be able to get the cows once one of the men got home. Now she could put the little ones to bed and go fetch them. She hoped her father wouldn't be mad that she hadn't gotten them earlier. She couldn't leave the little ones by themselves. Since she returned from Bailey's store five hours ago, her mother had been sleeping.

Mary heard him shouting upstairs and Ann crying out.

Without Uncle John or Grandma home to break up her parents' quarrel, it was up to her. Mary disentangled Harry's arms from around her neck and lay him down on the chair.

"What?" Little Helen asked sleepily.

"Nothing, sweetie. Here, you lay down on this chair beside Harry and I'll be right back."

Mary kissed her sister on the top of the head and covered both children with her shawl.

The noise inside the house was getting louder.

WILL SCOWLED WHEN HE CAME into the kitchen. No supper on the table. And where was everybody? A man comes home after working hard all week and where is his loving family to greet him, to welcome him home with open arms? His head was pounding. After he had awoken, outside the tavern, cold and hungover, with dirt in his mouth, he'd made his way to Hank Baxter's. The bootlegger had given him a bottle on credit.

"It's a wonder he did, the cheap bastard," Will told himself while opening the oven door and looking in. He'd spent the rest of the day walking home and drinking. He hadn't eaten a thing since yesterday.

"Other men have a wife and a decent meal to come home to," he muttered. "But where the hell is my woman? In the goddamn bed, that's where."

Will took the stairs two at a time. He slammed the door behind him, grabbed Ann, and started to pull her out of bed.

"Get up, get up, for Christ's sake, you lazy cow! Get some supper on the table. I'm just about starved and there's nothing cooked. The old woman's off God knows where and there's no supper on the table. So get at it. I'm goddamn sick and tired of you lying around."

Ann fell to the floor and lay there in a heap. He kicked her backside. She scurried away towards the bed as if to wedge herself beneath it .

"Oh, no you don't." He grabbed Ann by the ankles and dragged her towards the door. Her nightdress rode up her legs. "You're coming downstairs and making my supper, supposing I have to drag you all the way."

Halfway across the floor, Will dropped her legs and walked back over to the bed. He picked up the bottle on the side table, stared at it for a moment, then flung it against the wall. It broke and brown liquid splattered on the wall. He walked back to Ann and looked down at her, his legs wide apart, straddling her body. His hands were curled into fists.

"I should have known. You're half cut from all the trash you drink. Well, that's your last."

Ann sat up. "I need my medicine."

"Medicine, my arse." He grabbed her under the arms and forced her to stand up.

"Leave her alone."

Will raised his head.

"Leave my mother alone," Mary repeated.

Now there's the two of them against me, he thought.

Will released Ann and she fell back onto the floor, but just as quickly tried to scramble to her feet.

I'll get up, Will! Don't touch Mary."

He strode across the room and slapped the girl across the face.

"That's what you get for sassing me. I'm the boss around here."

No!" Ann limped over to her daughter, who stood holding her cheek, her eyes never leaving Will's.

"How dare you?" Mary whispered.

"I'll do what I like in my own house," He kept his eyes locked on Mary's while batting away Ann's hands.

"This is not your house," Mary corrected him. "This is Uncle John's house. You've never made enough money to have a house of your own. That's what everyone says."

"Is that right?" He pushed Ann away. She landed on the floor once more.

"Mary, please don't talk to your father like that."

"And who told you that, I wonder? Was it that young Reid asshole you've been whoring around with? Didn't think I knew, did you? I know a lot more than you think. He's one cocky little son of a bitch. He needs a good tuning up, and I'm just the person to do it. Be sure to tell him that the next time you see the little bastard. He won't always have his old man around to protect him."

Will grabbed Mary by the throat and backed her against the wall. Mary struggled to remove his grip. Will could see the colour rising in her face. His hand tightened.

"You know, you're just like your mother was at your age. You're turnin' into a right little slut."

Will bent down and kissed her hard on the mouth, then loosened his grip and backed away. She slumped to the floor, coughing.

Ann rushed toward her. "Forgive me please, Mary, forgive me."

Mary hid her face in Ann's nightdress.

Why did that girl always bring out the worst in him? All Will wanted was something to eat and his blasted headache to go away.

Why didn't everybody just leave him alone? When would he get any peace around here?

He started across the room again, towards Mary and Ann.

His fists are hard against my flesh.
I'm not strong enough.
I fall. I flounder. Beat the water, sink and rise.
My trial by ordeal, punishment for my sin.
He watches me, silent, curious.

ROCKLEY

Nova Scotia
September 9, 1877

WILL WAS LEANING AGAINST the kitchen stove holding a towel to his face. He had bloody scratches on both cheeks. John was seated at the kitchen table. Ann was in the parlour lying down. It was after midnight and the Dempsey kitchen and porch were full of men who had come, at the behest of Will and John, to look for Mary. Others stood in the yard and peered through the kitchen windows, their faces like full moons in the glow of the lanterns.

"It's like I told you all before, me and the wife sent her out to fetch the cows around seven and she never came back. We called and called for her and nothing. My punt's missing too, the stupid fool probably took off with it down the river."

"What happened to you?" Hiram Reid asked. "Looks like a cat got at your face."

"The wife went crazy when we couldn't find Mary. Started at me like it was my fault. Stings like hell, don't think it don't."

"Where have you looked?" Hiram asked.

"Down along the river, in the fields behind the house, and in the fishin' shacks, the ones that weren't locked."

"Locks never stopped you before," someone yelled from the porch.

Snickers rippled through the kitchen.

"What time did you say she went missing?" Hiram asked.

"It must have been around seven. I wanted to get the milking started. She's usually just wasting time, walking around and singing to herself. So me and the wife went looking. It was getting dark, so we came back here and brought the cows with us and I had to do the milking by myself. Then there was nothing doing, the wife got me and John to get people to come and help."

The crowd murmured.

"The wife's going crazy," Will continued. "I told her and told her that Mary would come back sooner or later with some story, but nothing doing. We had to start looking for her right away."

"Then we better get going," Hiram said, turning towards the kitchen door.

As the crowd pushed its way outside, rain started to fall and the wind gusted. Lightning flashed in the distance over Pugwash.

"I think we're in for a storm by the looks of it. We better get going before this rain gets worse," Calvin Bailey said.

Once outside, Will walked away from the others. Fred LeFurgey watched him go and shook his head. Hiram, shouting orders so everyone could hear, divided the men into search parties.

"All right, Fred, you, Frank, Ken, and Owen go walk along the Pugwash River as far as you can. Two of you on each side. Me, Jack, Smith, and Calvin will do the same along the river here. Dave, can your boy Harold drive to Pugwash and Wallace to ask about Mary? Good. John MacDonald, can you get your father's rig to drive into Oxford and do the same? Ask around about Mary and spread the word that she's missing. The rest of you stay close together, and start looking in the fields behind the house, then spread out to the woods, go around the school and up and down both sides of the road. Walk in the ditches. Don't know how much we can do tonight with the rain coming on but we'll do what we can. Watch the ground: there may be footprints, or she might have dropped something."

As the men dispersed, women, with their coats and shawls soaked through, pushed into the house carrying firewood, food, and tea. They kept the fire going, and made sandwiches with the ham and bread they had brought with them. Soon three pots of hot tea were steeping on the back of the stove. After the women arrived Ann began to pace back and forth, limping through the house, from kitchen to parlour, wringing her hands and sobbing. Her faded blue nightdress was torn in the back and covered with dirt and stains.

"I tried to get some tea into her but she keeps asking for her tonic," Elaine Clarke explained. "Does anyone know where it is? And where's Mabel?"

"John told me he took her to Oxford this morning to attend Kay Brown. She was planning to spend the night," Rita LeFurgey answered.

"Kay's having another one?" Freda Mills snorted. "That husband of hers never leaves her alone."

Elsie McDonald and Elaine Clarke tried their best to calm Ann. They got her to lie down in the parlour, again reassuring her that they would wake her the moment they heard anything. She lay back, wide- eyed, hugging a pillow.

"We'll need to keep an eye on that one," Elsie said as she came back into the kitchen. "Did you see the red marks on her neck? They look fresh. He likely laid a beating into her."

Elaine sighted. "Something went on here tonight, I don't know what."

"God knows," Freda replied. "I heard Mary's been running through the woods at all times of the day and night with that oldest boy of Hiram's. He's been shying around her for months."

"Smith Reid?" Elsie raised her eyebrows. "I never knew that. He seems like such a nice boy and he's been brought up right."

"Boys that age usually have only one thing on their minds, no matter how nice they are," Freda told them as she rose to check the fire in the wood stove.

"Oh Lord, poor Ann. No wonder she's the way she is." Elaine shook her head. "She just hasn't been the same since her fall last year."

"Lower your voice, she'll hear you."

"Not in the state she's in," Freda said.

"Mary'll turn up. Her parents were likely fighting and she got scared and ran off. I've often seen Mary out on the river in John's punt. She probably went for a ride and stopped somewhere along the bank because of the rain."

"All I know is if she was one of mine, I'd break her neck when she got back home." Elsie took out her knitting.

"I'm just grateful that I know where all mine are tonight. I can't imagine what Ann is going through right now," Rita said.

The others, silent, nodded in agreement.

HOURS LATER, HIRAM'S PARTY CAME across Will standing in the doorway of John's fishing shack, stubbing out a smoke.

"It's three in the morning," Hiram said. "I just talked to the others, there's no sign of her anywhere and this rain's not helping any."

Will nodded. "I'll go back and check at the house. You all might as well go home."

He spat in the direction of Smith's boots. The young man stepped forward, frowning. Hiram grabbed his son by the arm. Will turned his back and started to walk up along the river in the direction of the Dempsey farm.

"He wasn't even lookin' for her, Pa," Smith said. "Doesn't even seem to be worried or anything."

"That's because the bastard probably knows more than he's saying. I don't think Ann put those scratches on his face. Everybody knows she's been weak as a kitten for months."

Hiram swiped a match across the back of his pants and lit his cigarette. As he dipped his head, his hat brim poured rainwater at his feet.

"He wouldn't do anything to his own daughter, would he?" Jack asked.

"I'll kill him if he has," Smith said, his voice breaking. He turned his head away. "Something bad's happened. I just know it."

"I wouldn't trust Will Harney as far as I could throw him," Hiram told them. "Now let's get the hell home."

THE NEXT MORNING JOHN MCDONALD returned from Oxford. "Not a sign of her," he told Will, "but everybody says they'll keep an eye out."

Harold Mills had no better luck. "Went clear to Tatamagouche just in case," he reported to Hiram.

A number of men— volunteers from Pugwash and Wallace— had joined Harold on his return trip to Rockley to help with the search.

"And there's more on the way later today," he added proudly. "The whole county will be on the lookout for her by tonight."

Harold also alerted Constable Ryan, who said he would get in touch with the sheriff in Amherst about Mary's disappearance.

After church that morning Rita LeFurgey, Elsie MacDonald, and Elaine Clarke arrived at the Dempsey farm. Each carried a basket of food. Rita presented the cake she had made the night before and Elsie brought a large roast.

"This'll keep you from having to cook much," Rita told Mabel, who had arrived home a half hour earlier. Fred had gone to Oxford to fetch her.

Mabel shook her head and turned away, not wanting the other women to see the tears welling up in her eyes. Then she took a breath.

"I just don't know. If it wasn't for bad luck we'd have none at all. I'm much obliged for the food and the help. I'll have to tend the two young ones, and Ann besides, now. Where'd that girl get herself to?"

"Mabel, how's Kay doing? You spent the night I hear," Rita said.

"She's fine, had a healthy girl. If Caleb Brown was my man he'd be sleeping in the barn after this."

Elaine placed teacups and saucers on the table.

"Come and have a seat all of you," Mabel directed.

"You look worn out. You didn't have any sleep last night yourself, did you?" Elsie asked.

"Just dozed off and on after the baby came and they all got settled down. But there'll be no rest now until we find out what happened to Mary."

"It'll get sorted out in time. She'll be found, if not today, then very soon," Rita reassured her.

Mabel folded her shaking hands on the kitchen table. Rita reached out and covered them with one of her own. She had never seen Mabel so upset. With good reason, she told herself.

Harry and Little Helen ran into the kitchen from outdoors. Elsie grabbed the little boy and swung him up on her knee.

"Would you like a cookie, honey? There's some nice molasses ones right here."

The toddler nodded. He grabbed a cookie from Elsie with both hands and bit down.

Little Helen hid her face in Mabel's apron.

"You're getting tall, sweetie, and so pretty. What are you now, five?" Rita said, handing her a cookie. Little Helen hesitated and then gently took the treat and stood behind her grandmother's chair.

"And what do you say, young lady?" Mabel asked her.

"Thank you," Helen whispered.

"You're very welcome," Rita replied, smiling. "Mabel, can I get them some milk?"

"In the pantry behind the door. Glasses are in the cupboard there behind you."

Rita had just set the milk on the table when they heard someone thumping down the stairs.

"This'll be something now." Mabel shook her head.

Ann limped into the room. Rita got up to lead her over to the rocking chair.

"Have a seat, dear."

Ann still wore the blue nightdress and her hair was uncombed. Rita could see her hands trembling.

"Did Mary come home?" she asked, leaning on Rita.

"Not yet, dear. Can I get you some tea to warm you up? You're shaking." Rita took off her shawl and placed it around Ann's shoulders.

"Mary should be back by now. She's not far," Ann said, settling into the chair, looking at the others wild-eyed. She scratched her arms. Harry started to cry and reached for his mother while Little Helen sidled over from Mabel's chair to Ann's rocker. She patted her mother on the shoulder.

"Where's Will? Is he here? He knows where Mary is." Ann tried to rise from the chair, bracing her feet on the floor and bending forward.

"Stay put," Mabel commanded her. "Will's out looking for her right now. He'll be here later on."

Elaine rose from the table. "Ann," she said, "you need to get some food into you. You're white as a sheet." She helped Ann to her feet. Harry reached out to his mother again. Ann ignored them all and, turning, moved towards the porch door. "God, woman, you're stronger than you look," Elaine said, trying to steer her towards the table.

"I need to find Mary. Mary needs me."

"She's going out there barefoot. She'll catch her death," Mabel warned and got to her feet.

Ann moved her elbows away from her body and shook both women off.

"Let's just see what she's up to," Rita said, holding Elaine back. "We're right here. She won't get far."

"Crazy, crazy, crazy," Mabel said and sat back down.

Ann walked out into the yard. Little Helen and Harry, surprised by the novelty of their mother being outside, ran after her, dragging on her nightgown and begging to be picked up. Ann turned right, as if to walk out of the yard and down the lane, but then took another right and walked towards the back of the house, trailed first by her children and then by Rita, Elaine, and Elsie. In less than a minute, she had walked in a complete circle around the house and was at the porch again.

"She'll go back inside now," Rita reassured the others. "She just wanted some air."

But Ann began retracing her steps around the house. Elaine ran ahead and scooped Harry up into her arms.

"Here, little man, I'll carry you." She cuddled the crying boy.

"Rita, what's she saying? She's talking to herself."

"I can't make it out. We've got to get her back inside, enough's enough."

Rita ran ahead and grabbing Ann by the arm, swung her around.

"Come on back inside, it's chilly out here. You've had your air."

Ann struggled to get away from Rita's hold.

"I need to help Mary. She needs help."

"You won't help her by catching a cold," Elsie told her, grabbing her other arm. They pulled Ann towards the porch, while she begged to be let go.

"What a terrible thing for the young ones to see," Elaine said.

They finally managed to get Ann back into the porch and then the kitchen.

"For someone who hasn't been well, she's some strong," Elsie said, out of breath as they got Ann seated back into the rocking chair.

"Mabel, is there anything in the house to calm her?" Rita asked, practically sitting on Ann's knees to keep her down.

"If she hasn't already drunk it." Mabel went to the shelf above the sink, picked up a bottle with cough syrup written on the label, and shook it. "There's a bit left. I put some of it in here, hoping she wouldn't find it. The minute she gets hold of any, it's gone."

She scooped up some water from the bucket with a dipper, poured it into the bottle, shook it, and handed it to Rita.

"This should settle her for a while."

"Here you go, Ann. This will make you feel better. You need some rest." Rita gave Ann the bottle. She drank it down.

"All right. Let's get you to bed."

"I need to help Mary," Ann muttered.

"We'll help Mary, don't you worry," Rita reassured her as she and Elsie led Ann back upstairs. "You just have to rest now."

John came into the kitchen with an armload of firewood. He looked at Mabel and Elaine and forced a smile.

"Mrs. Clarke, it's nice of you and the other women to come and help Mabel look after things, but it will soon be over and Mary will be back home where she belongs. She's all right. Young people are headstrong by times," he said, trying to reassure himself as much as anyone else.

Throughout Sunday the search intensified. Men and boys walked shoulder to shoulder through brush and hayfields, sweeping long sticks before them and occasionally calling out. The Pugwash River and River Philip were both dragged. Three wagon wheels, the carcass of a horse, and old nets and fishing equipment were the only things found.

EARLY THE NEXT MORNING, JOHN rode into Pugwash and telegraphed Beatrice Hennessey.

"Her sister should be with her now," he explained to Mabel, who didn't think it was necessary.

"That's all we need, the two of them around here bawling. My nerves are on edge as it is."

"Nonetheless, her family has to know from us first before word gets to them another way."

While in Pugwash John stopped at the home of Philip Jones, the harbourmaster, to ask for his help. They stood on the veranda of Jones's house that overlooked the harbour filled with cargo ships and fishing boats.

"Yeah sure, I'll let people know. I'll tell them to keep a lookout for her or any signs of the punt. It's yellow, you say."

"I know there's little chance of her getting out of the river, let alone into the Strait. That little punt would be swamped in no time. But you never know," John said.

"She'd have to be awful strong," Philip said. "And it's a dangerous thing for anybody to do, never mind a young girl."

"I appreciate your help." John tipped his hat as he left.

"I'll do what I can. And God bless your family."

By Wednesday morning, with still with no sign of Mary, Rockley residents got back to their normal routines. Women worked in their kitchens and men dug potatoes and brought in their split wood for the coming winter. That afternoon Elaine Clarke, on her way to Bailey's store, stopped in to visit Freda Mills and to drop off some cranberries and an apron pattern she'd been meaning to return for months. Freda was on the doorstep yelling at her grandchildren, who were doddling along the main road on their way home from school.

"You two fly into this house."

She shook her head at Elaine and broke into a relieved smile.

"I don't like to have them out of my sight. Since Mary disappeared I don't have a nerve left."

"I know what you mean," Elaine said.

"I keep thinking Mary ran away on her own, but one never knows. Peter came home from Bailey's last night and said that word is going 'round that Will may have had something to do with her missing."

"Nothing surprises me anymore," Freda replied.

LATE WEDNESDAY EVENING, BEATRICE KNOCKED on the door of the Dempsey farmhouse. Fred LeFurgey, who had picked her up from the River Philip train station, stood by her side holding a large brown suitcase in each hand.

"You're not going into that place by yourself," he had told her as they drove up the lane to the house.

Mabel opened the door.

"So you're here," she said, standing aside to let Beatrice into the porch. She opened the kitchen door and nodded at the visitors to keep walking. She glared at Fred.

"I'm staying with her," he proclaimed, holding tight to the suitcase handles.

"Suit yourself." Mabel shrugged.

"Where's my sister?" Beatrice demanded, turning to the older woman. "And where are Little Helen and Harry? And what happened to Mary?"

Beatrice's eyes were swollen and red. She nodded to John, who, seated at the kitchen table, rose to greet her.

"The young ones are both to bed," Mabel said. "Been there for just a half-hour. Don't wake them up. Ann is up in her bedroom, lying around as usual."

Mabel pointed to the stairs. Beatrice started up.

"Just a minute," Will shouted. He had been out on the veranda and waited until Beatrice and Fred were in the house before following them. He looked at Fred first. "Get out."

"Go to hell."

Will grabbed Fred around the neck with both hands. Fred dropped the suitcases and struggled to remove Will's grip. At the same time John placed his arms around Will's torso.

"Jesus," Will cursed and let Fred go.

"Stop this foolishness," John shouted as Will made a move towards his uncle, but was prevented when Fred punched him in the stomach. Will doubled over, sinking to his knees.

"For the love of God, stop this," Beatrice yelled, her hands over her ears.

"You couldn't get Ann so now you're sniffing around the old maid," Will hissed at Fred.

Will looked at Beatrice. "You're not wanted here," he told her. "Ann doesn't need you skulking around here, nosing into our business."

"Ann is my sister and she and her children are my business."

"Mine, not yours," Will said, struggling to his feet. "Now get the hell out of my house."

Beatrice turned her back and made for the stairs again. This time John reached out and grabbed her arm.

"Miss Hennessey, I'm John, Will's uncle."

"Thank you for telegraphing me, Mr. Dempsey. I appreciate it."

Again she headed for the stairs.

"Just a minute."

She turned to John once more.

"It's getting late, Miss Hennessey, and everybody is tired. Is there a place you can stay this evening? Maybe you can see Ann and the kids in the morning."

"Over my dead body," Will told them.

"Miss Hennessey can stay with me and Ma tonight," Fred offered.

Will snickered.

"That's a good idea." John nodded and led Beatrice towards the door. "Fred, we're beholden to your family once again."

"Bu—" Beatrice started to protest.

John squeezed her elbow and walked her out into the yard. Will and Fred followed behind.

"It's better that you come back tomorrow, Miss," John advised her. "You'll not get anywhere with him tonight."

"Yeah, let's get the hell out of here." Fred placed the suitcases back in the surrey.

"Is there a hotel near here?" Beatrice asked as John handed her back up into the vehicle.

"You can stay with us tonight," Fred told her. "Ma will be pleased to have you."

"I'll talk some sense into Will. You'll see Ann and the kids tomorrow," John reassured her.

ON THURSDAY AFTERNOON, Mary's disappearance was reported in the *Chignecto Post*, and people from all over the county, throughout the province, and up into New Brunswick began to follow the story. Some of the curious attempted to get a first-hand look.

"Nosey bastards. Look at them, trying to see something as they drive by."

John, unlike himself, was getting crankier by the day, especially with the coach and wagon traffic clogging up the main road past his house.

"Some of them got enough nerve to drive into the yard and demand to see Mary's bedroom or want to give us their two-cents' worth on where she might be," Mabel said. "Come away from the window, John. Come and get some supper."

"One of those so-called mediums met me on the road coming home today and said that for ten dollars she would tell me where Mary is." John shook his head and wiped at his eyes with his sleeve.

BEATRICE AND ANN DID NOT see each other until Sunday afternoon. Will went off to Oxford for the day, warning both his mother and uncle not to let Beatrice near the house. But as soon as Will rode out of sight, John made his way over to the LeFurgeys' farm and brought Beatrice back in the express wagon. Mabel protested, but John escorted Beatrice up the stairs to Ann's bedroom. After he deposited Harry and Little Helen there as well, John stood with arms folded, guarding the door. Fred took up his post in the surrey, across the end of John's lane, determined that Will would not pass while Beatrice was in the house. Mabel stayed in the kitchen, rocking and scowling.

The sisters cried at the sight of each other.

"Oh, Ann." Beatrice crawled onto the bed and gathered her sister into her arms.

"What's happened to you? What's happened to Mary?"

Ann shook her head and tried to remove herself from Beatrice's grasp.

"Mary ran away."

"Mary wouldn't run away without letting someone know where she was. She's been gone for over a week now."

"I so wanted to come home when Mother died." Ann was sobbing again. "But I was so ill, and I still am."

"You don't look like yourself at all," Beatrice agreed. "And where's Mary? I don't understand what's going on."

"I fell down the church steps."

"Ann, for God's sake, I said, where's Mary, and—"

The door opened and Little Helen bounded onto the bed. Harry was too short to do so. Beatrice scooped him up into her arms.

"Oh, my dears. I could eat you up, I'm so glad to see you."

"Mary gone," Little Helen told her, and nestled down.

"Yes, I know, sweetheart, but we'll find her."

"Oh, Mary's hiding, but she's near," Ann said, placing a finger to her lips.

"Hiding, for God sakes, what's that mean?"

Ann snuggled down into the bed. "I need my medicine."

"Where is it? I'll get it for you."

"Mabel keeps it from me. I have to beg for it. I think there might be some in that top drawer over there." Ann pointed across the room.

Beatrice found a half empty bottle of whiskey among the clothes.

"This isn't medicine," she told Ann, holding the bottle in the air.

"Oh, yes, it is. Dr. Creed prescribed it for me himself." Ann motioned for Beatrice to come closer.

"Well then, I'll be talking to him, that's for sure." Beatrice put the bottle back and closed the drawer.

"Please, Bea."

"When did you start drinking, Ann?"

"Mummy drinks a lot," Little Helen proclaimed to no one in particular.

"God help us." Beatrice flung herself down on a chair and looked at the three of them on the bed. Ann began to cry again. Beatrice crossed the room, took the children up into her arms, and opened the bedroom door. She handed Little Harry to John and led the way downstairs.

After discussing Ann's condition with Mabel and John, Beatrice asked Fred to take her to see Dr. Creed. Then she booked herself into the Victory Hotel in Pugwash and telegrammed her father that she would be staying in Cumberland County until Mary was found.

"THIS MIGHT BE THE MISSING Rockley girl, if it's possible for a body to travel that far," Amherst Sheriff Dan Sherman said, waving a paper under his deputy's nose.

Lawmen and justices of the peace all over the Maritime provinces had received telegrams announcing the discovery of a young girl's body on a Prince Edward Island beach.

"It says she had clothes on when she was found. Get back to this Sheriff Flynn in Summerside, will you, and ask him to send me over a piece of clothing. And I'm going to send this message through to Ryan in Pugwash just to make sure he got it too."

Three days later a brown envelope containing a two-inch square of plaid fabric arrived on Sherman's desk. As soon as the sheriff received it, he took the train to River Philip.

Mid-afternoon the following day, Sherman and Constable Ryan rode up to the Dempsey farmhouse on horseback. Will, unshaven and shirtless, answered their knock.

"What can I do for you, gentlemen?" he asked, buttoning up his underwear and slicking back his blond hair with the palms of his hands.

"Mr. Harney, we'd like to have a word with you and your family," Ryan said, placing a foot inside the porch.

Will stepped aside to let them enter, then closed the door. "Have a seat." He gestured towards the kitchen table.

Both men removed their hats and placed them on their knees. There was a glass container of molasses and a large butcher knife on the table. Frowning, Sherman pushed away crumbs with his hand. He and Ryan nodded at Mabel who was sweeping the floor, and Sherman winked at Little Helen who was sitting in front of the open oven door on a braided mat, hugging a doll. As Will sat himself down at the table, the kitchen door opened again and John, who had seen the men ride up, came in. He greeted them then leaned against the wall beside the stove, with arms folded, and waited.

"Little Helen, go tell your Ma to get in here," Will told his daughter. "Now, what can I do for you?" He smiled.

Before either man could answer, Ann entered the kitchen, unsteadily.

"Do you have news of Mary? Have you found her? Where's Mary?" she demanded, wringing her hands in front of them. Her face was haggard and her hair hung in her eyes.

"Jesus Christ, woman, shut up and they'll tell you." Will turned to their visitors and rolled his eyes.

"Crazier than a loon," Mabel said.

"Shut up, Ma," Will barked.

Ann hung her head. "Forgive me."

"No need to apologize, ma'am," said Ryan. "Unfortunately, what we have to tell you is not good news."

Ann turned and grabbed her husband's arm. As he attempted to loosen her hold, she sank to the floor, folding up, as she fell, like a hinged wooden puppet. Ryan rose to help her but Will shook his head. "Let her be."

Sherman reached inside his long coat and placed a piece of faded red, black, and white plaid fabric on the table. Mabel stopped rocking and craned her neck to look while Ann grasped the table leg and attempted, laboriously, to stand once again. She snatched the fabric and held it close to her face as if struggling to see it.

"Last week, the body of a girl washed up over on Prince Edward Island. She was wearing a skirt made of this material. Does it look familiar to you?"

Ann stared at Sherman, her eyes glassy. Still clutching the fabric, she ran out of the kitchen and up the stairs.

"Hey, wait." Sheriff Ryan started up from his chair.

Will laid a hand on his arm.

"Let her go, man. That was Mary's all right and she knew it. That was a piece of the skirt she used to wear to church."

"It's evidence," Ryan warned. Sherman shook his head.

"Well, then you go after her." Will shrugged his shoulders and grinned. "It's Mary's all right. How did you get hold of it?"

"It was sent over from the Island," Sherman told him. "A young girl about the same age as your daughter washed up on the shore over there on the twelfth of this month and nobody knows who she is. They sent it after I requested a piece for identification. It looks like we got a match."

"But we need to find out for sure if it's hers," Ryan said, looking at Sherman.

John moved away from the wall and walked slowly up the stairs.

"Now what happens?" Will asked.

"Somebody's got to go over to the island with me to identify the body." Sherman got up from the table.

Will looked from one to the other.

"I suppose that's me," he sighed.

SUMMERSIDE

PRINCE EDWARD ISLAND
September 19, 1877

SHERMAN AND WILL MET Flynn at his office. The girl's garments were in a brown burlap bag. The first item Flynn removed from it was the brown belt.

"That was hers." Will jumped up off his chair, spilling his coffee. "Yeah, yeah, yeah, these were Mary's things, I'd know them anywhere. There's her skirt, see, with the piece cut out of it."

"You sure?" Sherman asked.

"Yeah, I'm sure. You know, I was kind of mad about having to come over here but it's proved to be a good time," Will said. "I'd never been on the ferry before, you know. And I've never been to the Island before. The place sure is green, even at this time of year, and I'd heard that the dirt was red but never realized how much until now."

Flynn and Sherman eyed each other across the room. The latter turned away, shaking his head.

"I thought that today we'd go out to the farm where she was found and talk to the family there and go look at the gravesite," Flynn said.

"What, she's been buried?" Sherman looked puzzled.

"Yeah, buried the day before I sent you that telegraph. Didn't realize they were goin' to do it so soon. It turned out all right after all since we know now who she is. No harm done."

"It's not right, though. The body should have been kept longer so it could be properly identified. It's not right," Sherman repeated.

Flynn threw up his hands.

"Look, I'm just as glad not to see a dead body," Will said. "These are Mary's clothes so that's that. What I'd really like to do now, if it's all the same to you, is look around town for a while, maybe walk down the street and take in the sights."

"Ah...sure, fine." Sherman nodded.

"But be back in a half-hour, then we'll take a drive out to the Bell farm. I'd like to have a talk with them even if you don't."

"Good. Can you point me in the direction of the harbour?"

Will started to whistle as he made for the door. While Flynn turned to the pot-bellied stove to refill his coffee cup, Sherman watched as Will proceeded down Water Street, tipping his cap to everyone he met along the way.

"WHAT TIME DO YOU THINK they'll be here?" Avard asked Gilbert as they sat down at the kitchen table. Catherine was ladling out boiled dinner for the noon meal. It was a windy and uncommonly chilly day for late summer and the ham, cabbage, and potatoes would taste good, Gilbert thought, after a morning of hauling and stacking wood in the shed.

"They're supposedly on the two o'clock train. Land here just at mealtime, I suppose."

"The poor man. I feel so sorry for him and his family," Catherine said, placing a bowl before her husband.

"Why they had to come here I'll never know," Gilbert said.

"The sheriff will have questions, and the father will want to meet the people who found his daughter. He's likely thankful that she was found at all. And we did give her a proper burial."

"Just cuts into the workday, is all."

"She's been buried," Eddie said. "How are they going to identify her now?"

"That's a good question," Gilbert said, fearing he knew the answer.

"Anyway, it may give the poor man some comfort to know she was found and where she's buried," Catherine said, carrying her own bowl over to the table and sitting down beside Jimmy, who was carefully eating around the cabbage in front of him.

FOUND DROWNED

GILBERT LOOKED UP FROM THE harness he was mending to see three men drive up in a buggy. The only one he recognized was Sheriff Flynn. A stocky man with a brown moustache jumped down from the left side of the front seat, followed by Flynn. The buggy's lone occupant, a tall, thin man with blond hair, was sitting in the back.

"Gil, I'd like you to meet Sheriff Dan Sherman from Amherst."

Flynn motioned towards Gilbert and then the stranger with his right hand. His left hand held a piece of straw he had just removed from his mouth.

"So that's the father?" Gil asked, raising his chin towards the buggy.

Avard and Eddy came around from the back of the woodshed, where they had been chopping and piling kindling.

"Do you know the name of the dead girl, sir?" Avard asked.

"Harney," Sherman told him. "Mary Harney from Rockley, just outside of Pugwash, over in Nova Scotia."

"Harney, eh? Never heard that last name before," Gilbert said.

"Originally from around Pictou way," Sherman said.

"There's been a bit of a misunderstandin'," Flynn told Gilbert.

"Oh, how so?"

"The sheriff here didn't realize that the body had already been buried. He wanted the father to identify it. But he's seen the clothes and they're hers all right. Took one look at them—I hadn't gotten them all out of the bag yet—and he said they were hers. So at least we know now who she is. So many that are washed up are never identified."

"Have you been over to the graveyard?" Gilbert asked.

"No, and I don't think we will. He's not really interested in seeing his daughter's place of rest." Sherman shrugged. "More concerned in smoking my cigarettes and when the next meal is going to be. He seems to be regarding this as one big holiday."

"Gil," Flynn said, "do you think that Catherine would have the teapot on?"

As they went towards the house, Avard and Eddie made their way over to the buggy.

"How many acres you got here?" Will asked.

"Pa has about a hundred," Eddie answered.

"I got two hundred acres back home. And got about twenty men working full-time at the place. Wouldn't believe it to look at me but it's true."

"We're really sorry about...about Mary," Avard told him.

"Thanks, boy. Yeah, it was a hard blow to both me and her ma. Mary was a good child. Prone to storytelling, but other than that she was mostly well-behaved."

"How old was she?" Avard asked.

"Eighteen come next January...I think. She was a bit slow-witted. It was hard to get any work out of her either."

"Did she have a beau?" Avard asked.

"One young fellow had been sniffing around her the last year or so. Had to keep my eye on the pair of them."

"Would you like to come in the house for some tea?" Eddie asked.

"Wouldn't mind." Will smiled. "It's been a long morning. It's been a nice trip but, like I say, it's hard to be away from the farm. I'm needed at home. By the way, could you boys point me in the direction of your outhouse? I drank a lot of strong coffee this morning."

"I'll show you," Avard offered.

As the boys moved to the front of the buggy, Will opened up a satchel on the floor and rummaged around inside. Avard saw him pick up a bundle, also from the buggy floor, and stuff it into the satchel.

"All right, where's the shithouse?" Will asked, jumping to the ground.

BACK IN SUMMERSIDE, SHERMAN PURCHASED tickets for himself and Will for the six-fifteen ferry crossing to Cape Tormentine. It was as they got ready to board the ferry, *Prince Edward*, that Sherman noticed the burlap bag was missing.

"What the hell, Flynn? I thought you told your deputy to put that bag in the buggy."

"I did. It should be there."

"Well, it's not. Do we have time to go back and get it?"

"You get aboard. It's getting late. I'll go back and ask Gerald what he done with it. I'll get him to run it down here to you before the ferry leaves."

"All right, but he'll have to be quick about it. I'll get the captain to hold the ferry if need be."

Will whistled as he made his way up the ferry's gangplank. "It's a grand day for a boat ride, don't you think?"

Sherman grumbled under his breath. He took tobacco and papers out of his jacket pocket and started to roll a cigarette.

"Could you spare one of those, Sheriff?" Will asked, walking back down.

Sherman sighed and passed over the newly rolled smoke.

"Thanks." Will grinned. "Think I'll take a turn around this tub and see what's happening." He flicked a bit of ash into the water and boarded the boat once again.

Sherman commenced to roll another smoke.

He was waiting on the dock when Flynn's buggy came into view in a cloud of dust. Gerald was driving as fast as he dared through town. He then reined the team in hard to avoid going over the side of the wharf. The horses tripped over their own feet in their attempt to stop. Gerald jumped out and ran up to Sherman, puffing. "I put the bag in the buggy. It should have been there. I put it in the buggy," he repeated while trying to catch his breath.

Sherman cursed. "Well, then, it's gone. If it shows up, which I doubt, send it on to Amherst."

He waved to the first mate, and hurried up the gangplank in search of his travelling companion as the steamer's engine rumbled to life.

WHEN THE *PRINCE EDWARD* DOCKED at Cape Tormentine, Sherman hired a wagon to take him and Will to Sackville, where they stayed overnight in a boarding house near the railway station. Throughout the trip Will denied seeing the burlap bag of clothes after they left Flynn's office.

"Honest to God. I don't remember the young fellow putting anything in the buggy and I was outdoors with him the whole time he was getting the horses ready," he claimed.

Sherman wrestled Will's satchel away from him but the only things inside were an extra shirt, two apples, and a newspaper Sherman himself had purchased in Charlottetown. He suspected Will of lying but didn't understand why he would take the clothing when he had already been told that it would be returned to the family. And if he did want them back right away, where were they now?

It just doesn't make sense, Sherman kept telling himself.

THE TRAIN CHUGGED INTO RIVER Philip at eleven o'clock the next morning. Will shouldered his bag and started walking north. After twenty minutes, a salesman with three steamer trunks in the back of a wagon stopped to offer him a ride.

"Women's clothes and dainties," he replied when Will asked what he was peddling.

He was going to Pugwash, as part of his monthly rounds through the county, and had a bottle with him. Will stayed on the wagon and was driven down the main road right past the farm. He saw John walking, stooped, to the barn and grinned to himself. He decided to go straight through to Pugwash, and make his holiday last a little longer. He was sure he'd get a ride back later in the day. The peddler let him off on Main Street and Will tipped his cap to his new friend and walked off in search of a drink.

Hank Baxter lived off Water Street, just behind Phoebe Carter's bakery. Phoebe let him stay in a room at the back of her building. It was an open secret that Hank and his brother Mac were bootleggers. Mac, who lived just outside town on the way to Wallace, supplied the liquor and Hank sold it. Phoebe didn't mind. Hank did odd jobs around the place and acted as a live-in night watchman. The Baxter brothers were well liked and many people appreciated the convenience of having a place to buy rum and whiskey on Sundays or after the Wharf Tavern closed for the night.

Will stopped at the bakery first and purchased two dinner rolls fresh out of the oven. Phoebe passed him the change from the ten-dollar bill he presented.

"I just got back from the Island," he announced, smiling.

"Oh yes, for a visit?" Phoebe asked knowing full well why he had been away.

"No, on official police business. Had to go over there and identify my daughter's body. She washed up over there, you know."

"Yes, I had heard about that, Mr. Harney. I'm very sorry."

"I appreciate your sympathies. Ever been on the Island ferry?"

"No."

"You should go some time if you ever get the chance."

The bell on the door jingled as Will closed it behind him.

Hank was sitting on the doorstep with a large German shepherd whose heavy head rested on its paws.

"Got any good stuff?"

"Sure, Mac came for a visit last night. Step inside and make yourself at home."

As he followed Hank inside, Will threw the uneaten bit of his roll at the dog, who snapped it between yellow teeth.

The room smelled of burnt beans and unwashed clothes and bodies.

Hank pointed to an unpainted ladder-back chair, its seat split in two, and Will sat down.

"What's your pleasure?"

"Can you spare two whiskies?"

"Yeah."

Will laughed when Hank pulled a wooden box out from under the unmade bed in the corner.

"I see you got a loan of some Huestis property."

The words Huestis Graystone Company, Wallace, NS, were stencilled along the side of the box. Its six-by-six-inch compartments originally held dynamite but now contained quart bottles of whiskey.

"Came by it honestly," Hank told him. "They were doing away with some of their stuff and Mac happened to be there."

Hank removed two bottles and handed them to Will.

"Here you go. That's a dollar twenty-five for both."

"That's a bit steep, Hank, but never mind. Can I have a couple sips before I go?"

"Fill your boots."

Will rolled one bottle up in the shirt he had in his bag. Then he unscrewed the top of the other and jerked his head back to take a long haul. His throat burned. He brought his head back down, removed the bottle from his mouth, wiped his lips, then handed it over to Hank who shook his head.

"It's a bit too early for me." He grinned.

"Go on." Will shook the bottle at him. "Have a drink courtesy of the Amherst sheriff."

Hank reached out for the bottle, took a sip, and handed it back.

"How's that?" he asked.

"Just got back from a paid trip to PE Island. They needed me to identify Mary's body."

"So it was her after all. God rest her soul," Hank said. "Now how did she ever manage to get way over there?"

"Well, my punt disappeared the same time she did. She took it to spite me and ran away from home. She probably was trying to get back to Pictou County to her mother's crazy family."

Will took another long drag on the bottle.

"It's a damn shame," said Hank.

"Mary was always a little simple in the head."

"So are you going to work today?" Hank asked, rising from the stool.

"No, lost my place there a while back," Will informed him. "That bastard foreman was always out to get me anyway. None of them any good, including those rich Seaman sons of bitches."

Hank gave him a puzzled look.

"It's a long story. Maybe I'll tell you sometime. But that dynamite box of yours just reminded me of the unfair treatment I got from that place. I think I might take a trip to Wallace today and give them a piece of my mind before I head home to my loving family."

Will took another drink.

Hank moved towards the door.

"That's probably not a good idea. Better just to get yourself home now, Will. Do you have a ride?"

"Nope." Will swayed to his feet. "Got the money to hire a drive but I'll be damned if I give any of it to that know-nothing Fred LeFurgey. I'd rather crawl home. It's a nice day and I might be able to hitch a ride with someone going out that way."

Will stepped out into the sunshine. He patted the dog's head as he clomped off the doorstep. He tipped his hat to Hank and headed down the road towards Wallace.

WHEN WILL ARRIVED BACK HOME at three o'clock the next morning, he banged on the door with both fists. Mabel eventually opened it and stood before her son with a metal poker in her hand.

"About time you got home," she said. "Scared me half to death with your knocking. Thought you were somebody come to murder us in our beds. Herself just about drove me and John crazy while you been gone. And wait until you see what she's done now."

"I CAN'T BELIEVE THAT POOR girl just disappeared into thin air," Elsie MacDonald said to Elaine Clarke as they sat, knitting, on Elsie's front veranda.

"Somebody's done something to her, I'd bet my life on it," Elaine said. "Heavens, I dropped a stitch. That's what I get for thinking ill of people."

"Have you met the sister yet?" Elsie asked.

"Yes, at Bailey's store the other day. She seems like a sensible person, very ladylike. I'm surprised she's not staying at John's, they have more than enough room."

"I see her walk past here every day from the hotel," Elsie said. "The first time I went out and introduced myself. I had heard she had come after Mary disappeared. She came in for tea. A lovely person. She's worried sick about Ann and Mary. Can't say I blame her. Her and Fred LeFurgey have taken up looking for Mary on their own. They're going all over the same ground where everybody else looked, and the rumour going around is that Will did away with her, his own daughter. I just can't believe it even though he seems to be little more than a brute. Remember that time he chased all of us out of the house?"

"I heard something but you've got to keep it to yourself," Elaine said, lowering her voice although there was no one else in sight.

"Cross my heart, I won't breathe a word to a soul," Elsie said.

"Well, Freda told me that Martha told her that word is out that it wasn't Will at all but Smith Reid who had something to do with Mary being gone. Folks are saying that she was in the family way."

Elsie nodded her head over her work. "I knew it, I knew it. Things aren't always as cut and dried as they seem. The truth will out, as they say. Of course, Mary just might have gotten it into her head to run away. Mabel said that the girl doted on her Aunt Beatrice, the one that's here now, and was always agitating to go and visit her."

"I don't believe that she just plain ran away," Elsie said. "I think that somebody needs to be held accountable for what's happened."

"YEAH, I'M PRETTY SURE THAT son of a bitch did something to her," said Hiram, leaning on the fabric counter behind him.

"Mind your tea around those prints," Calvin warned. "Jennie will skin me alive if they get stained."

Hiram raised the cup in his host's direction and grinned.

Hiram, Smith and Jack Reid, and Fred LeFurgey were meeting at Bailey's store to decide what to do about Will.

"Yeah, Harney likely did something. But what and how can we prove it?" Fred asked.

"The police didn't really do much, did they?" Smith growled.

Calvin snorted. "The police. Did you hear about the Huestis quarry in Wallace? Two of its warehouses burnt to the ground the other night. They're sure as shooting that it was arson but the police don't know who did it and likely never will. Their guard dog was found dead just inside the main gate. Beat to death. So it probably wasn't kids, killing a dog like that. But who knows. There's been lots of fires around over the last year or two. It's a worry to a businessman, let me tell you."

"Anyway," Fred said, "we might all think that Will did something to Mary but besides stringing him up ourselves, how can we get the authorities to pay attention?"

"We need to speak in one voice. They can't ignore a large group of people who want something done. And it has to be official," Hiram said.

"What about a petition?" Smith asked. "Last spring when the ladies' garden club in Pugwash wanted to have flower pots put around the post office steps, they got a petition going 'round for people to sign and sent it to the village council. They soon got their damn flowers."

"That's an idea. But what do we want?" Jack asked.

"I want Harney strung up by the heels," Fred said.

"Yeah, but we need to put it in a way that sounds legal and official. Something that the authorities will pay attention to," Hiram said.

"Then who would we send it to? Who would listen?"

"Send it to Halifax," Fred offered. "To the police. I remember reading in the paper not long ago that they have detectives down there specially trained, who will go outside of the city to look into crimes and to pick up prisoners. They've even gone up into Maine. Maybe we could get one of them to come here. We could send the petition to Hiram Black to sign himself and get him to mail it for us. He's the MLA, he'd know where to send it. He's a Liberal but he might be good for something."

"It's worth a try, that's for sure," Calvin agreed. "I'll go get a pencil and some writing paper."

"Who will we get to sign it?" Smith asked.

"Every man over eighteen," his father said, nodding.

"May as well let the women sign as well, the married ones anyway. We need all the names we can get," Calvin suggested.

"Miss Hennessey will want to sign it too, that's for sure. And she's not married," Fred said, looking sheepish all of a sudden.

"Heard you've been spending a lot of time in her company since she got here," Calvin said, raising his eyebrows at the blushing man.

"I want to sign it too," Jack piped up.

Petition
To the Chief of Police
Halifax, Nova Scotia
September 22nd, 1877

Dear Sir,

In the matter of the disappearance and murder of Mary Harney, the below signed individuals of Rockley, Cumberland County, Nova Scotia, and surrounding areas, request that the Halifax Police Department send a detective to Cape Traverse, PE Island, where a girl washed up on shore and was later buried. The dead girl might be Mary Harney.

The below signed individuals of Rockley and surrounding area accuse William Harney, the father of Mary Harney, of the wilful and wrongful murder of his daughter. We need the assistance of the police to bring him to justice.

Trust that we are your most humble servants,

Calvin Bailey
Hiram Reid
Fred LeFurgey
Smith Reid
Jack Reid

The stars blur above me. Then nothing.

HALIFAX

Nova Scotia
September 30, 1877

"EVER BEEN TO PE Island, Lew?" chief Ernie MacFarlane asked.

"No, I never have."

The Chief of Police motioned towards a chair and extended a cigar. Detective Lewis Hutt shook his head and sat down across from his supervisor. The desk between them was littered with papers, cigar butts, and ashes.

It's a wonder this whole building hasn't gone up in flames, Hutt thought to himself.

"Received a petition this morning by special delivery from Cumberland County. There's a missing girl up there and a body was found recently on PE Island. Might be the same person. People in... now what the hell was the name of that place again?"

Hutt watched with exasperation as Macfarlane rummaged around among the letters and posters in front of him. One of the many things the detective couldn't tolerate was disorganization. Finally, six long narrow pieces of sepia-coloured foolscap were retrieved from the mound.

MacFarlane blew out a smoke ring before continuing. "Rockley. Never heard of it. Anyway, a bunch of people up there are bound and determined that she was done away with. The father of the missing girl is named as the suspect."

He jabbed a yellowed finger at the document. "Look at all the names. Just about everybody in the place signed that murder has been committed and should be investigated. Their MLA sent it on. He and two justices of the peace signed it too. They want a detective to check it out."

"May I see that, sir?"

Hutt studied the list of names for a minute. MacFarlane began to drum his fingers on the desk.

"I should travel to this Rockley as well, sir."

"Go over to the Island and look at the body first. It's likely buried by now. You'll need a court order to get it dug up. I'll handle that for you. Talk to the locals. Get a better idea of what went on there first and then if things seem fishy, head for Cumberland County."

"When should I leave?"

"When can you leave is the question. Clear up what paperwork you got and head out right away."

"I'll have to go home and pack and telegraph Mrs. Hutt. She's gone to her sister's in Bridgewater for a few days."

"Fine, fine, no problem."

"Will—"

"Yes, Lew, the department will look after all your expenses. You'll be reimbursed when you get back."

THESE PLACES ALL LOOK THE same, Hutt thought as he stepped out of the hansom cab and down onto dusty King Street in front of the Cambridge Hotel in Charlottetown. Over the last fifteen years he had travelled, from time to time, throughout the Maritimes and New England, chasing criminals and looking for missing persons.

One case just runs into the other, he thought, sighing.

It was warm for the first day of October but to Hutt it felt good after the chilly steamship ride from Pictou. He retrieved his leather suitcase from the back of the cab and walked along the wooden platform to the door of the hotel. It was nice enough inside. The spittoons in the corners shone, the tidy counter stood in front of pigeonhole cupboards, neatly stacked with letters and telegrams. Hutt walked up and rang the bell.

A balding man stepped out from a small room and stood behind the counter.

"Lewis Hutt. I'd like a room for the night."

"Yes, sir. We have a number of vacancies. Our best room is six dollars a night. And every bed in the place, believe it or not, has spring mattresses."

"Do you have anything less expensive?"

"Got a nice little room on this floor. Four a night. Neat as a pin."

"I'll take it."

"Sign the register here, please."

Hutt carefully wrote his name and address in the thick green book on the top of the counter. The clerk swerved it around to read the entry and his eyes widened a little.

"Halifax. Any chance you're that detective I read about in the *Examiner* that's supposed to be coming to the Island about that Harvey girl?"

"Harney, her last name is Harney. And yes, I'm that detective."

"That was something. Imagine her getting over here all the way from Nova Scotia. How'd she ever do it?"

"That's what I've come to find out. My key, please. Thank you. And what time is supper served?"

"Starts at five o'clock sharp until eight, sir."

"Can I get a train to Summerside tomorrow morning?"

"At seven."

Hutt carried his suitcase down the hall and through the open door indicated by the clerk. After removing his coat and hat, he placed the suitcase on the bed. His shaving kit and brown leather collar box found a temporary home on the small bureau by the window. He hung his second-best brown travelling suit (he was currently wearing his third-best) on the peg at the back of the door. Hutt took off his spats and shoes, hung his hat and coat on the peg over his suit, then removed his collar and cuffs and placed them in the leather box. He hung his shirt and then his socks neatly over the back of the chair, which was placed before a small writing desk. Dressed only in his underwear, Hutt flung the quilt aside and sat down on the narrow bed.

Jesus, I'm tired, he thought. I'm getting too old to be traipsing around the countryside. Then, remembering, he rose once more and took his pocket watch out of his coat.

Four thirty-seven. He'd sleep until six-thirty and then go down to eat at seven.

Hutt reached into his case and extracted an oval frame containing a photograph of his wife, Annie. He set it on the bureau beside the collar box. He lay on the bed and stared at her face until he fell asleep.

He woke with a start. It was twilight. He reached for his pocket watch. "Damn," he muttered, rubbing his eyes. He'd overslept. That wasn't like him. Now he'd have to hurry if he wanted a decent bite before the kitchen closed.

When he arrived in the dimly lit dining room, all the tables were occupied. So much for a quiet supper. He'd have to ask someone if he could share a table. Two men, who looked like travellers themselves, were sitting in a corner hidden partially by a large fern. Hutt made his way over to them, squeezing between the tables. Yes, they would be pleased to have him sit with them. They turned out to be actors, members of William Nannery's Atlantic Victorian Theatre, currently on a regional tour, and were leaving for Fredericton in the morning.

Hutt was thankful his supper mates were more interested in recounting their own exploits than they were curious about him. The waiters shared sideways glances and whispered to each other, but they did not ask Hutt any questions either, beyond what he wanted to eat and drink. He was not averse to people knowing what he did for a living. It was usually to his advantage, however, not to have them know who he was when he came into town.

After an acceptable steak he said goodnight to his companions and went through the carpeted hotel lobby and out onto King Street. The first person he met was the young lad who worked in the hotel stables.

"Where can I find Sheriff Morris's office?"

"Just down to the next street on your left. Turn left and it's right around the corner."

Two men were seated on either side of a large wooden desk playing cards when Hutt walked through the doorway. A tall, pot-bellied man was leaning against the wall holding a cup of coffee. The oldest in the group, Sheriff Morris, put down his cards, shook Hutt's hand,

and introduced himself, his deputy, Scott Gordon, and Sheriff Darrell Flynn from Summerside.

"Would you like some tea?" Gordon asked him.

"No, thank you. I just finished supper at the hotel."

"They sent word over from the Cambridge this afternoon to let me know you'd arrived. The whole Island's buzzin' about the girl."

Morris motioned for Hutt to sit down in the chair he himself had vacated. The detective did so and crossed his long legs.

"What can you tell me?"

"The sheriff from Amherst was over here a few weeks ago with the father."

"Did you see the body yourself?" Hutt asked Morris.

"It was me who saw it." Flynn stifled a yawn and walked over to refill his cup. "The only mark on her was a round, deep hole over her right eye."

"What about the rest of the body? What did it look like?" Hutt asked.

"Doc Jarvis had it all covered by the time I got there. Said that there were no marks on her other than just some from being in the water."

"So you didn't see the body yourself, just her face and head?"

Flynn shrugged. "By the time I got there Jarvis had gutted her like a fish and she was all covered up. I didn't see the use of looking myself."

"Where's Jarvis now?" Hutt sighed.

"At home in St. Eleanor's," Morris answered. "I've been in touch with him about your trip over. He wanted me to let you know, he'll meet you at the station in Summerside and drive you out to Cape Traverse."

"Are you travelling with me in the morning as well?" asked Hutt.

Morris shook his head and pointed at Flynn.

"We'll meet Doc Jarvis tomorrow morning," Flynn told the detective.

When the Sheriff showed up in the hotel lobby at six-thirty the next morning, Hutt was already there. He dug out his pocket watch when he caught sight of Flynn. Together they walked to the station carrying their luggage then sat in the second-class smoking car. Flynn lit a cigarette and Hutt unfolded a copy of the *Examiner*.

"Looks like we might get some rain before the day's over," Flynn said between drags on his smoke.

"Hmmm," Hutt answered, wanting to discourage conversation.

By the time he was done reading the first article Flynn was snoring loudly, the butt of his smoke balanced on his bottom lip.

Dr. Jarvis met them at the station. He took Hutt's luggage from him as he stepped off the train.

"The buggy is just in the stables across the street. Only take us a minute and we'll be on our way."

The men passed through the busy station. Above the bustle of arrivals and departures, the cries of an unhappy baby echoed through the large room. Boys ran up brandishing the morning paper.

"Get away," Flynn said, waving his hand at them dismissively.

"Just a minute." Hutt fished into his vest pocket for a coin.

A boy handed him the *Summerside Journal*.

"You sure read a lot of papers," Flynn said, smiling.

"What better way to learn about a community?" Hutt asked.

The paperboy smiled and pocketed the money. Flynn gave him a swat on the back of the head. The youngster turned and stuck out his tongue.

"Nose wipes, the lot of them," Flynn said, and spat on the floor.

"That one's gainfully employed," Jarvis observed.

"Don't let that fool you. The wages he'd get selling papers is likely only a part of what he brings in. Pickpockets and thieves is all they are."

A stable boy led Jarvis's horse out into the yard and soon had it hitched up to his phaeton.

"Thank you, Heath," the doctor said, tossing him a coin, "for looking after my Betsy so well."

"Thank you, sir." The boy caught the money in mid-air, touched his cap, and smiled, showing deep dimples.

Jarvis swung up into the driver's seat. Flynn got into the back of the buggy and Hutt sat up front with the doctor.

"So she drowned, did she?" Hutt asked

Jarvis removed a piece of folded paper from his coat pocket and handed it to the detective.

"Thought that you would want to see this."

Hutt read the coroner's jury report twice and then looked at Jarvis.

"So her general condition was good?" he asked.

Jarvis nodded. "Her face and the front part of her body was banged up a bit. A number of scratches, but nothing out of the ordinary for someone who had been in the water for a few days."

"What about her extremities and her back?" Hutt enquired.

"Hardly any marks at all," Flynn spoke up from the back seat. "Body white as the driven snow."

Hutt turned around and fixed the sheriff with a stare then righted himself in the seat. Flynn smirked and reached for another cigarette.

"What about her extremities and back?" he repeated to the doctor.

"There were no lacerations on any other part of her body," Jarvis replied. "Her fingers and the tip of her nose and ears were eaten away a little."

"So the autopsy was straightforward?"

"Yes."

"What was the father like?" Hutt asked, now turning to Sheriff Flynn.

"Didn't seem too interested. Never went out of his way to see the grave or nothing."

"How old of a man would he be?"

"In his mid-forties, I'd say. Good-looking fellow, tall."

SHERIFF MORRIS HAD WIRED AHEAD. Avard and Eddie were standing in the barnyard when they arrived. Gilbert took his visitors to the house where Catherine served them lunch.

Jimmy Bell watched wide-eyed as Hutt quietly drank his tea and ate three doughnuts.

"Are you a detective for real?" he asked.

"Yes, son, I am."

"I'm a deputy. Sheriff Flynn made me one." The boy grinned widely, uncovering a gap recently vacated by a milk tooth.

"Good for you, son. Be sure to always be on the lookout for law breakers."

"Do you have a badge and a gun like Sheriff Flynn?" Jimmy asked.

Hutt took a leather pouch out of an inside coat pocket. From it he withdrew a gold piece with an embossed front. He outlined the words with his finger.

"See there, City of Halifax Police Detective Lewis W. Hutt. That's my badge number along the bottom."

"Wow, can I hold it?" Jimmy's eyes widened.

"Of course."

"Be careful, Jimmy," Catherine warned her son. She let him handle the badge a moment longer and then gingerly removed it from his chubby hands and passed it back to the detective.

"What about your gun?" Jimmy pressed him.

Hutt shifted his eyes from left to right then dramatically held open the right side of his long black coat, causing Eddie to laugh out loud. Jimmy was able to see a leather holster and the pearl handle of a revolver.

"Jesus Christ," Jimmy blurted out.

Everyone but Catherine laughed. She turned beet red. Hutt closed his coat.

"James Bell, your mouth's going to get a good washing out with soap." She pulled him towards her.

"Oh, he's all right. Leave him alone," Gilbert said and smiled.

Hutt reached out and placed Jimmy on his knee and handed him the badge once again. "Deputy Jimmy, can you tell me about the day you found the girl on the beach?"

The child turned the object this way and that as he related the story of his discovery once again.

"Your friend Tom, I'd like to talk to him as well," Hutt said.

"They're just up the road apiece, the McPhersons. I can get one of the boys to fetch him down here," Gilbert volunteered.

"No, that's fine. I'll drive over there a little later with the buggy. Perhaps one of your boys could go with me to show me the way."

Avard jumped to his feet. "I will, sir," he said.

"Good enough, now go outside for a bit, Deputy Jimmy. I've got to talk to the grown-ups for a while." Hutt retrieved his badge before letting the boy slide off his knee.

Jimmy looked at his mother, who nodded, and then he ran out to the porch and slammed the door behind him.

"Bright boy you have there," Hutt remarked.

"He is," Catherine agreed. "But he has to work on his manners."

She glared at Gilbert.

"All of you have a seat," Hutt directed. "Our first order of business it to get the body exhumed. I've got to have a look at it."

Catherine drew in a breath. "Can't we just let the poor thing rest in peace?" she asked.

Hutt looked around the table. These are good people, he told himself. Hard-working county people. This is the most excitement they likely have ever had. And they think it's sacrilege to disturb the body. But I need to do what I need to do.

"Unfortunately not yet, ma'am. We've got to find out how she died."

"But we already know that," Jarvis reminded him. "You just finished reading my report on the way over here."

"Yes, drowned," Hutt said. "I know. But there's a petition in Halifax with about two hundred signatures on it claiming that she was the victim of foul play. I've got to look at the body myself in order to fulfill my obligation to those people, who are taxpayers, don't forget, and to ascertain what happened before she landed in the water."

"She's been in the ground more than two weeks now," Gilbert pointed out.

"Oh God," said Catherine,

"You'll need a court order," Jarvis told him.

"Already have one. My captain wired Summerside yesterday. There was a telegram waiting for me at the hotel last night, giving me permission to exhume the body. I have it right here."

Hutt reached into a right-hand coat pocket and withdrew a piece of paper. Jarvis examined it for a moment and handed it to Gilbert.

"For the record, a signed permission form was also sent to the Charlottetown courthouse."

"We'll have to let Reverend Silliker know before we go in there tearing his graveyard apart," Gilbert said. "I'll go over and talk to him this afternoon."

"This is a police matter now, Mr. Bell. Whether your minister agrees or not, the body will be exhumed," Hutt said.

"He'll still need to know ahead of time. He'll have to get a couple of men to open the grave."

"Fine." Hutt stood up. "Have it dug first thing tomorrow morning. Now, young man," he said, looking at Avard, "let's go and visit the McPherson family."

Jarvis remained seated. "What do you hope to find that I overlooked?" he asked.

Hutt turned to him. "I won't know until I've seen the body." He looked at Flynn. "Get us a place to stay for the night."

"Somebody can stay here," Catherine volunteered. "We have room for one."

"Thank you, ma'am. I would be happy to accept your hospitality." Hutt smiled. "Flynn, find a place for yourself and the doctor for the night."

"There's a hotel up the road by the wharf," Gilbert said. "Likely to be a couple of rooms there for you."

"I'll stop in as soon as we're back from the McPhersons'," Flynn said cheerfully, rising from the rocking chair.

"No need for any of the rest of you to tag along."

Hutt and Avard disappeared through the kitchen door.

THE NEXT MORNING, WHEN DOCTOR Jarvis stopped his phaeton in front of the Cape Traverse Methodist Church, there were two mounds of freshly shovelled earth along the white picket fence at the rear of the graveyard. An apple tree from the adjoining property leaned over the fence, providing shade from the climbing sun. It was another unusually hot day for October.

"Guess that's the place," Hutt said as he stepped from the passenger's seat of the buggy. Flynn jumped out of the back.

Three men stood beside the piles of dirt, two of them leaning on shovels while the third held a folded newspaper under his arm. Hutt and Jarvis waved to the trio as they walked towards them over the crackling leaves.

Jarvis said, "There's something peaceful about graveyards."

"They hide lots of secrets, most of which remain that way," Hutt said flatly. "But hopefully we'll uncover one or two today."

Reverend Silliker stepped forward, switched the newspaper to his left hand, and extended his right. "This is a nasty piece of business we have here," he said. "It's most unfortunate that it could not have been avoided."

"Yes, it's very unfortunate that all this is necessary. Hopefully we can finish up fast here today."

"Gilbert told me about this yesterday afternoon. He promised to be a witness, a church representative, this morning, so he'll be here as well," Silliker told them.

"Yes, I know," Hutt said. "I stayed at the Bells' farm last night."

"Donald and Frank just finished about fifteen minutes ago." Silliker nodded towards the gravediggers, whose faces and shirts were beaded with sweat.

"Might as well get this over with," Hutt said walking towards the two men who raised their caps in greeting.

"We can lift the top off with a crowbar," Frank said. "You can hardly stand the smell. Donnie here near passed out down there in the hole."

"Good God, man, there's something spillin' out of the box. Gives me the heaves," his companion said.

"You'd better find yourself another line of work if a little thing like that bothers you," Hutt said, grinning.

"Thank you, gentlemen, that's enough," Silliker said, waving a dismissive hand. "We appreciate that this is an unusual situation. One of you please fetch a crowbar."

Frank loped over to one of the small sheds located at a back corner of the graveyard. He ducked inside and reappeared with the tool.

Squeamish lot, Hutt mused. I thought farmers had seen it all, what with hunting and butchering animals.

"Jump down there and open it up," he ordered, pointing.

Frank landed in the hole and quickly removed the cover from the rough box and handed it up to Donald, who laid it on top of one of the mounds of earth.

"Come back in a couple of hours...say, around ten o'clock," Hutt told them, checking his pocket watch. "We should be finished about then."

"Now what?" he demanded as the sound of a horse and wagon caused them all to look towards the church.

Gilbert and Eddie Bell jumped down from the wagon seat. Avard was sitting in the back. Gilbert yelled hello as he motioned for the twins to stay with the wagon. Other carts, wagons, and buggies followed Gilbert's into the churchyard. Men and boys walked up to the fence along the roadside in front of the church and leaned against it.

"Christ, doesn't anyone work around here?" Hutt shook his head.

"I guess word has gotten out," Jarvis said.

"Flynn, keep them back. Don't let those people any closer," Hutt said.

Flynn nodded and walked toward the crowd, moving his arms back and forth as if he were scattering chickens.

"Sorry, folks, can't let you get any closer than the fence here. Back up, back up."

He walked them to the church gate and then stood guard, arms folded, next to Gilbert's wagon.

Frank and Don leaned their tools against the shed and walked towards the disappointed onlookers who stood waiting to question them.

"I'll just let you gentlemen go about your business. I have correspondence to see to. Gilbert here will observe," Silliker called over his shoulder as he walked away. "I'll be just next door in the manse if I'm needed. Mr. Jarvis, Mr. Hutt, it was a pleasure meeting you."

Gilbert bent down on one knee and looked into the grave. "God, what a smell."

"Okay, let's get this over with. Let's get down there and cut that blanket off her," Hutt said, not taking his eyes off the box. Using his hands as a brace, he jumped feet first into the hole.

"Give me your bag," he said, flapping his right hand at Jarvis.

After handing the bag over, the doctor slowly lowered himself down into the grave. There was a small ledge of dirt around the box.

"They certainly didn't give us much room to manoeuvre," Hutt growled. He looked up at Gilbert. "Run and get those shovels, will you? We need to dig ourselves some more room around this box." He climbed back out of the hole.

Gilbert and Jarvis spent the next fifteen minutes removing the dirt from around the sides of the box. Hutt looked down at them, barking instructions.

"I'll go see if there's anything we can kneel on," he said, walking towards the tool shed.

He returned, shaking the dirt off three empty burlap feedbags.

"They'll have to do. All right, Mr. Bell, time for you to get out of there."

Gilbert threw both shovels up out of the grave then climbed out himself. Hutt handed the bags to Jarvis and eased himself back down into the hole. He and the doctor then knelt on each side of the box.

"All right, Doc, let's see what we got here. First thing to do is cut those blankets off her. You're not all that neat are you, Doc? What're all these lumps?"

"There's something wrong here," Jarvis said.

He twisted around to the right, opened his bag, and took out a pair of scissors.

"What?" Hutt asked, looking at him.

"These blankets are all twisted and bunchy. This isn't the way I wrapped her."

"Well, start cutting, man. Let's see what's going on."

Jarvis took hold of the top blanket and raised it from where it covered the chest area. He made a couple of cuts into the material.

"It's rotten enough now just to tear," he observed. Putting the scissors aside, he grasped the blanket at the top and ripped the fabric. Then he made a small snip in the second blanket underneath and tore it in two as well.

"What the hell...is this some new kind of embalming technique I've not heard of?"

Hutt looked up at Gilbert who was on his hands and knees, peering down in the hole.

"I didn't do this," Jarvis said. "I don't know what the hell is going on. This body was not touched by anyone but me."

"Well, then, you have a unique way of performing an autopsy."

Golden rod, brown-eyed Susans, daisies, and clover had been stuffed into the cavity Jarvis had created to examine the girl's internal organs.

"Jesus."

Hutt grasped handfuls of the wilted flowers and flung them over his shoulder.

"Jesus, what a mess."

Hutt expected to see the eyes big in their sockets and the prominent cheekbones of a body buried as long as this one had been. The rotting skin and green tinge was also usual. What had caught his attention was the throat clearly ringed with dark handprints. The girl's left wrist was also badly bruised; oval marks left by fingers that had gripped too tightly.

"What's that?" Hutt asked, pointing.

Jarvis stared at the body, then looked up toward Gilbert, whose mouth was hanging open. The detective knew that water arrested the severity of bruising on a body but had not seen it often and never to this extent.

"These bruises were not visible when I examined..." Jarvis's voice trailed off.

"Thank God I had the good sense to dig this girl up," Hutt hissed.

"Swear to God, she didn't have these bruises when we picked her up off the beach," Gilbert said.

Jarvis nodded in agreement. "I'm telling you, I never saw the likes of this in all my life."

Hutt brushed away the rest of the faded stalks from the girl's breasts and midriff. There were three huge round bruises there as well, all bisected by the path of Jarvis's scalpel.

Hutt's mind was racing. How in the hell could the doc have missed this? Was he totally blind, for Christ's sake?

"She was beaten up pretty badly by the looks of it," Hutt declared. "She has a few broken nails here and lots of bruising on her arms and hands. This girl fought for her life."

Jarvis cleared his throat. "There's something I have to tell you."

Hutt met the doctor's eyes and waited.

Jarvis continued. "There was something I never put in my report. I thought that it wouldn't make any difference in the scheme of things."

"Out with it."

"She was pregnant," Jarvis blurted in a loud whisper.

"Jesus. And you didn't think that was important! What kind of a doctor are you, anyway?" Hutt whispered.

Gilbert whistled and sat down on the ground.

"Lower your voice," Jarvis pleaded. "I know that it wasn't right. I've never done anything like that before. I've never falsified a report, never omitted a fact or added an untruth in my life. At the time it looked like her burial was going to be the end of it and I didn't want her to be thought badly of, being an unmarried girl and all."

"What made you think she wasn't married?" Hutt demanded. "Did you know this person?"

"No, no, of course not." Jarvis reddened.

"Well, this beats all. How in the hell am I supposed to conduct an investigation if I keep running into incompetence?"

"Just a minute." Jarvis stood up.

"No, there's no excuse for this." The detective lowered his voice. "How far along was she?"

"I'd say between three and four months. The fetus was tiny, she would hardly have been showing much, if at all."

"All right then." Hutt recapped aloud: "She was a few months pregnant and severely beaten just before drowning. Someone likely knew or suspected that she was in the family way and didn't like it. Perhaps a husband, a father, or a suitor."

"Have I done great damage to your investigation?" Jarvis asked. "I hope not."

"Well, I wouldn't have wanted to go back to Nova Scotia without knowing this." Hutt shook his head.

"I would never have kept it a secret if I had seen these bruises in the first place."

"Didn't your coroner's jury examine the body? This kind of bruising must have been evident by then. And what about all the flowers? Where did they come from?"

"We were all in Gilbert's barn and it was quite an overcast day. We had to use lanterns. I told them it would all be pretty routine. They weren't keen on looking at her too closely as it was. But the flowers weren't there then, that's for damn sure. As for the bruising, it just wasn't as defined as it is now. I didn't see it."

"You just better hope to God that I don't report you. You could lose both your license and your reputation for a stunt like this."

Hutt thought for a minute then looked into the doctor's eyes. "It doesn't pay to get emotionally involved with your cases, Jarvis. It goes hand in hand with a loss of judgment."

"I've been a physician for over thirty years. I've always done things by the book."

"Let's just forget it for now. That is, if you don't have any more secrets you'd like to share."

Jarvis picked up the torn blankets and covered up the body as best he could. "Let's get the hell out of here," he said turning towards Gilbert, not able to meet his eye. "Hand me down that damn lid."

Jarvis placed it back on top of the box and raised his right arm to Gilbert, who grabbed his hand and helped him to climb out of the hole. Hutt stood at the edge, bent over, and brushed the knees of his trousers. He motioned for Jarvis and Gilbert to come closer.

"Don't say a word about this to anyone."

"Won't tell a soul," Gilbert promised. He looked over his shoulder at the silent, waiting crowd. Avard, with hat in hand, jumped down from his father's wagon and walked out of the church yard.

THE FOLLOWING AFTERNOON DETECTIVE HUTT arrived in Amherst. He walked from the train depot to the Victoria Street police station and asked for Sheriff Sherman.

"I got your telegram yesterday. Come on back to the office and we'll have a chat. How did things go over on the Island? Want some tea?"

Hutt settled himself into a well-worn upholstered chair and looked around in approval at the neat office. Sherman served the strong tea in a china cup. There were hot biscuits and blueberry jam on the desk between them.

"The wife sent this over for the boys. Help yourself."

Hutt munched on a tender biscuit. The tea was scalding hot, just as he liked it.

"So what happened over there?"

Hutt recounted his findings of the exhumation, the bruised body and the pregnancy. Sherman whistled.

"You've spent time with the father. Do you think there's a chance that he's capable of harming the girl?" Hutt asked. "And she wasn't married, was she? No, I didn't think so. He'd be madder than hell with her for getting herself pregnant. And what about a beau?"

"Yes. Harney did mention a few times that there was a young man. But the locals sure think that Harney himself is the guilty party. According to Ryan, Pugwash and Rockley are in an uproar. They're all convinced that Harney's done away with her and they can't understand why he hasn't been arrested yet."

Hutt nodded, his mouth full.

"There's a couple of things I wanted to discuss with you. To me, they point the finger right at the bastard."

Hutt raised his eyebrows. "And they are?"

"When we visited the Island and he was shown the girl's clothes, he asked to take them to his wife. I told him I had to keep them as evidence until things got cleared up and then I'd personally see that they got back to the family. Flynn had them in a bag stowed in our buggy. We went from Bell's farm and then on to the ferry. When the time came to board, the clothes were nowhere in sight. At first I thought that they might still be in Flynn's office but they weren't. Couldn't figure it out but then, once I was home a day or two I remembered that when we stopped at the farm Harney got out of the buggy and Gilbert's boys showed him around a bit. I'm sure he threw the clothes away there. But I don't know why. Why would he want to get rid of them, not want them taken back to the family? He's hiding something."

Hutt put the teacup down and rested his head on his hands, considering.

Sherman continued. "The other thing that bothered me was that he was so calm, overly calm if you ask me, about the whole business. It's not natural. If one of my daughters was found dead I'd sure as hell want to know how and why. If anything, he seemed to be relieved."

"Nothing whatsoever left from what was found on the body?"

Sherman shook his head. "But I do have the list of the clothes that Flynn gave me."

"I would have liked to have seen them myself." Hutt frowned.

"Well." Sherman scratched his head. "All I can do now is copy out the list for you."

Hutt nodded. "Can you come with me to Rockley today? I want to talk to this Harney as soon as possible."

"I expected you would want me to go with you. We'll just wait for my deputy. His shift starts in half an hour, then I'll be free to go."

"What's the best way to travel?" Hutt asked.

"The train leaves here for River Philip in an hour and a half. That would get us there in a couple of hours. Then we'll rent some horses to get up to Rockley. There's been talk for years about extending the railway to Pugwash but God knows how long it will be before that happens. I'll send someone over to get me a change of clothes and tell the wife I'll be gone overnight."

"Good, I'll just go out for dinner and a shave. I'll come back in an hour."

"See you then. Best place for lunch is at the Lamy Hotel. They're a little more expensive but good."

Thirty minutes later, Hutt sat down at one of the dish-cluttered tables at White's Oyster Saloon on Victoria Street. He peered out the window, watching, as customers went in and out of Bird's Bookstore across the street.

Three dollars for lunch at that hotel. Not bloody likely, he thought. Even on an expense account, something like that would be questioned.

A young boy brought water to the table and cleared away what was left of the last customer's meal. There were a number of men seated along the long counter, teasing a young woman, who stood on the opposite side of it with a teapot in her hand.

"Don't any of you have a home to get to?" she asked in exasperation amidst their laughter. "I've got washing up to do in the back."

The detective grinned and opened the latest edition of the *Chignecto Post*. He scanned the advertisements on the front page until the boy placed a plate and a cup of coffee in front of him. Oysters were the specialty of the house but Hutt chose the boiled dinner.

HUTT AND SHERMAN ARRIVED IN Pugwash at five o'clock "I hope Harney won't be alerted ahead of time about our being here," Hutt said.

"Not much chance of that," Sherman reassured him. "He's lucky he hasn't been lynched by now. We've never gotten so much cooperation before. People keep coming out of the woodwork to tell Ryan about every move he makes and what kind of a son of a bitch he is."

Constable Ryan met them at the stables.

"Not a lot happening," he reported. "Harney's stickin' pretty close to home. Somebody told me he recently lost his job at the Wallace quarry. Probably just as well, he's got to stay home and keep that woman of his under control. By the looks of her she's crazier than three people. Don't think that head of hers has seen a comb in the last month. It looks like a hen's been in it. And she spends all day walking 'round and 'round the house. Pretty much worn a path 'round it. The two small ones trail behind her, bawling. Every once in a while Harney comes out and runs them all back in. She's pretty haggard and it looks like she's got a black eye."

Hutt and Sherman rode up the lane to the Dempsey farm on horseback. Ryan drove a buggy. No one came out of the house to meet them.

"What's wrong with the windows?" Sherman asked.

"That's somethin' else that's real odd," Ryan said. "It looks like they've been painted over. They've been that way since I got here anyways. Never could get a good look inside."

Hutt knocked on the door. He waited then knocked again. This time they heard a shout and a thumping as though someone was running downstairs. The door was flung open and Will stood before them, hair hanging in his face.

"Hello, Mr. Harney," Sherman greeted him.

"What can I do for you today, Sheriff?"

"This is Detective Lewis Hutt. He'd like to ask you some questions about Mary."

"Sure, let's just go out into the yard here."

Will made a move to step outside.

"No, let's go inside where we'll be more comfortable," Hutt said, pushing his way into the porch and then the kitchen.

Once inside Hutt immediately felt disorientated. It took the men a moment or two to come to terms with their surroundings.

"The goddamn house is yellow," Ryan blurted out.

The windows had been painted over, as had almost everything else. The kitchen table and chairs were yellow, and the thin kitchen curtains had yellow streaks through them. The stove was yellow as was the kettle on top of it. The colour extended beyond the kitchen into the hallway. The visitors stood, mouths open, looking around.

"It was her, crazier than a loon," said a voice from the yellow rocking chair beside the stove. An old woman rose to her feet to face them. "I hope you're here to take her away."

She sank back down into the chair.

"Why he ever married her is beyond me. My boy's a bugger for punishment, that's all I can say."

"Shut up, Ma. Have a seat, gentlemen." Will nodded towards the kitchen table then squatted down in the coal scuttle at his mother's feet.

"When I went over to PE Island with you," Harney began, looking at Sherman, "Ann went crazy. She got up in the middle of the night and painted the whole damn place yellow. I had some old paint out in the barn left over from when I painted the punt last summer, the one Mary stole to run away. Ann went over the whole house with it. We scraped a bit off the windows so we can see out. She's out of her head about Mary."

"She's always been that way, Mary or no Mary," the woman said.

Hutt began. "I want to talk to you, Mr. Harney, about the events leading up to the disappearance of your daughter last month."

Eyes too small and far apart, Hutt decided. Looks a bit like a fox, and he's got that smirk on his face that says he thinks he's just a bit smarter than anyone else.

"It's like I told the Sheriff here before. It was a Saturday night. I told Mary to go bring in the cows before it got too late. She went out but she never came back. The wife and I started looking for her later that night and all through until the next morning. Not a sign of her, queerest thing. Didn't hear anything about her again until the Sheriff brought out that piece of her skirt and took me off to the Island. That was a nice boat ride. I had never been in a big boat, you know...."

"Had Mary ever run away before?" Hutt asked.

"No. She'd go for walks a lot and take her time coming home with the cows," Will said, "but she never stayed away overnight. Mary was kind of not right in the head, you know."

"That's funny," Ryan said. "None of the people I've talked to around here said that. I've been told by most of them that she was smart as a whip."

"And lots of people around here think that you didn't deal with Mary fairly," Sherman added.

"What would people know?" the woman demanded. "And besides, it's none of their damn business anyway."

Will nodded. "People don't know what goes on in this house. Mary was always fed, had a roof over her head, and decent clothes to wear."

"Speaking of that, Sheriff Sherman tells me that the clothes that were taken off her body have gone missing," Hutt said.

Will nodded, looked away, then turned back to his visitors.

"Queerest thing. That's the law for you. Couldn't catch a cold, most of them. Sheriff Sherman, you're a good man but love a God, you couldn't even keep track of a little sack of girl's clothes."

Sherman turned scarlet.

"You don't have those clothes, do you?" Hutt asked.

"Jesus, no," Will said. "The wife cries every night. If I did, I'd let her have them to maybe comfort her a little. All we got is that patch of cloth. She sleeps with it under her pillow, when she does sleep, and won't let the rest of us even look at it."

"You didn't take the clothes and throw them away somewhere on Gilbert's Bell's farm?" Hutt asked again.

Will raised his eyes and let them travel from Hutt to Sherman and back again.

"Oh, so that's it. Blame me when something goes wrong. Why aren't you out tryin' to find out what really happened to Mary? Jesus, there's been a death here. Have you people no decency? Are you going to stop over at the Reid's and talk to that oldest boy of theirs? He's been sweet on Mary for months. And he's sneaky as hell."

The old woman was rocking back and forth as if preparing to propel herself from the chair. Then another woman, wearing an apron over a dirty nightdress, limped into the room and the rocking chair stopped.

She's a dope addict, Hutt thought. How many times had he seen the same skin colour and haunted eyes on poor creatures around the wharves in Halifax? He had never thought of it happening to a country wife.

"Have you come to tell us something about Mary? Have you found my Mary?"

"Mrs. Harney, we're here to ask you and your husband some questions. We're very sorry for your loss." Hutt rose from the table. "Your husband seems to think that Mary ran away. What do you think about that?"

The old woman snorted and commenced rocking.

"She got mad at me and ran away," Ann said.

"Why was she mad at you?"

"Those two fought all the time." Will shrugged. "If it wasn't about one thing it was the other."

"Was Mary sent out to get the cows the night that she disappeared?"

Ann looked at her husband then turned back to Hutt.

"Yes," she said slowly. "That was her job. And Mary loved the cows. It would take her forever to get them back to the barn. She would let them keep eating, make daisy chains to put around their necks."

"Were you surprised when she didn't come back?"

"It's the first time my baby was ever out all night in the cold."

"What was she wearing the last time you saw her?" Hutt asked

"She had on her plaid skirt and brown belt with her good jacket over it," Will said. "I asked her why she was so dressed up just to get the cows in."

"Is that true, Mrs. Harney?" Hutt asked.

At first Ann shook her head then she began to nod, her loose bun bobbing up and down.

"Well, which is it? How was Mary dressed?"

Will stood up. Ann started to cry.

"She used to say things about my husband." Ann swallowed hard and wiped the tears away with the palms of her hands. "I know they weren't true. Will said Mary was crazy, when she said things like that."

"Ann," Will said, stepping towards her.

Sherman and Ryan stood up and grabbed Will by the arms. He struggled against them.

"What kind of things did Mary say, ma'am?" Hutt asked.

He rose from his chair and escorted Ann to the table to sit down.

"Whatever she says, she's lying," Will warned.

Hutt took both of Ann's hands in his. "What did Mary say, ma'am?"

She looked at him and then down at their hands. "She told me that Will watched her when she took baths. She told me he was always trying to touch her and that sometimes he would sneak into her bedroom."

"Jesus Christ," said Will still struggling.

Hutt let go of Ann's hand and reached into his coat pocket for a handkerchief.

"She said that Will wanted her to touch him." She hesitated. "On... on his private parts," she blurted and covered her swollen eyes with her hands.

"But"–she grabbed for Hutt's hands again—"I knew it wasn't right. I knew that no husband of mine would do that. I told Mary to stop telling lies, making things up, and she never spoke about it again."

"The piece of cloth you have from Mary's skirt, will you show it to me?" Hutt asked softly.

"Oh, I could...couldn't do that," said Ann, looking at Will. "I'm saving it...I put it away for good. When Mary comes home, I'll sew it back on her skirt."

"Mrs. Harney, I'm sorry, but your daughter is dead." Hutt held her hands tighter. "She's buried over on Prince Edward Island. I saw her myself. She's dead."

"That's not my Mary," Ann said, opening her eyes wider. "Mary is someplace safe. Will said...she would always be near—"

"For Christ's sake," Will shouted. "Can't you see she's not right in the head?"

"Like mother, like daughter," said the woman in the rocking chair.

"Shut up over there," Hutt bellowed.

"How dare you speak to me like that in my own house. Get out. Get—"

"One more word and I'll arrest you for interfering with a police officer," Hutt said. "I'm trying to conduct an investigation here. Now shut up."

He turned again to Ann. "What did your husband say?"

"He said that it was better that Mary go away and that it was my duty, as a good mother, to let her go."

Will hung his head.

"Why did she have to go away?" Hutt asked.

Ann looked at her husband and then back at Hutt.

"Mary was bringing shame on the family."

She put her hand over her mouth. It took a moment for her to continue. "Will said she was a disgrace, just like me, that she was an embarrassment to us all. He said we'd have to leave Rockley, just like we had to leave Merigomish."

She fumbled in the pocket of her apron, brought out the piece of fabric, and passed it back and forth from one hand to the other.

"I have to go outside now," she said and moved towards the porch.

Hutt stood up.

"William Harney and Ann Harney, in the name of her Majesty the Queen, I am placing you both under arrest for the murder of Mary Harney."

Ann kept moving towards the door as if she had not heard. Ryan held her elbow and escorted her out. The woman sprang out of the rocking chair.

"You can't take my son away. He looked for her just as hard as any of the rest of them."

She sank down and started to cry.

"Ma, it's all right, it's all right. I won't be gone long. Don't worry. You'll be all right here with Uncle John and the kids."

Sherman took a pair of handcuffs off his belt and locked them on Will's wrists. As they walked outside to the buggy, Ryan came around from the back of the house still holding Ann gently by the arm.

"See what I mean," he said. "All she wants to do is go 'round and 'round the house in circles."

As she walked Ann spoke to herself and pressed the faded piece of plaid to her breast.

I drift with the current,
tossed to shore with the storm.

OXFORD

Nova Scotia
October 9, 1877

WILL SHARED THE VILLAGE'S tiny jail cell on two occasions: once with a man charged with vagrancy and then with a young boy arrested for setting fire to his grandparents' house. Ann slept and ate at the home of the jailor, Charles Murphy, in the custody of his wife, Myrtle.

"Please let Mrs. Murphy wash that filthy nightgown for you. It can practically stand by itself," Beatrice said to Ann, who was lying on the bed looking up at the ceiling.

"They took Mary's skirt patch away from me," she said, ignoring her sister's remarks.

"They need it for the hearing, Ann. You know that. They said you could have it back when it's all over."

"It's the only thing I had left of Mary." Tears welled up in her eyes.

Beatrice patted her sister's hand. "Right now you need to get some rest. You're exhausted. But first we're going to get you out of that thing and give you a bath. It'll help you sleep."

"I don't want to."

Beatrice left the room and went down the hallway. She returned a minute later with Myrtle Murphy on her heels.

"Now, Ann, there's a hot bath waiting for you in the kitchen. There's no men around, so there's no reason to be shy," Myrtle assured her.

Ann looked up at the two women defiantly and clutched the bedclothes beneath her.

"My dear, you're getting into that tub supposing I have to break your neck doing it," Myrtle said. "I've handled tougher customers than you, don't think I haven't. Miss Hennessey, you grab her lower limbs and I'll lift her up under her arms."

"No, Beatrice, don't! For God sake's let me be."

"It's for your own good, Ann. Please let us help you."

"We can do this the easy way or the hard way but we're going to do it," Myrtle said between her teeth as she grabbed Ann under each arm.

Ann yelled and kicked her feet, releasing her legs from Beatrice's grasp.

"Don't bother being gentle, Miss Hennessey. Like you said, it's for her own good," Myrtle said as she heaved Ann up into a sitting position.

"She's not very heavy. We can get her down the hall and into the kitchen. She'll squawk but between the two of us she'll get a half decent wash."

AN HOUR LATER, ANN WAS back in bed, sleeping in a fresh nightgown. Myrtle had burnt the old blue one up in the kitchen stove.

"It's little more than a rag," she proclaimed, stuffing it in with the poker.

Myrtle and Beatrice sat at the kitchen table drinking tea. The younger woman tried, unsuccessfully, to hold back tears.

"I've lost my mother, my niece, and now my sister just like that. I'm ashamed to say it, but I'm glad mother's not alive to witness all this," she said, taking a handkerchief out from under her dress sleeve.

"You'll get through it, dear. It'll all get settled."

"Ann arrested for murdering her own daughter! How is that possible? How could they ever think she'd do such a thing?"

"It'll be all right dear, you'll see." Myrtle patted Beatrice's hand and refilled her teacup. Beatrice whispered, "I feel like everything's crumbling around me. My father shouldn't be left by himself with only the help to look after him. I'm caught in the middle."

"My dear," Myrtle said, "don't fret about things that you can't control. It does no good. You need rest. Go back to the hotel. The hearing starts tomorrow morning. Both you and Ann will need all your strength for that. She'll be fine with me. I gave her something to calm her down. She'll sleep like a baby until morning and if not I can control her. Don't worry about that."

Beatrice made her way back to the Starr Hotel. She would wait and write to her father after the hearing. She collapsed on the bed fully clothed and slept the rest of the day.

THE PRELIMINARY HEARING WAS HELD in the main room of the Oxford Odd Fellows' Hall. It was a large space that took up the entire length of thc building, with a low ceiling and three large eight-over-eight windows running down its length. Two more windows flanked its front double doors. Plaques engraved with the names of local honoured members of the International Order of Odd Fellows decorated the walls. Queen Victoria, hand to her cheek, looked down upon the room from a sepia photograph. Beneath its massive frame, in the middle of the back wall, four men were seated behind a ten-foot-long table.

"Thank God all the windows are open," a woman in a tight dress commented to the friend beside her fanning the air with a doubled-up copy of the *Chignecto Post*. "Not that it really makes a lot of difference," she continued, "with all those fools plugging them up, it's a wonder we have any air in here at all."

Men, boys, and a few young girls not able to fit inside the crowded room were indeed peeking in the hall windows. Some were perched on the shoulders of friends. Others stood on ladders braced against the outside wall. Inside, all the wooden chairs facing the four justices were occupied. Everyone was eager to hear, first-hand, what had happened to Mary Harney. People from as far away as Halifax and Saint John were among the onlookers. Besides those seated inside and pressed against the windows, a group of latecomers crowded around the front door.

It was noisy and Justice Joseph Oxley, the chairman for the hearing, was not in a good mood. He didn't like to be rushed, and that's exactly the way he felt. His tongue protruded out of the corner of his mouth as he concentrated on the notes in front of him. The swell of talk was making his head ache all the more.

The door opened and Sherman and Ryan walked into the room. Oxley leaned over and whispered to the man seated next to him at the long table.

"Tom, it's goin' to be a long day."

"Morning, gentlemen." Sherman walked along the front of the table, shaking the hands of each of the justices. Oxley introduced them in turn, Thomas Black, Harry Carter, and Howard Hingley.

"Should I bring them in now?" Sherman asked.

Oxley nodded, then, looking over the top of his spectacles at the crowd before him, he motioned for Sherman to step aside, and raised both his gavel and his voice. "Ladies and gentlemen, if you want to stay here and observe this hearing, you'd all better quiet down, and I mean right now!"

The crowd came to attention as the gavel fell.

Oxley nodded his head in approval.

"Gentlemen, let's proceed," he said, looking at his watch. "Hopefully the clerk will show up soon. Until then, I'll take notes myself."

"Bring them in." Sherman nodded to Ryan, who had been waiting at the door. The constable touched his hat, turned, opened, then closed the door behind him, causing the noise level emanating from the crowd outside to rise and fall. A few minutes later, he returned with the prisoners. A woman limped slowly into the room. Ryan, his hand on her elbow, pointed her towards the justices. She wore an emerald green dress too large for her, and her eyes were red and swollen. A smartly dressed woman walked beside her with her arm around her waist, squeezing through the crowd. After them came a man with blond hair, his head bowed. His shackled hands and feet caused him to shuffle, and his appearance drew immediate reaction from the onlookers.

"There he is."

"Murderer!"

"Should be strung up."

"Shut up or I'll clear this room." Oxley pounded on the table with his gavel again.

"Constable, tell that bunch outside to quiet down too or I'll have the lot of them thrown out," Oxley commanded. "My damn head is pounding enough as it is."

Ryan nodded and went back out the door.

"Pipe down, all of you."

While Ryan retraced his steps, the trio had stopped and waited for him. Ryan led them to the three ladder-back chairs which faced the justices. The limping woman stopped in front of the middle chair, turned, and dropped herself into it. The shackled man sat on her left with the other woman on her right. Ryan walked back to the door and stood with his rifle resting over his right arm.

Before anyone had a chance to speak, there was a tentative knock. Ryan moved aside and a tall, skinny man with a notebook, pen, and inkwell came into the room.

"My apologies, Justice Oxley, gentlemen," he said. "Trouble with the milking this morning."

"That's fine, we're not started yet." Oxley pointed towards a desk and chair to his right. Eamonn Walsh took off his coat and hung it carefully over the back of the chair. He sat down, rolled up his sleeves, opened his notebook, and placed his pen and inkwell on the desk beside it, then he folded his arms and looked at Oxley.

Justice Oxley began. "This is a very serious matter and needs to be dealt with promptly and carefully." He nodded at the clerk, who dipped his pen in the inkwell. "This is the preliminary examination of Michael William Harney and Ann Helen Harney, who have been brought before us on the suspicion of murder of their daughter Mary Harney."

The woman in the green dress lifted her head. Tears spilled out of her closed eyes, over her cheeks, and fell off her chin into her lap. She did not make a sound or move to wipe them away. The other woman dabbed at her own face with a pink, monogrammed hanky.

"This examination will be conducted by myself, Justice Oxley, with Justices Black, Carter, and Hingley, here in Oxford, Cumberland County, Nova Scotia, on this, the tenth day of October in the year of our Lord eighteen hundred and seventy-seven."

Oxley waited a moment for Eamonn to catch up. "The purpose of this preliminary examination is to ascertain whether there is sufficient evidence to bring Michael William Harney and Ann Helen Harney to trial for the murder of Mary Harney. There's a number of people to hear from today, so let's get started."

Sherman was the first witness called.

Oxley began. "We've looked over Detective Hutt's report as well as the coroner's report. They're both very thorough."

Sherman nodded.

"Is there any proof besides the say-so of William Harney that the body on Prince Edward Island is that of Mary Harney?"

"We have a positive identification of a patch taken from the skirt worn by the victim, sir," Sherman said. "The father identified it as such and the mother becomes frantic at the sight of it."

"Do you have it in your possession?"

"Yes, sir. After the mother was incarcerated, the jailor's wife was able to get it away from her."

Sherman took a small brown envelope out of his vest pocket and handed it to Oxley. He extracted the fabric from it, looked at it for a moment, and passed it down the table.

Justice Carter spoke up. "Any other proof?"

"No, not right now," Sherman replied. "As Hutt's report says, the body was just in too bad a state of decomposition to travel, and the rest of the clothes are missing. We had men over on the Island looking for them and they'll continue to keep an eye out. There were certainly signs of struggle on the body, indicating that she'd been badly beaten and had fought back."

Justice Carter asked, "What happened that the girl's clothes are gone?

Sherman spent the next ten minutes retelling the story of the missing clothes.

Oxley called Freda Mills as the second witness.

"How long have you known the Harney family?" Oxley asked.

"About sixteen years."

"What can you tell us about the relationship between Michael William Harney and his daughter Mary?"

"I didn't see them together very often. Sometimes in church. Sometimes in Bailey's store over the years. I found him surly a lot of the time. Mary always minded when she was out in public. She was well behaved. I'll say that for her parents."

"What can you tell us about the relationship between William and Ann Harney?" Justice Carter asked.

"In her day Ann was a lady. I believe that she came from a good family down Pictou way, but that man of hers just beat her down over the years. The poor thing never had a life with him. If it wasn't for John Dempsey the whole bunch of them would have starved to death years ago. That man of hers is just no good. I don't think he's ever worked hard enough, in a single day, to break the Sabbath. Always losing one job after the other and didn't do much of anything around the farm."

Freda looked at the prisoners for the first time and nodded her head for emphasis.

"Mrs. Mills, were you at the Harneys' home the night that Mary disappeared?" Justice Black spoke for the first time.

"Yes, sir. I was there about midnight. A group of us women, mostly from the church, went over to bring food and to help Ann and Mabel."

"How did Mr. and Mrs. Harney act on that night?" Black asked.

"Poor Ann was beside herself. She had to be forced to go lie down. I didn't see him. But I heard from other people that he didn't seem too worried about the whole thing. I heard that said on the night she went missing and in the days after."

"Do you think that Mr. and Mrs. Harney killed Mary?" Justice Carter asked.

"Oh no, not Ann. But I'm positive that he's done something."

"Why would Harney kill his daughter?"

"I don't know, but I know he did. He—"

"What proof do you have?" Justice Hingley interrupted.

"I have no real proof, just the way he acts, how he is. I've heard stories about him. Other people can tell you first-hand. It's just the way he is. Something about him is sneaky."

"Mrs. Mills, you don't like Mr. Harney, do you?" Hingley asked.

The witness shook her head. "To be perfectly honest, sir, no I don't."

"Does anyone else have any other questions for this witness?" Oxley asked, looking down the table at his colleagues. "No? All right, thank you, ma'am. You may go."

She nodded, rose, and returned to her seat.

The questioning commenced again with Calvin Bailey, the storekeeper.

"Harney is as mean a son of a bitch as I ever come across," Bailey commented halfway through the interview.

"Have you ever seen Mr. Harney in a violent mood?" Hingley asked.

"One time last year in my store. He went after Jack Reid for making fun of him. He would have beaten him real bad if I hadn't been there. As it was he broke his nose and it ain't been the same since."

The next witness walked with a pronounced stoop to the chair.

"Mr. Dempsey, you are a relative of Michael William Harney?"

"Yes...yes, sir, I'm his uncle."

"And you lived in the same house as Mr. and Mrs. Harney and their children?"

"I still do, yes."

"Do you think that Mr. Harney has anything to do with Mary Harney's disappearance?" Oxley asked.

"I don't know, sir, I just don't know...I hope not."

"Why do you say that?"

"He's my sister's only child, and I don't like to say anything for her sake. But I can say for a fact that he's lazy and one of them that thinks that the world owes them a living and a coffin thrown in at the end."

"Laziness doesn't make someone a murderer, Mr. Dempsey," Hingley said.

"No, sir, it don't," John agreed. "In fact, if he is innocent, laziness would likely be the reason why."

The crowd snickered. Oxley threw them a stern look and reached for his gavel as he asked the next question. "Where were you when Mary Harney went missing?"

"Early that morning I brought my sister Mabel here to Oxford to sit with a woman. Mabel's a midwife. We got to the Browns' about one o'clock in the afternoon and had dinner with the family. Then I tended to some errands and went to see Bradley Davis about getting some pigs from him next spring. On the way out of town one of my horses threw a shoe. I went to a blacksmith here. What's his name? Frank Smith, that's it. Took a while for him to fix the shoe and then I stopped by at the Victoria Hotel there and ate my supper late before starting home. By the time I got back to the house it was about half past nine."

"So where was everyone in the house when you got back there?"

"Ann was upstairs, lying down as she usually was. The two youngest ones were running through the house with nobody minding them. Will was out on the veranda, smoking, when I drove up."

"Had the alarm already been raised about Mary when you got home?"

"No, it hadn't. By ten o'clock I was really worried. Will came in a few minutes after I had first got home, complaining about how he had to milk the cows 'cause Mary wasn't around. He went on about that for a while. And he had these four godawful scratches down each side of his face. He said it was Ann gave them to him. They were bad, they kept bleeding and he was carrying a towel around and wiping at them every once in a while."

"So no move was made to look for Mary before that time? Doesn't that seem like a long time after to start looking for her?"

"Yes, it does."

"And who finally decided that it was time to go look for the girl?"

"It was me. Will told the sheriff that it was him but it was me who started the search. I went out around to the back of the house and hollered for her. One thing I can tell you is that we often had to call Mary when she went out on errands."

"Why was that, now?"

"Mary often forgot about the time. She loved being outside. In the last year or so she seemed to spend as much time away from the house as possible. I think that she just didn't want to be there any more than she had to."

"Do you know why that would be?"

"I think she just wanted to stay clear of him and his mother as much as possible."

"By that you mean Mr. Harney and his mother, Mabel Harney?"

"Yes, my sister Mabel. They were always at the poor soul. Complaining and criticizing."

"Is it true that Mary had a beau?"

"Yes, young Smith there. They used to meet in the evening when she went for the cows. I followed her and it was innocent enough between them."

"Did you follow Mary every night she went to bring in the cows?"

"No, sir, not every night, just twice. Once I seen that Smith was meaning no harm and seemed genuinely fond of her, I left them alone."

"And Will Harney knew about these meetings?"

"I think he must have seen them one night when he was coming home from work or something. He let on that he didn't know but I'm pretty sure that he did. I'm surprised that he never went after the boy about it. But then Smith beat him in a fair fight one time last year."

"What happened when Mary didn't show up after you called for her?"

"I went back in the house and told Will that I hadn't found her. Then I went back out and started down the river calling for her. That was when I noticed that my punt was missing. I figured that she had headed up the river with it. I walked along there for a bit in case she came back. I wasn't too worried, she mostly took the punt in the afternoons and sometimes in the evening. After about an hour of that I went back to the house."

"So now it would be half past ten or more, is that right?"

"Yes."

"What were Mr. and Mrs. Harney doing when you returned home?"

"Ann came downstairs and I told her Mary wasn't home yet. She looked like hell, even worse than usual, and she had been crying. I never saw her move around the house so fast as she did that night. She's been sickly for quite a while, you know. She sat at the kitchen table while Will and I argued back and forth about what to do. He kept saying that she would show up sooner or later. He got mad when I told him about the punt being gone. We talked for about a half hour until Ann jumped up from the table and grabbed a hold of Will, demanding that he go get Mary. He put her off for a while but finally the two of us set out, me in the wagon and him on horseback, each going a different way, up and down the main road, to ask people if they had seen her and if they would help us look for her. Everybody gathered at the house and we split up into groups to start looking."

"So that would be around half past eleven by then, Mr. Dempsey?"

"Yes, at least that, I'd say."

Smith Reid was called as the next witness.

Oxley got right to the point. "Is it true that you were Mary Harney's beau, Mr. Reid?"

"I never came right out and asked Mary if I could be. We just fell into a pattern. We only saw each other in the evenings whenever she went to get the cows in. And that wasn't every night. She wouldn't let me see her any other time."

"Why not?"

"She said that her father didn't want her keeping company with any young men. And especially not with me."

"Why not you?" Hingley asked.

"Mr. Harney and the Reids don't see eye to eye. He beat up my brother Jack a while back. Then me and Harney got into it."

"So you and Mary were seeing each other behind her parents' back?"

"Yes, sir."

"How long was it that you were keeping company?"

"About eight months, I'd say."

"Detective Hutt's report says that the girl who was found on the beach on the Island was...er...with child," Carter said.

Smith reddened.

"Were you and Mary Harney intimate at any time?"

"Not in that way, sir. Mary was a lady and I respected her."

"Are you sure?"

A ripple of laughter went through the audience.

"Yes, sir. I'd swear to it on a stack of bibles."

"Perhaps Mary was keeping company with more than just you," Black suggested.

"She was a lady," Smith repeated, red in the face again. "She wasn't that kind of girl."

"Tell us where you were the night that Mary went missing," Carter said.

"I didn't go to meet her that night. I had some lessons to get ready. I'm teaching this year at the Rockley School. And then I was helping Pa with shoeing the horses. I might have been able to prevent this from happening if I had gone. But it's too late now."

Smith wiped an arm across his eyes.

"Can anyone vouch for you? Swear that you did not meet Mary that night?"

Hiram Reid stood up.

"I can swear that he was with me. All the afternoon and evening. We were just finishing up in the barn. It was quite late and John comes running in asking if we had seen Mary that day."

"Is there anyone else, besides a family member, who can vouch for you, Mr. Reid?"

"Not that I know of. But I was with my father at the time when Mary usually went for the cows. If I had been there that night it would have been Harney who'd be missing right now, not her."

"When was the last time you saw Mary?" Black asked.

"The night before she went missing. I had told her I likely couldn't come the next night due to the shoeing. I said that I would if I could. I wish...."

Tears welled up in his eyes.

"That's all I have for you. Do any of my colleagues have any questions for this young man? No. All right, son, that's it. Thank you."

Smith nodded his head and walked back to his seat beside his father.

"It's just past noon," Oxley observed, looking at his pocket watch on the table top. "I call for a two-hour adjournment. The hearing will commence again at two o'clock."

"Four and a half hours and only through four witnesses. This is going to take days," Oxley told his three companions as they walked towards the American House Hotel for their dinner. He hoped some food would help ease his headache.

The men had just seated themselves and ordered their steaks when they were approached by a man who doffed his hat and wished them a good day.

"Robert White from the *Chignecto Post*. Would it be possible to get a quote or two from you gentlemen on how things are going?"

"No, it would not," barked Hingley. "As a newspaper man, you should know better. We can't make a statement to the press with a hearing in progress. Leave us alone, and go do your muckraking somewheres else. I've got a good mind to speak to your employer about this." Hingley turned back to the table and lit a cigar.

Carter shook his head and took a drink of water. "I'm sure there's a lot of individuals over at the hall who would be happy to give you their opinion on this. Leave us to eat our dinner in peace."

White, still smiling, tipped his hat again and made his way to the other side of the room. He ordered the oyster stew, watched the justices, and took notes.

TWENTY-EIGHT WITNESSES WERE QUESTIONED DURING the four-day hearing. Most were adamant that Will had done something to Mary. Many simply came out and proclaimed that he had indeed killed the girl. All agreed that her disappearance was the result of foul play. Mabel Harney was the only witness who spoke in Will's defence.

Justice Oxley, in the afternoon on the last day of the hearing, turned to Will Harney and asked if he wanted to make a statement. He nodded.

"Go ahead, then."

"Me and the wife never killed—"

Ryan stepped forward, grabbed Will under his left arm, and pulled him to his feet.

Will began again. "Like I said all along, me and the wife never killed nobody, your honours, especially not Mary. Truth be known, she was the wife's favourite child, Ma always said so. We had to treat her a little rough sometimes in front of the two little ones so as not to make them jealous. We never killed her. We sent her out that night like we always did to get the cows and she just never come back. Simple as that. The wife has been heartbroken ever since. Can't talk any sense into her. She's soft, you know. Ain't nobody like her going to kill nobody, especially her own kid. And me, Judge, you don't have to worry about me. I run off at the mouth a bit by times, but I've never done no one any real harm. I just try to provide for my family, that's all. It's been hard on me. Things haven't gone like I thought they would years ago. Being a family man got in my way lots of times. Ann and me, we're planning to move on now, maybe go to the States and start again, maybe out west. We'll go away and never come—"

"Mr. Harney, where were you on the night that Mary disappeared?" Oxley interrupted.

"I was home, your Honour. After supper I was sitting in the kitchen reading the paper and yelled to Mary to go get the cows for milking. She walked down the stairs from her room, passed me, not speaking, belligerent as usual, and all dressed up in her best clothes, and out the door for the fields. Like I said before, that was the last time I saw her. I swear to God I never hurt Mary. I had nothing against her. She got on my nerves from time to time but that was it. I'm telling you straight, I didn't touch a hair on that girl's head."

Will sat down. Ann, with her head bowed, was crying silently. Justice Black rose from his seat, took a blue spotted handkerchief out of his pocket, shook it, and walked over to Ann.

"Mrs. Harney, is there anything you would like to say now?" Oxley asked.

Ann started to rise from her chair.

Oxley put his hand out. "You may remain seated, ma'am."

"Will never touched Mary. She lied when she told me that. I should have sent her to her Aunt Beatrice's like she wanted."

Ann started to cry again.

"Eamonn, get Mrs. Harney a glass of water."

The clerk laid down his pen and moved towards the pitcher at the centre of the table. Beatrice rose from her chair and, taking the water from him, nodded her thanks.

"Just take your time, ma'am, there's no hurry whatsoever."

Ann gulped the water greedily and used the blue handkerchief to blow her nose. Beatrice kept one arm around her.

"I'm so sorry, may God forgive me. I am not a fit mother. I was never fit." She gulped again. "I just hope that God will forgive me."

"Why do you ask for forgiveness?"

Ann hung her head and slumped back. Beatrice placed a shawl around her sister. While the crowd murmured in sympathy, Justice Oxley brought them to attention with a loud bang of his gavel.

"All right, this ends the examination part of the hearing. We're adjourned and will meet back here as soon as a decision has been made."

The audience began to rise.

"Well, gentlemen, what are your thoughts?" Oxley asked as he moved his chair closer to the table. It was six-thirty and the four justices were just settling down to supper back at the hotel. They had the dining room to themselves to discuss the hearing and come to a decision.

TWO HOURS LATER, THE JUSTICES, with Eamonn Walsh trailing behind, filed back into the Odd Fellows Hall. Little boys, stationed as lookouts on the streets, either ran into buildings or let out loud whistles. People all over Oxford poured out of homes, stores, hotels, and Russell's Tavern and hurried to the hall. It took a while to get everyone settled back into their places. Lanterns were set up throughout the building, and since it was such a warm evening some of the windows were left open. Many resumed their positions on the ladders outside. Every chair was taken and bodies crowded three deep around the perimeter of the room.

"I see none of them went home to stay," Black said. "There's even more here than this morning. And this being a Sunday and all."

"Sheriff Sherman and Constable Ryan, bring the prisoners in, please," Oxley directed.

The sheriff led Ann and Beatrice back to their chairs, followed by Will, still in shackles. Constable Ryan, and then Fred LeFurgey and John Dempsey brought up the rear. John braced himself against the closed door with his head bowed and Fred stood beside him.

Oxley lowered his gavel on the table.

"Okay, let's get back into order. This preliminary examination of Michael William Harney and Ann Helen Harney, on the suspicion of murder of Mary Harney, will now resume."

Oxley, clearing his throat, looked around the room. The *Post* reporter, Robert White, was looking up expectantly, clutching pencil and pad.

"Damn papers, looking to pick the bones," Hingley whispered in his ear.

Oxley nodded and cleared his throat again.

"After careful deliberation, my colleagues and I have come to the following conclusion."

He paused. There was not a sound in the room.

"After careful deliberation—"

"Yeah, yeah," someone in the crowd scoffed.

"After careful deliberation we have come to the conclusion that there is not sufficient evidence to warrant this case going to trial," he spat out hurriedly.

Groans and shouts rose throughout the room. Beatrice threw her arms around Ann and began to cry. Will relaxed back into his chair and John bolted out the door, slamming it behind him.

"What the hell does that mean?" Calvin Bailey shouted, rising to his feet.

"It means that the prisoners are free to go."

There was more shouting. Sherman and Ryan positioned themselves in front of the justices' table with rifles visible in their crossed arms. Fred walked over and stood beside them.

"This ain't right, Oxley, and you know it!"

"There's just not enough evidence to hold them," Carter said. "Not enough for a lawyer to make a case."

Most of what he said was lost in the noise made by the yelling and by a spray of broken glass. A young man carrying a stick jumped through a window and ran towards Will, who put his arms up to his face to ward off attack. Beatrice screamed and threw her arms around Ann.

"All right, all right, that's it." Sherman grabbed the man by the arm and held him fast. "You're under arrest," he told his captive, whose face was scratched and bleeding.

Sherman nodded at Ryan who hurried towards the door, opened it, and stood in the entryway.

"Okay, everybody," Sherman shouted above the noise, "we're all going to slowly move towards the door in single file and leave the building quietly. Any problems and you'll find yourselves either under arrest or with your kneecaps shot off, women and children excepted, of course. And any firearms in this room better stay where they are."

With Fred's assistance, Sherman placed handcuffs on the man in custody.

Children were crying and three women collapsed back into their chairs. Their companions reached into bags and pockets for smelling salts.

The crowd filed out but not without protest.

"This isn't the end, Harney," someone shouted. "You're going to get what's coming to you."

"The law won't be here to protect you all the time, you bastard."

"Something funny's going on. Her family probably paid them off."

"I heard that she did come from money."

"Shut up and move along," Ryan ordered.

I don't hear the shouts of the approaching boys
or feel the stones.

ROCKLEY

Nova Scotia
September 8, 1877

"MUMMA, WHY DO YOU let Pa do things to me?" Mary wiped her mouth on her mother's nightgown to remove the feel of her father's kiss.

"It's because I'm not your pa. No one knows who he is, not even your mother, I don't suppose."

Mary looked from one to the other.

"I'm not your father, you stupid cow. I married your mother out of pity and for money. I couldn't stomach her otherwise. Neither her ma or her pa could handle the thought of a scandal. Scared them to death, the old hypocrites. That old bastard Hennessy promised me a lot of money for my troubles, but after we married it stopped coming. Ma told me to walk away at the first. I should have."

"Mumma?"

Ann was leaning against the doorjamb with her hands over her eyes.

Will forced her to look at Mary.

"Tell her. Tell her."

"Yes, it's true. Will's not your father."

"I hate you. I hate the both of you."

Mary ran from the room and down the stairs. She fled out the kitchen door, leaving behind Harry and Little Helen still sleeping on the veranda. She tripped over a doll's carriage on the doorstep, her mind whirling as her feet flew over the uneven ground.

Not her father. He was not her father. All the times that she feared what he might do and thought her mother didn't care.

Well that, at least, was true, Mary thought to herself: she didn't care.

Mary heard the door slam. She slowed down and looked back. Will was on the doorstep. She could see her mother through the kitchen window, lighting the lantern on the table. She turned and ran down the lane.

ANN FOUND AN OLD PAIR of boots in the corner of the porch and struggled to get them on her bare, swollen feet. Carrying the lantern, she hurried out the door and down the lane, in the direction she had seen Will take. She stumbled along in the gathering darkness crying, her mind racing. I should have told her...that Will saved me. Shame to the family...music teacher...ruined. Had a wife...said to get rid of it.

Ann was half walking, half running now. The backs of her ankles were raw from the tight boots. The wind blew the tears down her face and neck. The muscles in her right arm ached from carrying the lantern. My poor mother...assumed Mary was Will's.

Ann's thoughts were interrupted by a scream. She listened, then hurried on again, stumbling and shivering down the lane in her thin blue nightdress.

SHE WOULD GO TO MERIGOMISH, right now, tonight, even if she had to walk every step of the way. She'd go to Mrs. LeFurgey's. She'd let her stay there tonight.

The wind picked up, swaying the trees. The dark air was warm on her face. She reached the main road, ran across it and over the narrow strip of grassland leading to the river. She stumbled down the short bank, scuffing her boots on the way down to slow her progress.

She'd never have to do anything that he told her to do again. She'd never have to see him again.

But I'll never see the little ones again either, or Uncle John, or Smith, she reminded herself.

Tears welled in her eyes and she clutched at the locket around her neck. They'd expect her to come back after a while with her tail between her legs but they'd soon find out she was gone forever.

She stopped and looked out across the river. The moving water was the only sound in the night. The moon peeked in and out behind the gathering clouds.

"And where might you be going?"

Soft words, little more than a whisper, in her left ear. Mary screamed and jumped away.

He had followed her.

He was smiling.

Fear froze her, then Mary turned to run. He grabbed her hair. As pain shot through her head and into her neck, she felt a spike of anger rising.

"How dare you?"

Mary slapped him across the face.

"Oh, sassy, eh? You're not accomplishing anything, just making me madder than I already am. You'd better quit while you're ahead."

Mary spat in his face.

"You're not my father. Where is my real father?"

He grabbed her throat and brought her face up close to his, their noses touching.

"I said, quit while you're ahead. You're never getting away from me."

He hauled his arm back and hit her in the mouth. The pain of it almost made her pass out. There was blood and a tooth. She felt her knees buckle. Regaining herself, she reached up with both hands and raked her fingernails over his face. Four red welts appeared on each of his cheeks and down his neck.

"Jesus Christ!"

Mary ran. Then something heavy caught her in the back of the head and brought her to her knees. She looked around and saw him walking towards her through the dusk.

Got to get away from here, she thought, her mind straining to focus. Got to get away.

Will bent down to pick something up, then kept coming.

Got to get away. Her body had a strange coldness.

She was on her feet when she saw, beyond his approaching figure, a light bouncing closer. A lantern. Someone was coming. Mumma. Mumma was coming to help her, to save her. And someone was yelling something, or was it she herself who cried out, making a sound that was carried away on the wind. Then pain surprised her.

"I told you, told you, told you a hundred times not to make me mad," Will yelled in rhythm with the blows he brought down upon her head.

Mary's face was sticky with something that was making it hard to see but she sensed that the lantern had stopped in front of her. She could see the hem of a nightgown and heard screaming again.

"Mumma," she whispered. "Mumma."

BELL'S POINT

Cape Traverse, Prince Edward Island
May 1891

"DADDA, THERE'S MEN HERE to see you," Elizabeth called, running into the barn.

"Thanks, Puddin', tell them I'll be right out."

Avard emerged to find two men standing in the barnyard in front of a horse and buggy. They both smiled and extended their hands as he approached.

"Mr. Bell?"

"Yes. What can I do for you?"

"I'm Charles LeBlanc. This is my friend Henri Cormier. He doesn't speak English too good, so I'll talk for the two of us."

Avard nodded at Cormier.

"We're from Richibucto, over in New Brunswick. We're hoping you can help us."

"I'll try. Come on into the house," Avard offered.

"Non, merci." Charles shook his head. "It's better if we talk here."

"Puddin', you go and see what your brother's up to."

The child skipped across the barnyard.

"We were told that there was a girl found on the beach near here."

"Yeah, there was, a long while ago now, just down here at the point. My younger brother Jimmy found her. He doesn't live here now. Works on a farm over in St. Eleanor's. Just got married last week."

Charles translated Avard's words to his friend.

"Henri's sister disappeared back in '77, when she was just seventeen years old," Charles said. "He has been trying to find out what happened to her ever since."

"Oh well, the girl we found was from Nova Scotia."

"Can you tell us what she looked like?"

"Well, she was small and had blond hair. She's buried up in the Methodist churchyard. I can show you where. There's a wooden marker."

Charles spoke in French once more. Henri nodded and asked a question.

"He wants to know if there was anything found with her. I know it was a long time ago now."

"There was. Come with me." Avard directed them to a small tool shed on the other side of the yard.

"Haven't been in here since the old man passed away," he said, placing his left shoulder to the door of the shed and giving it a shove. "I'll see if I can find them."

He emerged ten minutes later with a faded burlap bag and handed it to Charles.

"These were what she was wearing. Her father threw them in the woods behind our outhouse when he was here," he said. "I watched him and picked them up after he left. Should have given them to Sheriff Flynn when he came back around looking for them. But I was kinda sweet on the girl even though she was dead, and I wanted to keep something of her for myself. Here they are."

Avard didn't tell them about stuffing the flowers into the girl's body. He had never told anyone about that. His father had never asked him about it though Avard was sure he suspected.

Charles set the bag on the ground, reached in, and handed the items, one by one, to Henri, who began to nod.

"Oui, Natalie, Natalie."

"T'es-tu sûr?" Charles asked his friend each time he spoke.

"Oui, oui."

Henri was on his knees beside the clothes now, touching each item. Then he jumped to his feet, took a tintype out of his coat pocket, and handed it to Avard. A girl seated on a wicker chair was wearing the same garments that now lay crumbling at their feet. A solemn young man stood behind her.

"I'll be...damned." Avard shook his head.

"Ah, bien, dis-y!" Henri grabbed Charles by the arm and pushed him around to face Avard.

"Natalie disappeared the same day this picture was taken," Charles began. "She was going to be married. Her fiancé said that she must have ran away because she didn't want to marry him. He married somebody else just two months later. The police looked for her but never found anything. Don't think they tried very hard, being that she was French and them English. Henri's been looking for her off and on ever since. He's never given up. He heard a story a year ago about a girl turning up over here and finally saved enough money to make the trip."

"What did he say her name was?"

"Natalie. Natalie Cormier," Charles answered.

Henri stood still, clutching the garments to his chest, tears running down his face.

"Come on into the house," Avard said gently. "The wife will make you a cup of tea, and I want you to meet my mother, Catherine. She often speaks of the girl, especially in the fall. Then I'll take you to the graveyard to visit your sister."

ROCKLEY

NOVA SCOTIA
August 15, 1952

"HOLD IT, A HALF turn at a time, remember. It has to stay level." Edgar Fraser, down on his hands and knees, yelled while eyeballing the structure. There were four men at each corner of the building, and another four underneath it working the screw jacks. "Hold it a minute, not yet. Cecil, don't get so excited."

Fraser raised one hand and shook his head amidst laughter.

Ian Gordon and Barry Fraser sat in the long grass under a spidery apple tree and watched. They were two of the many boys, on a hot, humid day, who had come out to watch the old Dempsey house being lifted from its quarry stone foundation and placed on the new concrete wall, just down the lane and across the main road. The Rockley Baptists had purchased the building from the landowner in the States and paid to have it moved. They were going to use it as their new church.

The farmhouse's lane and yard were grown up in alders, grass, and thistles, the barn was gone. The remaining grey outbuildings were in varying stages of collapse and the gardens had long since weeded over.

"The building isn't in too bad a shape; it needs some work, a new roof, but it can be used again," Barry's father had said last night at the supper table.

The Dempsey house had been vacant for a long time, longer than either of Barry's parents could remember.

"My old man says this place in haunted," Ian told his friend. "Said that when he was a kid, people used to see a light moving around at night down here and along the river and hear screaming and crying something awful."

"Yeah," Barry said. "Me and Nan were walking to the store one night last winter and we heard something. She ran all the way home." He grinned at the memory. "Some girl's supposed to have been killed around here a long time ago. Look, they're starting to take the booms out now."

It was another two hours before the timbers were removed, the float backed up into position, the jacks lowered, and the house eased onto the flatbed. As the float slowly made its way to the new site, the boys walked over to where the building had stood.

"Look at the hole it left," Ian said, standing at the edge. "Bet you there's some interesting stuff down there. Remember that film at school about the people who dig in the ground for old things? We could do that here."

Barry jumped into the hole, and walked around jabbing at rocks and clumps of dirt with his feet. Then something he kicked free flew up in the air, catching Ian's eye.

"What's that?" he called jumping down next to Barry. "I saw something just now."

He walked over in the direction the object had fallen and got down on his hands and knees, sifting through the dirt with his fingers.

"I'm sure I saw something. Yeah, look at this."

"It looks like part of an old locket," Barry said. "Nan got one of those for her birthday last year."

Ian rubbed it on his pant leg.

"Have to take it home and clean it up."

"It's a treasure! Bet it's worth millions," Barry whispered.

Ian took out a red and white polka-dot handkerchief, wrapped his find in it, and placed it inside his pocket. They scrambled out of the hole and mounted their bikes to catch up with the float. Then, like the other boys, they made a game of throwing stones at the windows, trying to shatter the few remaining panes of yellow glass.

IN SEARCH OF THE REAL MARY HARNEY

FOUND DROWNED IS A novel, but it is based on a series of events that really happened. I first heard of Mary Harney's disappearance as a ghost story and became fascinated with her. I researched through a number of sources to find out more. The only archival information I was able to track down concerning the case was contained in newspaper articles. Then I built Mary's story around them. Here are some examples of those news stories.

The Patriot (Charlottetown, PEI)
Saturday, September 15, 1877
It is reported that the dead body of a young and good looking woman partially dressed and bearing marks of violence was found on the shore at Cape Traverse the middle of this week, and that none in the vicinity recognized the remains. Is it another mystery of the dead or will the coroner's inquest clear it all up?

The Examiner (Charlottetown, PEI)
Monday, September 17, 1877
Body Washed Ashore – A Mystery
The body of a young woman, apparently about 18 years of age was washed ashore on Bell's Point, near Cape Traverse on Thursday afternoon. She had every appearance of being a lady. The body was scantily dressed- a chemise, one skirt, and one jacket, with a belt around her waist. There was a mark or dent over one of her eyes, as if it had been done with a hammer. It is supposed by appearance not to have been long in the water. A coroner's inquest was held on Saturday. The whole affair is thus far a mystery which calls for thorough investigation.

A dispatch to the *Moncton Times* from Cape Traverse, says, "The body is that of a young woman, picked up in tide wash on the 12th. Could have been no time in the water, as it was not decomposed or eaten by fish. No marks of violence on the body. The Coroner's Jury returned a verdict of "found drowned." The body was not identified.

Summerside Journal (PEI)
Thursday, September 20, 1877
An inquest was held Thursday last by Dr. Jarvis, coroner, upon the body of a female that had washed ashore near Cape Traverse on the day previous. The body was that of a young woman somewhere between 17 and 20 years of age. She was slimly clad, having nothing but a cotton chemise and a flannel petticoat upon her person. Her face was considerably disfigured. She could not be identified and a verdict of "found drowned" was returned. Her remains were interred in the Wesleyan Burying Ground, Cape Traverse.

The Wesleyan (Halifax, NS)
September 22, 1877
The body of a young woman apparently about 18 years of age, was washed ashore on Bell's Point, near Cape Traverse, PEI on Thursday afternoon. She had light hair, small hands and feet and every appearance of being a lady. The body was scantily dressed – a chemise, one skirt and a loose jacket, with a belt around her waist. There was a mark or dent over one of her eyes, as if it had been done with a hammer. It is supposed by appearances not to have been long in the water.

Summerside Journal (PEI)
Thursday, September 27, 1877
The body of a girl found at Cape Traverse not long ago is said to be that of a foolish girl from Pugwash who had started out in a small boat, for what purpose no one knows, and the supposition is that it capsized with her, as girl and boat were missing about the same time.

Chignecto Post (Sackville, NB)
Thursday, September 27, 1877
The missing girl, Hurley [*sic*], who disappeared from Port Philip some days ago, it is believed is one and the same with the corpse of a young woman picked up two weeks ago at Cape Traverse. The girl had always been mentally clouded, and it is believed she went across the strait in a punt. A relative of hers has gone over to establish the identity if possible.

The Examiner (Charlottetown, PEI)
Monday, October 1, 1877
Detective Hutt of Halifax was in town yesterday. He leaves for Summerside this morning.

Chignecto Post (Sackville, NB)
Monday, October 11, 1877
The Girl Harney!
Foul Play Suspected!
Our readers will recollect that some weeks ago a girl aged about 16, was discovered missing at Port Philip, NS. An alarm was raised and parties of men searched the woods in the vicinity for some days, but finding no trace of her, the search was abandoned. About four weeks ago, the body of a girl was picked up at Cape Traverse PEI. An inquest was held on the remains but no evidence being forthcoming as to their identity, the jury returned the verdict of "found drowned" and the body was buried. The identity of the girl Harney and the body found was at once surmised by the people of Port Philip, and indeed the suspicions of certain persons that the girl had not been fairly dealt with found currency in rumors, which resulted in Detective Hutt taking up the case. He went to PE Island, had the body exhumed, established by the dress etc. to his own satisfaction that the deceased was the Port Philip girl, and then returning to Port Philip, had Mrs. Harney the girl's mother, and Harney, the stepfather, arrested for murder. The preliminary examination took place yesterday in Oxford.

By telegram this morning
The examination of William Harney and wife, charged with murder of Mary Colburn, daughter of the latter, took place yesterday before Justices Oxley, Black, Carter and Hingley. Twenty-six witnesses were examined, none of whose testimony in any way implicated them.

ACKNOWLEDGEMENTS

IN THE TWO AND a half decades it took me to complete this book, many people assisted and encouraged me along the way. My thanks and gratitude go to:

Robin Sutherland, former UNB instructor, who read an early version of the manuscript; Peter Dickinson, former Research Historian, Kings Landing Historical Settlement; Barry Cahill and Philip Hartling, Provincial Archives of Nova Scotia; Heidi Coombs, UNB Library; Dr. Sasha Mallally, Dept. of History, UNB; Jean McKay and Fred Horne, MacNaught History Centre and Archives, Summerside; Robert Hawkes, Physics Department, Mount Allison University; Rick Cotie, Canadian Coast Guard; Kelly Langille, Archives Assistant, Pictou County Genealogy and Heritage Society; the late Dave Dewar, Director/Curator, Wallace and Area Museum; John Boylan, Public Services Archivist and Jill MacMicken Wilson, Systems Archivist, Public Archives and Records Office of Prince Edward Island; Joseph Wickens, W.K. Kellogg Health Sciences Library, Dalhousie University; Dr. Allen E. Marble; Wayne Wright for information on PEI doctors; Bill Fairbanks, QC, for advice on preliminary hearings; the late John MacKay; writer Gerry Beirne for his helpful criticism; my sister-in-law Louise Ploude for translation assistance and my niece Elizabeth Glenn, who, with me, placed flowers on what we believed to be the drowned girl's final resting place in Cape Traverse.

ARTSNB for providing me with a much needed Creation Grant in 2013; the anonymous reader with the Writers' Federation of Nova

Scotia Manuscript Review Program who made great suggestions; my best friend, Barb Thompson, who tramped the woods with Grace and me during hunting season and later shared her expertise on nineteenth-century clothing; writer Sara Jewell and her husband, Dwayne Mattison, who advised me about the River Philip and provided a lovely tour of the Rockley area; the long-suffering Fredericton Fictional Friends writing group charter members: Ana and David Watts, Josephine Savarese, Carla Gunn and Kathie Goggin, who read parts of the manuscript over and over and over again for so many years; and my online writing group friends, Nadine Dolittle and Kathy-Dianne Leveille, who gave me lots of great advice over many drafts.

My sister, Maureen Glennie, who aided me in the early stages of research; my father, Reg Glenn, for providing information on all kinds of useful things like express wagons, horses, mauls and other farm tools, how to raise and transport a house, and lots about life in general.

Grace Trenholm Speth for preserving Mary's story in Lore of North *Cumberland* all those years ago, which captured my imagination and led to this book. I'll always be grateful.

Whitney Moran at Vagrant Press for giving Mary and me a second chance. It was so nice to work with you again, Whitney, sorry about the sunburn; my editor, Kate Kennedy, whose patience, keen eye for detail, and deep knowledge of her craft made this a better book and me a better writer; Nimbus art director, Heather Bryan, for the wonderful cover.

Barry Norris, my sweetie, husband, and safe harbour, whose love and support enable me to write.

And my late mother, Annie Glenn. It's because of her that I write.